Janet McNaughton

The Raintree Rebellion

Published by Harper*Trophy*Canada™,
an imprint of HarperCollins Publishers Ltd

Originally published in trade paperback by
Harper*Trophy*Canada™: 2006
This mass market paperback edition: 2007

HarperCollins Publishers Ltd
2 Bloor Street East, 20th Floor
Toronto, Ontario, Canada
M4W 1A8

www.harpercollins.ca

Canadian Cataloguing in Publication Data

McNaughton, Janet, 1953–
The raintree rebellion / Janet McNaughton.

ISBN-13: 978-0-00-225529-5
ISBN-10: 0-00-225529-4

I. Title.

PS8575.N385R33 2007 jC813'.54 C2007-
904522-7

IMS 9 8 7 6 5 4 3 2 1

Printed and bound in the United States
Set in Monotype Plantin and Franklin Gothic

Excerpt from "The Grandmothers of Argentina"
by Enos Watts, on page vii, reprinted from *Spaces
Between the Trees* by Enos Watts
(St. John's: Flanker Press Ltd., 2005) by permission
of the publisher.

For Alison Mews and Heather Myers,
children's librarians of
Newfoundland and Labrador

They were the young,
who survived,
swallowed up
by their own cities,
vanishing into strange houses, stamped
with counterfeit names
There must be a thousand
in Buenos Aires alone,
no one knows

from "The Grandmothers of Argentina"
by Enos Watts

1

My name is Blake Raintree. I was born on July 14, 2352.

For the first sixteen years of my life I didn't know those things about myself. Not my name or my birthdate or my age. I didn't know who my parents were, or how I had been separated from them. I didn't know if I was lost or thrown away.

—From the victim statement of Blake Raintree

"Look at the city!" Erica says. She makes for the nose of the airship, lurching a little as it dips into its descent. Her voice is full of wonder and regret. She hasn't seen Toronto for more than fifteen years.

I trail her through the empty observation deck. Most people are already below, vying to be first off, but Erica wanted me to see this. "Look," she says again. Tall buildings rise directly in front of us in the bright morning sun, towers of glass and stone and steel, faceted to catch the light. Most have roof gardens. It's amazing. And it fills me with overwhelming disappointment.

"I don't remember it," I tell her. "I thought there would be . . . something. Recognition or a feeling of coming home. I don't feel anything."

She puts her arm around me. "Of course you don't, Blake. Sixteen years is a long time and you were barely two when you left. How could you remember?"

I don't say anything. I was born here. Something about this place ought to resonate with me. I believed it would.

"You were up and gone before I woke this morning,"

Erica continues. "Was it the nightmare again?" I nod. "Can you tell me about it?" she asks. "Come and sit down."

"I'll try," I tell her. I take a deep breath. "It's a short dream, just a moment, really. I'm with my mother, but I'm very small, I barely reach her waist. It's night and everything is soaked in dread. The worst part is my mother's voice. That's what makes it so awful."

"What does she say?"

"She's begging me to keep up with her, over and over. My arm aches right into the shoulder socket, she's pulling so hard. The pain seems very real. And I know it's all wrong. My mother isn't supposed to ask me to do more than I can. That's not really a thought, but it's in the dream. You know?" Erica nods and I continue. "I want her to pick me up, so I can go to sleep. I dig my heels in and take a deep breath, and a howl starts inside me, swelling and swelling until it finally breaks out. But it's more than a sound. It fills everything. My ears, my eyes, the world. When the howl starts, the dream ends. Waking is like falling. My whole body jumps."

Erica shudders. "No wonder you didn't want to talk about it. But now we're here, maybe the nightmare will stop. Maybe this trip caused it."

"What do you mean?"

"We've been following the route you took all those years ago, down the St. Lawrence to Nova Scotia and across to Terra Nova. It's the same journey, in reverse. At some point when you were travelling with your mother you must have felt the way you do in the nightmare."

"I probably did. But when I'm awake, it's easier to imagine what it was like for her, how scared she must have been, with the technocaust starting, my father and so many others just arrested because of their special knowledge. She was so brave to make that trip alone with a small child. I would have been a dead weight, too heavy to carry and too little to walk any distance by myself. Without me, she might have survived. And look what happened. A few weeks after we made it to Terra Nova, I was stolen from her by a homeless child and she never saw me again. And then, because she went public to try to get me back, she ended up dying in a concentration camp. Maybe that's why I'm trying to stop her in the dream."

Worry lines Erica's face, making her look her age. I usually forget she's almost sixty, about ten years older than my mother would have been.

"I wish you wouldn't torture yourself like this, Blake," she says. "I almost wish we hadn't found out so much about your past sometimes. Don't you think your mother would be happy to know you've found people who love and care for you?"

I put my hand on her arm. "Of course she would. She'd love you and William. You're my parents now. I learned so much about her, these past two years, living in St. Pearl with people who knew her."

"They knew a lot about her, didn't they? You have a lot of time to talk in a concentration camp." A shadow passes over Erica's face. Because her life was torn apart, too. If the technocaust hadn't happened, she'd probably still be teaching history at the university in Toronto. Instead, she was forced to run, just like us, but a year later. I sometimes forget she lived in the same camp my mother died in—but after, near the end of the technocaust, when it became possible to escape.

"And your mother would be so proud to know you're coming back to Toronto to work with people who are trying to put everything back together again," Erica continues. "I'm happy you agreed to come with me, Blake, even if it does mean interrupting your education. This Justice

Council is going to be so important. If we make it work, if hearings about past injustices can be held, the victims of the technocaust will be heard. Maybe we can even make elections possible." Her eyes shine. Getting the Justice Council to function is going to be a challenge, but Erica is undaunted. She looks to the future, never dwelling on the past, no matter how bitter it might have been. But whenever she talks this way, I add a few wishes of my own. Yes, we can see that justice is done. And, while we're at it, we can punish the people who ruined so many thousands of lives. I want the ones who took my parents away from me to pay. This anger is a wheel inside my heart that never stops turning, the thing that makes it possible for me to breathe, to think, to be. Without it, I might cease to exist.

Of course, I never say that to Erica. She would try to take my anger away, and it's what keeps me going. That, and the thought that I will eventually be able to make a victim statement before the Justice Council myself. I'm already working on it.

William, Erica's husband, was my first science teacher. The idea that I would interrupt my education upset him at first, but when he realized how important it is to me to explore my past by coming here, he relented. Before we left home he gave me two presents for the journey. One was a portable holo-lab, to let me continue my science education, and the other was a notebook. It's the ancient kind, made of paper with a red metal coil binding so it lies flat when it's open. And it's divided into sections. "So you can think about the past and the future all at once," William said when he gave it to me, smiling. At the time, I didn't know what he meant, but now I do. In this book I can write about all the new things that happen, but I can also work on my victim statement. I lie awake at night, thinking of things I want to say, and in the morning I write them down in the notebook so I won't forget. My victim statement is the most important thing I will ever write. It has to be perfect.

Erica has gone to the windows again. "Look, Blake, a jet plane!" She points to a long, slender silhouette in the distance, low in the sky. "It's landing at the airport north of the city." Erica sighs. "We could have made this journey in just a few hours in one of those, instead of three days. If I'd known this trip was going to be so hard on you, I might have let the Transitional Council pay the extra money for the plane tickets."

"I'd never expect you to do that for me," I say, but I'm touched. The fuel cells that power these airships are too weak for planes. The jets need ancient technology, internal combustion engines that use rare and costly fossil fuel. There are huge taxes on anything that creates so much pollution, so travelling by jet is expensive. The temporary government in Toronto that is bringing us here, the Transitional Council, would have paid the fare, but Erica couldn't bring herself to travel in one of those CO2-spewing monsters. "Throwbacks from the old days when we ruined the earth," she said. Erica lives by her principles.

When I look ahead again, we seem uncomfortably close to the buildings. "It looks like we might crash."

"Don't worry," Erica says, "we'll move out over Lake Ontario soon."

I get a hollow feeling in the pit of my stomach as we descend even more rapidly. The tall buildings seem to swing to our right. The city beneath us is so vast. Just before we reach the lake, we see something strange in the streets below—crowds of people who seem to be wandering aimlessly.

"That's odd," Erica says. "Excuse me," she calls to a cleaner I hadn't even noticed, a woman silently making her way through the compartment, picking up garbage. "What are all those people doing down by Front Street?"

The woman comes over to look. "Oh, *them,*" she says, her voice thick with disapproval. "They really shouldn't be there."

"Who are they?" I ask.

"Debtors who left the forced labour camps in industrial zones after the Uprising. You know, the Protectors used to send them there when they failed to support themselves. No one knows what to do with them now. I think they should be forced back where they belong," she says. "Without their labour, we just can't get most manufactured goods. It's getting bad." She goes back to work, grumbling.

"That explains why there's so little pollution," Erica says. "I knew about those debtors, but I didn't realize they were camped downtown."

We've already left them far behind. I know they must be a problem, but I'm glad they escaped from the forced labour camps.

"See that green space?" Erica says. She points inland to a large patch of treed land that looks almost wild. "That's High Park. We'll live a few blocks from there. And there's the mouth of the Humber River. The docking port is just on the other side. We'd better go below." She gives me a look that seems to go right into my heart. "Are you all right?"

"I guess so," I start to say, and then I shake my head. "Not really. I'm scared."

She squeezes me with one arm, a half-hug. "Don't worry, Blake. I'm sure you'll be perfect as my aide."

"It's not that." Without meaning to, I grab my left wrist and wring it, giving myself away. I can't actually feel the micro-dot in there, but at times like this, it seems as if I can.

Erica looks puzzled. "Your micro-chip?"

I nod. "When we found it, we learned so much about what

happened to me and my mother, just because I finally knew my real name. We can learn a lot more from the ID code, and the people who can make sense of it are here, in Toronto."

"But Blake, you made up your mind about that two years ago, after the Uprising, when they opened up access to the ID codes. I wasn't sure you'd made the right choice, but once you decided not to submit that code you seemed to find some peace. Why change your mind now?"

"Erica, how can I live so close to those offices without looking for answers? What if my father is out there, waiting—" I stop, unable to continue.

Erica takes my left arm and rubs it, as if she could soothe the phantom pain. And somehow, she does. "Blake, sweetheart, your father was taken very early in the technocaust. People like him didn't survive." She says this as gently as she can.

"I know. We've been through this before. I didn't get my mother back, but at least I know what happened to her. Maybe I learned enough to give me nightmares, but it's enough to let me make a real victim statement, too. Most of the street kids who were my age when the techoncaust hit can't make victim statements because they don't know if the technocaust caused what happened to them." I square my shoulders. "I'm ready for the other half of the story. I don't expect to find my father, but I want to know who he was."

"All right," Erica says. "Tomorrow, I'll find out where the ID office is located and—"

I interrupt. "I already know. I checked as soon as I knew we were coming here."

She smiles through her doubts. "That's my girl," she says. And I smile back, because, no matter what happens now, that's what I am.

2

The greater Toronto area is expected to reach a population of 800,000 before the end of 2370.

—Newscast on *The Solar Flare,* August 29, 2370

It takes forever to get off the airship and pick up our luggage in the vast docking port because of the crowds. St. Pearl is the only city I've known. I expected Toronto to be similar, but it's much larger, and I can already see that living here is going to be different. When we finally get outside, Erica raises her hand for a taxi and gives the driver our new address.

"I can't get over how clean the air is," she says after a few minutes.

"It's great," the driver says, "except for the shortages. But it's been like this for a long time now. You must be visitors. Where do you come from?"

"Terra Nova Prefecture," Erica says. "I live in a small village on the west coast, Kildevil, but Blake has been studying in St. Pearl."

"That's so far away. What brings you here?"

"I've come to sit on the Justice Council," Erica says.

Her words have an immediate impact on the man. He sits straighter. When we stop at a traffic light, he turns for better look at Erica. "You've really come to serve on the Justice Council?" I hear the awe in his voice. "Do you mind if I ask why you were chosen?"

I know Erica won't tell him. All those years of secrecy are still ingrained in her. It's easier for me to remember we can speak openly now. I was only involved in the struggle to change the government near the very end. "Erica helped lead the resistance in Terra Nova," I tell him.

The driver gives a low whistle of disbelief. "It's an honour to meet you. People are so sick of waiting for elections. Two years now. Those riots last spring were inevitable. The Justice Council is the first hope we've had." Erica smiles. Whenever the traffic stops us, the driver glances back, looking at Erica as if she's rare and special. Which she is.

The busy auto-route soon gives way to quiet streets. Houses are sparsely scattered among grassy lots that show faint traces of foundations. Most of the houses are new, but some are strange. "I've never seen houses like those," I tell Erica.

"This area has a lot of the older houses. They're early- to mid-twentieth century, more than three hundred years old. It's an odd quirk of history. Houses were built soundly in the nineteenth century and the first half of the twentieth, so many survived. After World War II, builders weren't so careful, and the later houses barely lasted a century. Of course, the ones that survived have been retrofitted to use advanced technology like any other house."

I smile. Erica sounds like a historian today, more than she did when we were home. Coming back to Toronto must make her remember the life she once had here. "But how did they survive the Dark Times?" I ask.

"People might have lived in them, or maybe they were abandoned and rebuilt after civilization was restored," she replies. "We don't know much about the twenty-second century—that's why it's called the Dark Times. But most of the older houses are gone. All these empty lots had houses on them once. The city supported a much larger population, too; three times as many people lived here before the eco-disasters of the twenty-first century."

We leave the pretty houses and trees behind, turning onto a broader road. "Bloor Street," Erica says. "This is one of the main streets in the city. Look at all the shops, Blake."

"This isn't the most direct route," the driver says, "but I thought you'd like to see the neighbourhood."

Street vendors have set up carts on vacant lots. We pass the facades of a few bigger buildings that must be malls. Suddenly, we're stopped by heavy traffic. Ahead, I hear drums and whistles.

"Oh, man. Is this Saturday? I should've remembered to stay off Bloor." The driver hits the steering column with the heel of his hand.

"What is it?" Erica asks. "It sounds like a parade."

"We'd be lucky if it was. At least parades move. It's the ghost library. We could be here a long time."

"What's the ghost library?" Erica asks.

"People want a library. So, every Saturday they protest in High Park." He sighs. "They're supposed to stay in the park, but they always spill over into the street and block traffic."

"Is this allowed?" I ask.

"Yes," Erica says, very quickly. "All forms of protest are tolerated as long as they are peaceful. That's in the preliminary edicts of the Transitional Council. "

I've struck a nerve. A lot of people think the Transitional Council is just holding on to power now. When Erica was invited to be on the Justice Council, she agonized for weeks before accepting, pouring over the edicts the transitional government had issued. She only accepted when she decided she could trust them to move toward democracy. Not everyone has reached the same conclusion.

"What's a library?" I ask.

"It's a place where people can borrow books. When I was young, they were everywhere, but, near the end of the technocaust, the old Protector governments closed down all the libraries to limit access to information. Now, we could set up biblio-tech units all over this city—they'd cost less to operate than a library. But that technology doesn't bring people together, it keeps them apart. You just download your book and go. A library is more than books. You can hold meetings at a library. You can run programs for children. It creates a sense of community," she sighs. "These people want information again, but they also want places where they can meet and talk. And they have every right, but it's going to take time. So many things have to be fixed. Libraries may have to wait."

After about forty-five minutes, we finally pass the ghost library. I was expecting some kind of angry protest, but it's more like a party. Small groups listen to people reading from books, but there are jugglers too, even one with flaming torches. I see a girl in a bright velvet dress standing beside a booth that looks like a small stage, talking to an audience of children. Suddenly, a puppet pops up, squirts her in the face with water, and quickly disappears inside the booth. Even from inside the vehicle, I hear the children squeal with laughter. They make me smile. The girl puts her head down into the booth, apparently talking to the puppet. The children lean forward to see what happens next. I do too, but then we drive away.

On the crest of an embankment, I glimpse a tall man with long silver hair, dressed in odd, flowing clothes. Somehow he draws my attention. He's looking around with satisfaction, as if all this belongs to him.

"It looks like a circus," Erica says.

"It might as well be," the driver replies. "It's run by this radical who calls himself Prospero. He's done a lot of good, even before the Uprising. His group takes homeless kids and teaches them how to support themselves by performing circus tricks in the streets. But the ghost library always messes up traffic."

It looks so intriguing. "Can we stop and have a look?" I ask.

Erica shakes her head. "We've got to unpack. Anyway, we're going to be here for months. You'll have plenty of opportunities to see the ghost library."

"You sure will," the driver says. "The address you gave me is only a few blocks from here."

Soon after, we stop on a side street. The park is close enough to see when I look back. "This is the house?" I ask Erica.

She laughs. "I wanted to surprise you. Let's have a look."

We climb out. It's one of the old houses, red brick, with three storeys topped by a sloped roof with black shingles. Two large white dormers set with little windows are flanked by tall brick chimneys on the outside walls. There's a big wooden door in the middle sheltered by a curving porch roof. Big windows with white wooden trim look out from either side of that door. It's not a grand house but it's dignified. I never imagined living in such a place.

"How could anyone give this up for us?" I ask Erica.

"They didn't, exactly, Blake. The owner, Rebecca Mendorfsky, is a judge. She's gone to Vancouver Prefecture to do what I'll be doing, helping to set up a Justice Council there. Her family went with her, so she offered us the use of the house. Let's have a look. I've got the codes."

The driver won't accept payment. "I don't want your money," he tells Erica. "It's not every day I get to drive someone who's going to be on the Justice Council." She finally makes him understand she has a travel stipend. I'm glad he's been so respectful. I know Erica was braced for hostility.

We drag everything up the steps to the porch, then Erica keys in the codes. I feel a shiver of anticipation. It's like opening a huge present.

3

When I came to Toronto, so much of my story was still a mystery. If I had known what we would discover, would I have submitted my ID code? I still can't say.

—From the victim statement of Blake Raintree

Erica and I are standing on a corner at Bloor Street, waiting for a minibus to flag down. Part of me wants to run back to that beautiful house where we spent all day yesterday getting settled, to hide in my lovely new room with walls that can change colour and a ceiling that mimics the sky, but I take a deep breath and root myself to the spot. It's Monday morning and we are going to the ID codes office.

"Maybe we should have called a cab. Maybe this won't be safe. Maybe I can flag a cab down. Do you see one?" Erica is nervous too, but for other reasons.

"We went through this yesterday," I remind her. "We'll have to use the minibuses if you want to keep your expenses down." But I can't resist adding, "I'm sure a lot of your colleagues will use taxis without even thinking about it."

Erica flushes. "That's the point, isn't it? If people never think about their privilege, how can we hope to change things?" She sets her mouth in a tight line. "Using minibuses will make me more interested in restoring public transportation."

But I know she's scared, in spite of her principles. "I'm sure it'll be safe. It's been months since passengers were killed by rival companies. Is this one now?" It doesn't look like any vehicle I've ever seen. It's half the size of a standard bus, painted bright green with big pink and yellow patterns stencilled all over it.

"That's a minibus," Erica says, and she flags it down with grim determination.

"Welcome, pretty ladies!" the driver cries as Erica hands him her script card. His skin is the colour of a cup of very fine tea without milk. His eyes are quick and clever. He has no accent, but the quaintness of his speech makes me smile. I've never heard anyone use the word "ladies." "Are you visiting my fair city?" he asks as he returns Erica's card. "I've never seen you before."

"No," Erica says. "We will be living here awhile."

The driver is delighted by this news. "I'll give you my disk. You can use it to coordinate your travel with my schedule. I am Hanif, your dedicated driver. Achmed's Minibus is the finest service in Toronto. We have never lost a single passenger. Not one! No rival dares challenge us." I don't know whether to be amused or alarmed. Erica grabs my elbow as the vehicle lurches forward and we half fall into some seats. We're going very fast. I look around for seatbelts. There aren't any.

After a few minutes, we stop at a traffic light. "Where are you going, new ladies?" Hanif calls back to us.

"To the ID codes office on Grosvenor," Erica replies. "You can let us off at University."

"No, no. I'll take you there. Drop you right on the doorstep." Erica tries to protest, but he won't hear of it. "Special service for new regular customers," he says. When he turns his attention back to the traffic, Erica shakes her head with a rueful smile. He is certainly dedicated.

I look around, trying to keep my mind off the reason for this trip. Erica is right about one thing: travelling like this will make it hard to forget the people who don't have our privileges. There are young women with small children, old women with carts of groceries. A man sits talking calmly to a companion who isn't there. Everyone has big, dark circles under their eyes. Can living in a city like this make people tired?

Sooner than I expect, the bus stops and the doors fly open. "Here you are, ladies, the ID codes building," Hanif says with a flourish. As we get off, he adds, "I hope you find what you're looking for."

"How did he know?" I ask Erica as the minibus pulls away.

"Everyone who comes here is looking for something. My, what a place."

I look up. The building is made of smooth grey stone, with huge supporting pillars. It must be very old. Inside, there's a big lobby with marble floors. A guard beckons us over to a security device. "Residency cards," he says, his voice flat and bored.

I never needed a residency card in Terra Nova. I didn't even have one until we prepared for this trip. The guard studies ours, then says, "You're visitors. Why would you need to come here?"

"We were both born here," Erica says in a clipped, efficient way. "We're going to Code Tracking." This seems to satisfy him. He scans our cards and gives us directions.

The office is large, but only a few people are working behind counters. More wait in chairs. "Your number is thirty-four," a disembodied voice says as we enter.

"We'd better sit down," Erica tells me.

While we wait, I pull my scribe from my bag and bring my ID code up on the screen. Looking at it reminds me how we found the micro-dot in my arm, just by accident, because it set off the kitchen scanner in Erica's house every time I went near it. Then an old techie in Kildevil,

Lem Howl, reconfigured a spare scanner so we could read the information hidden in my arm. That was just before the Uprising. The micro-dot gave us my birthdate, my name, the fact that I was born here, and the ID code. Those few clues allowed Lem to discover so much about my mother and my past. But the ID code has always been a mystery. How much more will we learn now?

I'm so lost in these thoughts, Erica has to nudge me when my number is finally called. I take a deep breath and step up to the counter. "I'd like to have the information for this ID code," I say, passing my scribe to the woman across the counter.

She shakes her head. "You can download the forms, but we can't work from your information. You'll have to have your micro-chip scanned."

I wasn't expecting this. "But why? The code is correct."

"We can't assume that. If we start with wrong information, we'll waste our time."

"All right, you can scan the micro-dot if you want to." I hold out my arm.

"We can't do that here. This is Code Tracking. Code Scanning is on the third floor. They'll provide you with an official download. We work from that."

"So I can do that now, and bring the download back to you?"

She gives me a look of pity mixed with exasperation. "You can make an appointment with Code Scanning today. I'm not sure how long the waiting list is right now. After you've been scanned, file your documents with us and we'll get started." She takes my scribe. "I'll load the forms and a map to show you how to get to Code Scanning."

When she passes my scribe back to me I quickly ask, "How long will it take, after I file the documents, to get the information from my ID code?"

"A few weeks at least," the woman says. "Number thirty-seven," she calls over my head.

The conversation is over.

An hour later, we are back on the street. "I have to wait a week for my appointment, and then even longer for them to trace my number. Those records could be accessed in seconds. Why does it take so long?" I ask as we walk away.

"There's a political reason, like just about everything else," Erica says. "After the Uprising, the bureaucracy was purged of anyone who seemed too closely connected with the Protectors. Then the Transitional Council decided to reduce the bureaucracy to save money. This was detailed in reports I read over the summer. There are half as many people working in government offices now as there were before, and that's not enough. They'll have to hire more people before things work efficiently again." She pats my arm. "Try not to be discouraged.

"Now, we have an appointment with Security at the headquarters of the Transitional Council to get our clearance," she continues. "The building's just a few blocks from here."

I follow Erica, suddenly wishing we could just go home to Terra Nova. I hate the crowds, the noise. The city is never silent. Even at night, lying in bed, I hear it hum and throb. I long for the silent green of Kildevil, for the space that gives me room to think.

We cross the street and Erica takes me through a maze of buildings that look newer than most. Suddenly, we're facing one of the prettiest buildings I've ever seen, a red stone structure, absolutely massive, with peaked roofs and domed towers, arches and round windows. But one wing is completely burnt out, the windows empty, the roof gone.

"What is that?" I ask.

"Queen's Park. Long ago, before the Dark Times, it was the legislature building, back when there was democracy.

For all of my lifetime, it was the seat of government as well."

"The Commission, you mean?"

"What we called the Commission in Terra Nova was called Queen's Park here. Collectively, all those dictatorships were known as the Protectors. Since Queen's Park fell in the Uprising, these buildings have been used by the Transitional Council. That burnt-out wing was destroyed in the riots last spring because people were afraid the Transitional Council wasn't going to hold elections. The destruction upset people, sobered things up a bit, maybe. No matter what governments do, the building is a symbol of this community. Luckily, most of it is still fine. We might be working here. I'm not sure if they've decided where our offices will be yet. But that's where Security is. Let's go."

We pass under the huge, red sandstone arches of the main entrance. The lobby is cluttered with security guards and their equipment. Once again, we present our residency cards and Erica explains why we are here.

"We need to record some information, to create a profile for Security," one guard says. "Step over here, one at a time." He points to me. "You first."

I've had reason to fear authority in my life. My heart pounds, but I obey. He puts my residency card in a slot, then positions me in front of a device. "Look straight ahead, don't move, don't blink," he commands. The device hums. "Keep still a bit longer," he says, as a beam of blue light scans my entire body. "You next," the guard says to Erica. She steps forward as he hands me my card. When he's finished, he says, "Your retinal scans are recorded now, but you won't have access to the buildings until your security badges are ready tomorrow morning."

"What was that about?" I whisper to Erica as we leave.

"That device recorded the patterns of the retinas in your eyes. It's a very effective way of identifying people."

"What about the blue light?" I ask.

Erica shrugs. "They're always coming up with new forms of security. It could have been anything. The university is very close." Erica points west. "Would you like to see it?"

"You mean the one where my mother worked? Where my parents met? Of course."

She smiles. "Are you hungry?"

I hadn't realized I was until she asked. "I'm starved."

"Follow me," she says. "I used to buy the best noodles from a cart in Queen's Park."

I look back at the building. "In there? They said we couldn't go inside until tomorrow."

Erica laughs. "I guess the Victorians who built this place weren't very imaginative. Queen's Park has been the name of all the governments who used this building, and the name of the old building itself, but it's also the name of the park. I'll show you."

Behind the stone building, we find a lovely park in the shape of a large circle, dotted with trees and benches, vendors' carts and statues. The traffic flows around us at a distance on either side, but the fuel-cell vehicles aren't bothersome. We must have driven past here in the minibus this morning, but I was too distracted to notice.

"There's the noodle cart I was thinking of," Erica says, "just where it used to be." She sounds delighted.

The smell of food makes my mouth water. A young woman with jet-black hair smiles at us from behind a rising curtain of steam. She looks too delicate to be working out here. In response to Erica's request, she quickly ladles hot broth and noodles into two big bowls on the spotless steel counter of her cart, then adds unusual foods—steamed greens, a sprinkling of green onions, I recognize those but not much else. "Don't eat the lemon grass or the chilies," Erica warns. "They're just for flavour." Then she hands me two sticks. "Chopsticks. Eat with these."

I search her face. "You're joking, aren't you?"

She laughs. "It's easier than it looks. I'll show you."

When I manage to get the food into my mouth it's delicious, hot and spicy, full of complex flavours. But I'm glad we're outside, because more than one noodle lands on the ground. Erica handles the chopsticks with ease, chatting with the vendor. She's delighted to discover this girl is the granddaughter of the woman she remembers.

About halfway through the meal, the chopsticks finally start to work. "It's not a bad way to eat," I say when I finish, quite awhile after Erica.

"If you're ready, the university's just over there." Erica points west.

"Can we see the labs?"

She looks puzzled. "What labs?"

"My father had a laboratory. It could have been there. Maybe I can see it."

A shadow passes over her face. "There were so many labs, Blake, and most of them were shut down. We don't even know if your father worked at the university. If we had his name . . ." she trails off, defeated. My father's name—the one piece of information my mother's friends couldn't give me. I only know it wasn't the same as my mother's or mine.

"It's all right," I tell her, quickly. "It was just a thought." Just a thought I've cherished ever since I knew we were coming here, but I don't say that.

"Let's go," Erica says. "It's a pretty place, you'll love it. After, we'll take a taxi home. We've had enough adventure for one day."

Before we can leave, a little girl sidles up to us. She might be seven. Her clothes are dirty cast-offs, her brown hair is matted. Her face is marred by an angry eruption. She stands in front of us and composes herself in an oddly formal way, clasping one hand with the other. Then she starts to sing:

I am a poor, wayfaring stranger
Travelling through this world of woe,
But there's no sorrow, no pain, no hardship
In that far land to which I go.
I'm going there to see my mother,
I'm going there, no more to roam,
I'm just a-going over Jordan
I'm just a-going over home.

Lots of street kids perform for money. For most, it's just a way to dignify begging. But this child's voice is sweet and true. The melody is haunting and her lyrics touch me to the core.

"Erica," I say when the song is finished, my voice weak.

"It's all right," she whispers quickly, and she crouches down. "Are you hungry, sweetheart?" The child nods.

Erica turns to the noodle cart, but the vendor protests. "You shouldn't encourage them," she says.

"Please," I say, "we just want to feed her." I've said "please," but I realize I've shouted.

The woman looks frightened for a nanosecond, then her faces goes blank. She does not want the trouble I'm causing. She quickly scoops noodles into a disposable container, covers it, and gives it to Erica, who pays. The child is gone the instant the container touches her hand.

I watch her scamper across the park. But when she stops, my heart does too. Some older kids are waiting for her. Even at this distance, their deliberately shredded clothing and elaborate hairstyles show they are Tribe members. The one with tattoos on her face is a leader. She says something to the child, who puts the bowl of noodles behind her back in response, as if trying to hide it. Older kids laugh and grab the bowl. Then the leader stands over the little girl, hands on her hips, and starts to lecture. We're too far away to hear words, but the tone of voice carries, angry, hectoring.

Erica starts forward but I grab her shoulder. "Don't," I say quickly. "This is their turf. We're outnumbered and they won't hesitate to come at you." Erica stops, reluctantly. She knows I'm right. "We'd better get out of here," I say. As we leave the park, I take a quick look back, just in time to see the child take a cuff on the ear. I'm sorry we tried to help her now.

4

The homeless kids who run the Tribes are very strict and brutal. When they tell you to do something, you do it. That was the most difficult year of my life. I did things I still can't talk about, things I have to shove into the darkest places in my mind so I can pretend they never happened.

—From the victim statement of Blake Raintree

Erica is subdued in the taxi home, disturbed by what we've witnessed. The child haunts me, too. "What was that song?" I ask.

"'Wayfaring Stranger.' I think it was sung by the African-American slaves, back in the nineteenth century," Erica says.

Well, that's appropriate. That little girl is a slave to her Tribe, just as I was, once.

Afternoon light floods the hall when we get home. The university was a disappointment. Against all logic, I'd hoped to find something that would connect me to my past, but it wasn't there. Still, I feel a lift as soon as I walk through the door. "Do you think houses have personalities?" I ask.

Erica smiles. "I think they might. What kind of a personality does this one have?"

I look around. The house has been retrofitted with the latest technology, but it looks exactly as it would have when it was built in the early twentieth century, with bookcases full of real books and overstuffed armchairs. This style, Erica has told me, is called Early Consumer, named after the ones who consumed the resources that should have sustained the lives of those who came after them.

"If this house were a person, it would be an old aunt, like someone out of a book, generous and welcoming, with just a few quirks. Someone who would give tea parties."

Erica laughs. "I think I know what you mean. This place fits like a slipper. Have you decided on a colour for your room yet?"

"I'm down to two, a light yellow and a light blue. I'll show you how they look after supper. I still can't believe the wall colour changes so easily. How does it work?"

"It's biotechnology, I think. I seem to remember something about cells taken from giant squid, but you'd really have to ask William."

I feel a pang of homesickness. "I wish he could be here," I say.

Erica sighs. "So do I. We've never spent so long apart. But he's doing good things in St. Pearl, sitting in the new House of Assembly. It's so strange, neither of us living in Kildevil. I hope we get a holo-conference line connected soon so we can at least see one another."

In the kitchen, Erica prints the schedule for the minibus on the network console. It comes out in a wildly elaborate font, with graphic flourishes. "I'll post this and put the micro-disk in here in case you want to download the times to your scribe. Now, I'll just check the console for messages." After a moment, she smiles. "William sends his love. He says Fraser would like to hear from you."

My shoulders tense involuntarily. "I know," I say, too quickly and too forcefully. Then I recover myself. "I do know." Fraser is working as William's parliamentary aide, so news of him is inevitable. Fraser swears he fell in love with me the first time he saw me, when I was sixteen and he was fifteen. I don't understand how anyone could do that. I don't really understand that kind of love. It makes me want to run away. When I came home from St. Pearl to Kildevil to prepare for this trip, I avoided being alone with Fraser as much as possible. I'm terrified of needing anything or anyone as much as I might need him. And yet, if his love vanished from my life, I'd be devastated.

Erica notices something's wrong. "Is he pressuring you for some kind of commitment, Blake?"

This is one reason I feel so badly. He isn't. Fraser never pressed me, turning away to hide his disappointment when I pretended to be too busy to spend time with him. "Not really," I tell Erica, "I just—I'll talk to him when I'm ready, but not yet. Could you tell him for me?"

"I'll tell him something. I think you're being very sensible." Erica approves, but I'm not sure I do. What looks like maturity to her seems more like cowardice to me.

Erica keeps checking messages. A few minutes later, she says, "Here's one from the Transitional Council. Our office is in the Queen's Park legislature building, a suite of offices actually, so we can hire more people when the work gets heavier. They want us to start setting up tomorrow, probably so they can say they've accomplished something before the reception tomorrow evening. Have you decided what you're going to wear yet?"

I groan. "I've been trying not to think about it. Those dresses the weavers made for me are beautiful, but they make me feel like an imposter. I don't belong in clothes like that." I don't tell her how nervous I am about meeting the other people on the Justice Council.

"Nonsense. You look lovely in them."

I knew when I took this job I'd have to meet new people, and sometimes dress in expensive clothes, but inside me there's a street kid who can't believe anyone would take me seriously in this new life. It's not like being a student in St. Pearl, where I dressed as I pleased. I'm dreading tomorrow.

We eat supper in comfortable silence, but when we finish, I'm too restless to sit still. Except for the grocery shopping we did on Sunday and our trip today, I've been in this house constantly, getting things unpacked and organized. I'm starting to feel trapped.

"Erica," I say as we finish eating, "I'd like to go out for a walk."

"Oh, Blake, I'd love to, but I have so much reading to do."

We have to have this conversation sometime. "That's fine. I can go alone." I brace myself.

Erica frowns. "I don't think it's safe—" she begins, but I cut her off.

"Erica, I'm eighteen. I lived in St. Pearl for two years. I'm used to being in a city." I don't even mention all the years I spent fending for myself.

Erica wavers. For a moment, I'm afraid she might try to forbid me to go out alone. I really don't want this to turn into a fight, but I can't be trapped inside.

"I don't want you out after dark," she says.

"That's fine. I still have a couple of hours." I'm trying to show I'm willing to compromise.

She stands and picks up her dishes. "Take your scribe and use your common sense." She sounds a little sharp. Then she looks helpless. "I suppose I'll have to get used to you going out without me. You're too old to be treated like a child. I'll watch for a message in case you need me." I can see she's fighting the desire to keep me home. She takes her dishes to the kitchen. "When you come back, we'll decide which dress you'll wear tomorrow. Go now, while there's still lots of daylight."

I wouldn't mind helping her clean up, but I know she'd rather have me back before dark, and I don't want to give her time to reconsider.

Being out in the city without Erica for the first time makes me feel giddy. I go to the end of our street and walk north, toward Bloor, retracing the route we've taken before so I don't get lost. The scribe in my pocket has maps for Toronto, but I want to see how long I can navigate without help. High Park is just across the road; the sun slants low through the trees beyond the far side. What should I do? Maybe I can see where the ghost library was.

At Bloor, I cross the road heading west along the north edge of the park. The sidewalk on this side is empty, but across the street people are walking, loitering, talking in groups. I'm so interested, I forget it's unwise to look around too openly. Before I know it, I've caught the eye of a man in tattered clothes who is lounging against a post. I look away, but not quickly enough.

"Hey, sweetheart," he calls across the street. "Wanna have some fun?" His speech is slurred. He starts to follow me. The busy traffic divides us, but there are traffic lights ahead and behind where he could cross. I don't want to show how frightened I am, so I keep walking, even though each step takes me farther away from Erica and safety. Maybe I could escape by going into the park, but it's already darker than the street. I feel like I'm trapped in a nightmare.

Then, incredibly, by the main gates ahead, I see someone I know. It's Hanif, with a pretty young woman by his side and a turbo-pram between them. I'm so relieved, I greet him like an old friend. "Hanif, do you live around here?"

He doesn't answer me directly. "The park is pleasant for the baby. This is Shauna." The woman smiles shyly at me, but says nothing. From the corner of my eye, I see the man who was following me turn away.

"Would you like to join us?" Hanif asks. Away from the minibus, he seems like a different person, more serious and formal.

"Yes, I would," I say.

Just inside the gates, I catch the smell of cooking food and I see a kind of camp under the trees, with tents, lines of laundry, even a few vehicles. I had assumed no one from the ghost library would be here, but I was wrong. There are adults, but many more children, some sitting in small groups, others juggling clubs and balancing on a slack rope. They look well fed and clean. Everyone seems busy, happy. I stop to watch.

"No tourists," someone says in a commanding voice. It takes a moment to find him. He's sitting with a child on a bench under a tree. This is the man I saw in the centre of everything when we drove past the ghost library. Everyone turns to stare at me, following his gaze.

"I'm not a tourist," I say. I want to sound bold, but my voice is timid. From the corner of my eye, I see Hanif and his family slip away. But I can't join them. I can't back down.

The man passes the strings on his fingers to the child beside him. He rises and comes toward me. He's an imposing figure. My heart pounds but I find I can't look away. His voice is angry. "No tourists, no gawkers, no children of the privileged come to see how the homeless survive. Away." He dismisses me with a theatrical wave of his hand.

When I speak, my words sound choked. "Who are you to call me privileged? I spent most of my life homeless."

He looks shocked, then skeptical. "I've seen every homeless child in this city at one time or another. I've never seen you."

"I lived in St. Pearl, in Terra Nova. My mother went there to escape the technocaust, but she died in a concentration camp." I stop in disgust. "This is crazy. I don't need to explain myself to you." I turn away.

"Wait, wait," he cries behind me. "I have misjudged you."

I turn around, still furious. I'm unwilling to leave, but I seem unable to forgive him. I throw him a challenging look, but his eyes are filled with compassion now. "I call myself Prospero," he says, "and these are my children. I make a place for all who have suffered as you have. Come, join us." He holds out his hand. He's magnetic. I can't stop myself from going to him. "Who are you?" Prospero asks. "And what brings you here?"

"My name is Blake Raintree. I saw the ghost library on Saturday, when we arrived, and I wanted to see it again."

"Come back next Saturday and help, if you like. We always need volunteers. But why are you so far from home?"

I tell him briefly about the Justice Council and Erica. "She was a leader of the resistance in Kildevil," I tell him.

"Is Kildevil near St. Pearl?" he asks.

"No, it's on the other side of the island, about seven hundred kilometres away."

"How did you get there, then?"

"When the government opened up work camps for homeless children I gave myself up. They moved me to a work camp in Kildevil. That was how I got away from the Tribe that had me in St. Pearl. Life with the Tribe was too . . . difficult." I falter. Even the memory still frightens me.

Prospero nods. "We try to find our children before the Tribes get them."

I remember the little girl by the noodle vendor. This place would be perfect for her. "What if they've already been taken by one?"

He frowns. "That would be more complicated. So, you lived in the work camp until the Uprising?" It seems he would rather talk about me.

"I was taken out of the work camp before the Uprising by Erica and her husband. I was almost like a servant at first, but then we found there was a micro-dot in my arm.

That helped us find out how I lost my mother in the technocaust. They made me part of their family, because they'd suffered in the technocaust too." He's such a sympathetic listener, I'm telling him things I would never normally tell a stranger. "After the Uprising, we helped run the work camp when the government staff abandoned it. We turned it into something like a school, then we tried to find homes for the children. Most of them have families now."

"A victim of the technocaust," Prospero says, almost to himself. Then he smiles, and his face is like a beacon of light. "But you found your way and you helped others. That's what I like to hear. Let me show you around."

He makes a sweeping gesture. "Our children are becoming performers. We teach them to juggle, tell stories, work with puppets, mime, do magic tricks. We give them food and shelter while they learn to make a living. Anything they earn while they live with us is saved until they're ready to set out on their own. Then we send them off with a bit of money. Many travel to other cities. The most talented stay here to teach others."

We watch the children for awhile. Everything is so interesting, I'm surprised when I notice it's almost dark. "I'd better go. Erica expected me home before now. She'll be worried."

"But you'll come back, " Prospero says.

I smile. "I'll come to help with the ghost library on Saturday."

"Good," Prospero says. "I'll be waiting for you."

The streetlights are already on. At the park gates, I fumble with the scribe and send Erica a message to tell her I'm on my way, wondering how I'll get home safely. Then I see Hanif and his family. They almost look as if they were waiting for me.

"We'll walk you home," Hanif says.

5

. . . even now, when I meet new people, I expect them to despise me because of what I have been.

—From the victim statement of Blake Raintree

"If you really want me to tie your hair back, Blake, you'll have to stay still longer than ten seconds."

I know I'm trying Erica's patience, but I can't actually make myself sit still. I smooth the fine woven cloth on my knees in an effort to calm myself. "Are you sure this colour looks good on me?"

"It's perfect. The red makes your hair look almost black."

All day, setting up in Queen's Park, I tried not to think about this evening. Our suite has five offices and a reception area, all accessed through a main door, so it was easy to spend all day in there, hiding from everyone else. I even packed a lunch. I'm not looking forward to meeting the other aides. My experience with the children of privilege has not been good. I'm sure they will look down on me when they know I was homeless.

"There," Erica says, stepping back to examine her work. "What do you think?"

"You've done a good job," I tell her. I wish I could sound more enthusiastic.

She gives my shoulder a quick squeeze. "You're going to be fine. Now, I have to dress."

Am I so transparent? Erica sees my anxieties even when I try to hide them. I take a deep breath and look around my new room. I loved it the moment I first saw it. I've settled on pale yellow for the walls now, and the skymaker has created the illusion of a dome-shaped ceiling. I've set it to project the sky as it would actually appear over Kildevil far to the east of us, so it's already starting to deepen into night. The evening star shows near the virtual horizon.

I want to turn off the lights and lie back on my bed, to watch the stars appear, faint lights that seem to wish themselves into being, but I'll wrinkle my dress if I do. Tomorrow, I tell myself, I'll be able to do this tomorrow. In fact, I could reset the program to start again when I come home tonight, but somehow, that seems like cheating. I like to think I can see exactly what people in Kildevil will when they look up tonight. I don't allow the thought of clouds to interfere with my fantasy.

Finally, I force myself to go downstairs. Erica joins me, wearing the beautiful blue skirt the weavers made for her and a white silk blouse. We both look like other people. I glance out the window. "There's a vehicle outside."

"That's our driver," Erica says. "Let's not keep him waiting."

The vehicle they sent for us is finer than anything I've ever seen. The driver actually opens the door to let us in and closes it behind us. The seats seem to be covered in leather.

"Erica," I whisper quickly before the driver gets in, "this is ridiculous."

"I'm afraid most of the evening will seem that way to you, Blake. The Transitional Council is accustomed to doing things in style."

"But what are we supposed to do tonight?"

"Nothing, really. There might be a few speeches, but mainly we're just supposed to mingle."

"What does that mean, 'mingle'?"

"It means we try to meet people we'll be working with and have light, meaningless conversations. The last thing anyone wants under these circumstances is a disagreement. Even a serious discussion is considered in poor taste."

In Kildevil, where Erica and I lived, people only talk when they have something to say. "I'm not sure I can do that for a whole evening."

Erica gives me a grim smile. "Neither am I. We'll have to do our best. If you notice me shouting at anyone, come over and spill a drink or knock over a tray of hors d'oeuvres."

"Of what?"

"Little snacks. You'll see." Erica laughs, but this reception sounds more and more intimidating. I sink back into the soft, deep seat, wishing we could spend the evening at home.

This is the first time I've gone right into the heart of the city. Buildings get higher and higher as we go, the streets more crowded. The city at night, seen from the inside of this luxury vehicle, looks like some sort of exotic jewel. I'm sure the same streets would look tawdry, even dangerous, from Hanif's minibus. Or walking alone. Suddenly, I'm glad of this luxury.

We turn into a curved driveway and the door beside me flies open. I instinctively shrink back, but Erica whispers, "Don't worry. It's just the doorman. We're here."

We are ushered through huge glass-and-gold doors into a large, busy room. "Where are we going?" I ask.

"The main ballroom," Erica replies. "According to that display, we go this way."

"We're going to watch a ball game?"

Erica laughs. "No history lesson tonight. Remind me to explain another time."

The ballroom turns out to be a large hall full of people. No balls in sight. The entrance is crowded with serious-looking men in black uniforms speaking quietly into audio implants. Erica goes to a table covered in little cards and tells the woman who we are. She picks cards with our names printed on them. "Just let me activate them," the woman says. "Oh, you're from Terra Nova! How lovely." The cards have some kind of display built into them. They've begun to show images from around Kildevil behind our glowing names. I stare at mine, fascinated.

"You're supposed to pin it on, dear," the woman says after a moment, not unkindly. Then I notice the line of people waiting for name cards that formed behind me while I stood gawking at the technology. I retreat to Erica, blushing.

"Well, they are amazing," Erica says. "I've never seen anything like them."

Not exactly a good start. Inside the ballroom, I immediately notice that the other women look nothing like us. The garments the weavers have made us are colourful and textured. These women wear sleek, microfibre dresses in dark, subdued tones. Some have dyed patterns on their arms and necks that blend seamlessly with their clothes. "Erica," I whisper, "we look like we just stepped out of a time capsule."

A young man with a tray of glasses goes by and Erica helps herself to two, giving one to me. She's not fazed. "We look like ourselves, Blake. That's exactly what we are. I think those people over there are members of the Transitional Council. I should introduce myself. Do you want to come?"

The thought of speaking to such important strangers scares me into complete silence. I shake my head.

Erica notices my alarm. "Do you mind if I go?" she asks. She sounds concerned.

"No, of course not," I manage to say. "I'll be fine."

I was hoping she'd understand I don't really mean it, but she smiles. "I'm sure you will. Try to make some friends."

She might as well tell me to try to fly. When she walks away I stand alone in the middle of the room, probably only for minutes, but it seems like hours. I'm seriously wondering if I could hide in a washroom when someone speaks close behind me.

"That dress is beautiful. It must have cost a fortune." The voice is soft, with a hint of laughter in it.

I swing around to find a girl about my age who is dressed like a butterfly herself, or at least how butterflies would dress if they wore clothing. She's wearing a long, coat-like garment, mostly dark blue, covered in bright flowers, with a big pink sash around her waist. The sleeves are huge and drape gracefully toward the floor on either side of her. Her black hair is swept up neatly, and her brown eyes twinkle. She seems to expect an answer from me.

"I didn't buy it," I tell her. "The weavers made it for me."

Her eyes widen. "Oh, you're the girl from Terra Nova. Blane?"

"Blake."

"Right. Blake Raintree. This is fabulous. I've never met anyone who actually knows weavers. I just love the cloth they make. My name is Kayko Miyazaki. I'm an aide, just like you, to my uncle Ken. He's over there." She waves vaguely in the direction Erica went. Her sleeve flutters like a banner.

"Where do you come from?" I ask.

"Here. Toronto. Uncle Kenji is from Winnipeg. I know everyone working for the Justice Council is supposed to be from somewhere else, but I begged and begged to be allowed to work for him. Finally, they got tired of listening to me and gave in."

"But you seem so . . . exotic." I'm afraid I've insulted her, but she just laughs.

"Oh, the kimono? It's Japanese. My family has lived here for hundreds of years, but I still think it's one of the prettiest ways of dressing, and I can get away with it, so why not? People have actually tried to speak Japanese to me a couple of times. Too bad I don't understand them." She laughs again.

I'm trying to take all this in. Kayko is like a storm of butterflies, but she seems friendly.

"Have you had anything to eat yet? There's great stuff over here." She leads the way. Several people turn to smile at us when we pass. I no longer feel hopelessly out of place. With Kayko, I'm suddenly special.

"Look," she says, "samosas, my favourite."

"I don't recognize any of this food," I tell her.

"Well, these are pot stickers from China, and chicken satay from Thailand." Then she points to tray of little rolls, beautifully arranged to make a flower pattern. "And this is sushi, from Japan." She lowers her voice to a whisper. "Don't tell anyone, but I don't really like most sushi. It's the seaweed." She shudders. "I can't believe nobody else is eating," she says, without pausing for breath. "I guess they're too sophisticated to be hungry. I'm starved. Help yourself."

Kayko heaps a small plate with a mountain of food. I take less, afraid of taking more than my share.

She finds a place to sit and attacks her plate with delight. "What's your town called?" she asks between bites. "It looks so pretty on your name tag."

"Kildevil," I tell her. "It's beautiful. All ocean and trees and mountains with the tops cut flat by glaciers thousands of years ago. It was a national park once, before the Dark Times."

"And you lived with weavers? Now that's exotic." The idea that someone dressed like Kayko might find the weavers exotic makes me smile.

"They're just sensible, hard-working women, really. I tried to apprentice as a weaver, just before the Uprising."

"Really? You know to make cloth like this?" Kayko reaches over and lovingly strokes the sleeve of my dress. It's such a friendly gesture, I'm suddenly happy I came here tonight.

It would be nice to tell her stories about weaving, but I can't lie to her. "Kayko, I was awful at it. Everything I did was wrong. I was just lucky we discovered I have a talent for working with ideas. Then, they let me leave my apprenticeship and go to St. Pearl to study."

"That must have been a change. What did you study?"

I hesitate. Even though the technocaust has been over for years, people were taught to hate the victims. There's still a permanent distaste for science and technology in the hearts of many, all tangled up with guilt now and very difficult to overcome. But it's an important part of what I am. She'll find out sometime. It might as well be now.

"Science." I throw the word out bald, to see her reaction. "Geology, cybernetics, nanotech, biotech. I'm going to be a scientist."

Kayko doesn't miss a beat. "Well, good for you. Uncle Kenji is a potter. He makes brilliant stuff. He was protected during the technocaust because pottery was classified as an ancient craft, but he's a scientist too. Everything he does with clay and glazes, with firing the pieces, it's all pure science. There's no guesswork, he understands the chemistry and such. He's always trying to interest me, but I'm such a bubblehead." Kayko laughs at herself. "And my parents use science too. They run a huge bakery company. Half the bread sold in Toronto comes from their factories. And nobody wanted to go without bread, of course, so they were protected too. The directive that protected us said bakeries have existed since ancient times, but our bakery used all the latest technology."

I smile when she says this, but I feel a pang of envy. Her family was so lucky, to have such knowledge and come through the technocaust unharmed. And they must be wealthy, too. We're very different.

Kayko is busy with her plate of treats and doesn't notice my sudden silence. "So what did you do for fun in Kildevil?" she asks.

"Fun?" The note of disbelief in my voice is unintentional. She took me by surprise.

She raises an eyebrow. "You're familiar with the concept? People doing things that don't serve any particular purpose, just for enjoyment?" But her sarcasm is tempered with humour.

How do you explain a whole way of life to someone? I'm so overwhelmed by the challenge that I fall silent.

"I was joking," Kayko says, a note of apology in her voice. She thinks I'm offended.

"I know. I'm just trying to think where fun fits into Kildevil. The kids play, of course, like any other kids." As I say this, I realize this isn't exactly true. I never played when I was a kid; everything I did was aimed at survival. Just for a flash, I wonder what Kayko will think when I tell her about my past. Not yet, I tell myself, don't push your luck, and I force my thoughts back to Kildevil. "But the adults work really hard to make a living off the land, and the weavers' work is very formalized. Then, of course, there was so much to do after the Uprising, organizing new forms of government and everything."

Kayko nods. "People are really impressed, you know, by how smoothly and quickly that happened in Terra Nova."

"Well, the weavers had been waiting for democracy to return, and it's easier in a place where everyone is connected," I say, but I glow with pleasure anyway. We have done well, and it's nice to know that's recognized.

"But that sort of life doesn't leave much time for fun."

"Well, this sort of life does. What have you done since you got here?"

"No much yet. Last night, I met a man named Prospero in High Park. That was fun."

"You mean you *saw* Prospero," Kayko says.

I can't imagine why she'd contradict me. "We saw him at the ghost library on Saturday, but I met him last night. He showed me around and told me I could come back anytime."

"That's amazing. Prospero's very difficult. We've been giving him money for years to help those kids and he still won't even talk to my father. It must be because you were a street kid yourself."

My head jerks back as if I've been slapped. "How did you know that?"

Kayko doesn't seem to notice my reaction. She smiles, pleased with herself. "When I finally got this job, I set out to learn as much about the other people on the Justice Council as I possibly could. I want to be a journalist. I've always dreamed about it, but now there's a free press again, it's like a dream come true. I already have my own holo-zine."

"You do?" My voice is filled with disbelief. Her family can't possibly be *that* rich.

She laughs. "Well, not a real one. It's not on a holo-display network. You have to download it from the net." Her face puckers as if she's just bitten something sour. "In fact, I've had to shut it down because of confidentiality. I can't write about anything I learn while I'm working with the Justice Council, and I can't imagine writing about anything else. In the meantime, though, I'm going to learn a lot that will help me cover stories in the future." Her eyes shine. "I thought I was going to be so bored tonight. I'm glad you're willing to talk to me."

"What do you mean?"

Kayko lowers her eyes. "A lot of people resent my family because we came through the technocaust unharmed. Nobody was even arrested." She lifts her chin. "It wasn't as if my family collaborated with Queen's Park like some people did, betraying friends and neighbours. The Miyazakis never did that. We were just lucky. Some people hate us anyway. I know a little bit about what happened to you. I thought you might hate me too."

"Kayko, when I came here tonight, I was afraid someone like you would look down on me because I've lived on the streets."

We both laugh.

"It's strange, isn't it?" she says. "We were just babies when the technocaust happened, but it just goes on and on. Maybe it's time everyone left all this stuff behind."

"Maybe," I reply cautiously. In fact, I can't imagine ever feeling that generous. But tonight, for the first time, I wish I could.

6

The newly formed Justice Council meets officially for the first time today. Rumours of serious conflict among the councillors already swirl through the corridors of Queen's Park.

—Editorial comment, *The Solar Flare,* September 3, 2370

This morning I wake up feeling happy for the first time since we arrived here. At first, I can't even think why. Then I remember Kayko. The Justice Council is having its first formal meeting today. I'll have to face a lot of strangers, but I'm eager to get to work anyway. I couldn't have imagined feeling like this yesterday.

At work, just before we reach our offices, someone calls my name through an open doorway.

"Blake, in here." It's Kayko. Inside, I find her wielding a dustcloth on the end of a long pole. The ceilings are high, and her cleaning method looks a little dangerous. She talks without looking down. "Expecting us to do our own cleaning is ridiculous," she grumbles as the pole wobbles back and forth. She makes a swipe, loses her grip, and almost drops the pole. "I guess I'd better stop," she says, to my relief. Then she notices Erica. "Excuse me, I thought Blake was alone." She pulls off her work gloves to shake hands while I introduce her.

"I'm pleased to meet you, Kayko," Erica says. "I met your uncle last night."

"This isn't the work I imagined when I begged him for this job," Kayko says. "I could bring staff from home and they'd do everything for everyone in a day, but the Transitional Council says it's too much of a security risk. Honestly."

"Kayko-chan, it will do you good to clean up after yourself for once in your life." The voice belongs to a man standing in the doorway of one of the inner offices. He is tall and slender, his hair slightly grey. The angular features of his face are touched with an affectionate smile.

"After *myself*?" Kayko says. "Uncle Kenji, this dust has probably been here since the Dark Times." He laughs. I can see how comfortable they are together.

After Kayko introduces me, Erica says, "I'll go check my mail, Blake. Why don't you stay and visit for a few minutes?" She seems to understand how much Kayko's friendship means to me.

"You'd better not use that dusting pole while Blake is here," Kenji says when Erica leaves. "I'll feel responsible if you injure her."

"Very funny. Why didn't they retrofit these walls with biotech? Dust is so—so retro," Kayko says as she tackles the storage units with a duster.

"This is a historic site. They don't want to lose the architectural detail."

"Oh, look, a spider," Kayko says happily. She coaxes it onto her duster. Then she says,

Don't worry, spider,
I keep house
casually.

Her uncle laughs. "Very good, Kayko. Issa is my favourite haiku master." He's delighted.

"I'll find a window for it." Kayko disappears into an inner office.

"Was that a poem?" I ask.

"Yes, a haiku. It's a Japanese form, a short poem usually about nature. That one was written over five hundred years ago."

Kayko returns without the spider. "I try to write haiku, but all my poems turn into senryu."

"There's nothing wrong with senryu," Kenji says. "Yours are quite good. You could write haiku if you'd just learn to leave yourself out of the poem."

"But that's harder than it sounds," Kayko says. She turns to me. "Do you like poetry?"

"I love it. It never occurred to me that there might be literature in other languages."

Kayko laughs. "Of course there is, silly. Japan is famous for its poetry. People all over the world write haiku."

My cheeks burn with shame. My knowledge of poetry comes mainly from the bibliotechs in the work camp. I must seem completely ignorant to these people.

"Kayko, try not to overwhelm your new friend," Kenji says. A hint of caution in his voice shows he's noticed my embarrassment.

And Kayko responds, making her voice more gentle. "I'm glad you like poetry, Blake. I've never had a friend who was serious about literature." This kindness soothes away my awkwardness. "Eat lunch with me," she adds. "It will fortify us for the afternoon ahead." She's herself again, cheerful and adventurous.

"If Erica doesn't need me," I say.

"The Council is meeting informally over lunch. Erica will find out when she checks her office memos," Kenji says. "We won't require our aides, so you're free."

"I know just where to go," Kayko says. "I'll come for you at noon."

I'm smiling again as I enter our offices. Erica looks up from the network console. "Blake, I won't be able to eat lunch with you today. Will you be all right on your own?"

"Kenji Miyazaki told me. I'll be fine," I say, and I tell her about Kayko's plan.

"Oh, that's good," she says, but she frowns.

"What's wrong?"

"Maybe nothing. It's just that, well, the Miyazakis are very wealthy people. Kayko has always lived an easy life, to say the least. I can't imagine anyone less like you. This work is going to be tedious and sometimes downright unpleasant. She might not be up to it."

"You think she'll get bored and quit?"

"Exactly. If you get attached to her, well, she might let you down."

I want to argue, but I don't know Kayko well enough to defend her yet. She might be frivolous. "Maybe you're wrong," I say without conviction.

Erica softens. "I hope so. Let's try to get organized."

I sit at my network console and begin sorting files from the Transitional Council. Maybe I should take Erica's warning to heart, but I can't. Kayko makes me happy. I'd have to work hard to be cautious of her, and I'm just not willing to do that.

I can hardly believe it's noon when I look up and see Kayko standing in the doorway.

"Let's go," she says. "We'll have to be quick to get back before the afternoon meetings start." Two beefy men follow us out of the legislature building. Kayko doesn't seem to notice them. "You don't mind walking, do you? I could have ordered a car, but it's just a few blocks and there's no parking over there anyway."

"A car?"

She points to a passing vehicle. "What do you call that?"

"A vehicle, of course."

She smiles. "That is so quaint. That must be because technology was so disrupted in Terra Nova during the Dark

Times. I did a whole course on the Dark Times once."

"At school?" I ask.

She looks embarrassed. "With a tutor, actually. My parents didn't send me to school."

We've been walking for blocks now, and the men who left Queen's Park when we did are still behind us. "Kayko," I say, "I think those men are following us."

"They are. Just ignore them." She sighs. "They're my bodyguards. I'm not allowed out without them. Actually, I'm surprised the Transitional Council didn't assign you a bodyguard."

I laugh. "I'm not important enough."

She shakes her head. "I'm sure that's not true. It must be an oversight."

"Well, I'm glad. I don't think I'd feel comfortable being followed all the time."

"I understand. I've had bodyguards all my life, and I still wish I didn't." Kayko navigates the busy streets, talking all the while. "I can't believe this is finally happening. It took forever to put the Justice Council together," she says.

"Do you know the other Council members?"

"Erica is the only one I've met so far, other than Uncle Kenji, I mean. But I know who they are and a bit about their backgrounds. And I think I know their positions."

"Their positions?"

"You know, where they stand on forgiveness and retribution. Or, at least, where they're likely to stand. That's what makes this so interesting. Nobody knows exactly what the Justice Council is going to do. Punish or pardon? We've been talking about it for months."

"You and your uncle, you mean?" I ask. I'm startled to discover I'm not the only one thinking about punishment. I never imagined anyone talking openly about it.

"My parents, too. Some families follow sports. In our family, it's politics. We're so excited to think that democracy may be restored. Oh, here we are. I reserved a table so we won't have to wait. I don't want to miss anything this afternoon." Kayko leads me into a beautiful room, everything decorated in red and gold. Thick carpets muffle conversation at dozens of tables. Servers, men and women, move through the room with carts.

Kayko's arrival causes an agreeable flutter. We are quickly whisked to a quiet corner and a server approaches. Kayko points to little bamboo baskets which are placed on the table for us. Not enough to make a meal. "Try these," she says, "*cha shu bao*—steamed buns filled with barbequed pork. You do eat meat, don't you? I forgot to ask."

I hope we're going to have more to eat, but I can't think of a polite way to say so. "I eat anything."

Kayko laughs as if I've made a joke, not realizing how true this has been in my life. "Well, this is dim sum. It's a very old Chinese style of food. You just choose what you want off the carts. Everything is little treats, but we won't eat the chicken feet."

"You're joking, aren't you?"

"Not about the chicken feet."

The men who followed us here are gone. "Kayko, where did the bodyguards go?"

"To an observation booth. This place is completely wired. If anything unusual happens, they'll be here in seconds. It's nicer than having them hover around, don't you think?"

I silently agree. As we eat, I'm glad for Erica's lessons with chopsticks. I'm not as out of place as I would have been a few days ago. I start to relax and enjoy myself. The food is strange but delicious, and Kayko seems delighted to show me each new delicacy. Then I recall what she said when we were walking. "Do you really know how everyone on the Justice Council is likely to think?"

Kayko nods. "There are three other Council members.

Monique Gaudet from Quebec. She is an important social theorist who fled to Haiti during the technocaust. Now she's back in Montreal. She's mostly likely to side with Uncle Ken and Erica. Her aide is Griffin Stockwood. I'm not sure how they're connected." She frowns. "I hate not knowing things like that.

"Then there's Daniel Massey from British Columbia. He made his fortune designing navigational technology for the Northwest Passage. What happened out there in the technocaust was particularly bad, so he's likely to be interested in revenge. His aide is Astral Robertson. I read that Daniel Massey is an old friend of Astral's family."

"Her name is Astral?"

"No, *his* name is Astral." We both giggle, then Kayko looks more sober. "It's a Truth Seeker name. I suppose I understand why he'd be good for this work. The Truth Seekers managed to stay clear of the technocaust. They didn't try to stop it, but they didn't involve themselves either, they just sat around in their divining parlours, trying to communicate with the spirits of the dead." Her tone is scornful. "They are not known for intellectual rigour. Our Astral is probably going to be a bit of a bubblehead." She gives me a wicked smile.

"The final Council member is Paulo de Lucas, who comes all the way from Cuba. Cuba has a longer tradition of democracy than any other part of North America, dating all the way back to the twenty-first century. They even managed to keep their parliament going through the environmental disasters and the Dark Times. We're not sure if that will make him moderate, or if he's more likely to be outraged by what happened here. The Cubans have their own history with dictatorship, long ago, and that may colour his feelings." The bubbleheaded butterfly is gone. This Kayko is deadly serious and full of information. I wish Erica could see her now.

"And his aide?"

"His aide is his only child, Luisa. She's seventeen. Last year, she eloped with the son of their driver. Their security people tracked the couple down and the marriage was annulled."

I'm astonished. "How do you know all that?"

Kayko shrugs. "It was an international scandal, all over the HD tabloids. The family is very prominent. Paulo de Lucas has been a senator, and his wife sits on the supreme court. I'm sure the de Lucases want Luisa to assume a leadership role in her country. Working for the Justice Council here would help those ambitions. Plus, she's far away from the unsuitable lover."

I try to imagine behaving so impulsively. I can't. I'm the sort of person who always wants my emotions to be tightly reined. I'm curious to meet Luisa.

"Which leaves my uncle and Erica," Kayko continues, drawing me back to the present. "Uncle Kenji's whole philosophy of life is about balance and moderation. He's not likely to suggest anything that would upset anyone, and he'll work toward compromise and consensus, you know, getting everyone to agree. He's very interested in healing the rifts of the past." She pauses to take a bite of a custard tart. "Now, Erica Townsend isn't exactly a moderate. She's always been passionate in her political life, a dedicated member of the resistance during the technocaust and after." It's strange to hear Kayko talk about Erica as if she were a stranger, but what she says is true. "She was a major force in the Uprising in Terra Nova. She and her husband worked to ensure that democracy was restored peacefully and relatively quickly, and that's what we need here, so she's a natural."

"Can I ask you a question?"

"Of course."

"I've been wondering for months why Erica was chosen for this Council. Is that why? What you just said?"

"Oh, there are dozens of good reasons. Her grasp of history, her experience as a leader. But maybe the most important thing, my parents said, is the fact that she suffered in the technocaust."

This surprises me. "Really? Why?"

"We have prisons full of people who were important in the government before the Uprising. Most of them had been in power since the technocaust. If someone like Uncle Ken calls for forgiveness, it's easy to dismiss him. No one in our family suffered. If someone like Erica asks, though, people will be forced to listen."

Forgiveness. Kayko just assumes I agree with Erica about it. Erica does too. "So that's why Erica was chosen, even though she was directly involved?" I ask.

Kayko smiles. "Exactly. And she and my uncle are what you'd call natural allies. Which is great, because otherwise you and I could never be friends."

The pot sticker I've just picked up stops halfway to my mouth. "What did you say?"

"If Erica didn't think the way my uncle does, I'd have to avoid you."

I'm glad Kayko is talking about Erica and not me. If she asked me directly, I couldn't lie. I'd have to tell her how I feel about the people who caused the technocaust. I put the pot sticker down. "Is that why you like me? Because we're on the same side?" I feel oddly empty.

Kayko laughs. "Of course not. I like you because you're bright and interesting. If you were boring, I'd still be nice, but I wouldn't want you for a friend." She changes the subject without taking a breath. "Look at the time. We'll have to hurry to get back before the afternoon session starts." Kayko flies from the table, stopping long enough to have our meal placed on her parents' account. I can only follow, wondering how I'll manage to keep up with her, in every way imaginable.

7

Will this new Justice Council resolve the tensions in our society? Or will we lapse into chaos once again?

—Editorial comment, *The Solar Flare,* September 3, 2370

"Goodness, Blake, I was getting ready to leave without you."

I feel the sting of disapproval in Erica's voice but I know it's really not aimed at me. I wish I could tell her Kayko is more than she seems, but I only have time to scoop up my scribe on the way out the door. Erica's anger is like a cloud passing over the sun on a windy day, though. It's gone almost before you feel it. So, when we meet the Miyazakis in the hall, she smiles at Kayko and falls into conversation with Kenji. Kayko and I follow behind.

"Give me your address," Kayko whispers, "so we can message while the meeting is on."

I know Erica would disapprove but I don't want to draw her attention, so I quickly whisper the address to Kayko.

The meeting room is right out of the distant past, with wood panelling, a high ceiling, and a bank of huge windows on one wall. It's a much larger room than we need. The Council members sit at a heavy wooden table, and we aides take our places in a second ring of chairs behind them. Kayko sits behind her uncle, opposite me. A chair at the head of the table is empty.

I quickly glance around. It's easy to figure out who the other Council members are from Kayko's descriptions. The man beside us with a girl sitting behind him must be Paulo de Lucas. Both have the same dark eyes. I was expecting Luisa to look remarkable, passionate, and beautiful I suppose, or tragic. Instead, she has an open, pleasant face. I want to know how anyone could be so impulsive, but her appearance gives no clue.

Across the table, beside Kenji Miyazaki, is Monique Gaudet, an elegant woman, small but slender, dressed in a carefully tailored grey microfibre suit. Her blond hair is cut in an elaborate geometric pattern. An older man across the table with curly grey hair must be Daniel Massey. That leaves the two male aides. There's a slight, blond man in his early twenties sitting behind Monique Gaudet. His fair hair is already thinning. He looks serious and scholarly and I suppose he must be Griffin Stockwood.

I've already formed a picture of Astral Robertson because of Kayko's description. He should be young and inattentive, someone who will constantly forget everything he's just heard. But the aide behind Daniel Massey looks nothing like this. He is older than the other aides, in his late twenties. He's tall enough to drape over his chair with a studied casualness. A shock of dark hair falls over one eye. He radiates concentration. He must sense my stare, because he looks directly at me and raises one eyebrow in a silent question, as if to challenge my foolish preconceptions about him. His eyes are ice-blue, searching, and intelligent. I force myself to hold his gaze and give him a weak smile, totally unnerved. This is Astral Robertson?

"We're just waiting for Dr. Siegel, head of the Transitional Council, to arrive," Kenji Miyazaki says. "His staff has been trying to get answers to some questions that arose over lunch. I believe some of us have not met yet. We should go around the table and introduce ourselves while we're waiting."

Monique Gaudet introduces Griffin Stockwood as "one of my most promising students at the New Sorbonne in Port-au-Prince." In response to her praise, Griffin looks at us all with such trust and enthusiasm that I like him immediately. Kayko smiles with satisfaction as she is finally able to understand the connection between Monique and her aide. But Daniel Massey is a man of few words, it seems, introducing the man behind him simply as "my aide, Astral Robertson." An older, balding man enters the room and quietly takes his place at the head of the table, nodding to indicate we should continue without interruption.

When Paulo de Lucas introduces his daughter, his pride is evident. In response, Luisa smiles at him. If there was strife between them, it seems long past.

Erica refers to herself only as "a historian whose life was changed forever by the maelstrom of the technocaust." She says nothing about her role in the resistance. I notice several people at the table smile at her modesty. I am afraid she will embarrass me by talking about my life, but her introduction is brief. "Blake's story is complex," she ends. "I'm sure you'll learn more as you work with her."

Which leaves Kenji Miyazaki. "I am a potter, originally from Toronto, but living in Winnipeg for more than twenty years and active in the Potters' Guild. My aide is my niece Kayko, who hopes to become journalist. And now, as Dr. Seigel has joined us, perhaps we can begin." He continues without pausing. "Over lunch, we all agreed that this society will never be ready to move ahead until we can address the horrors of the technocaust." A look of frustration passes over his face. "Beyond that, we've hit a stone wall, it seems. There is no consensus on what should happen to those who caused the technocaust. Should they be tried for crimes against humanity? Should they be charged with crimes against the individuals who suffered at their hands? Should they be required to make a full confession of their wrongdoings? Will victims be allowed to sue individuals for compensation, or will the state make reparation? Today, we only know that we are very far from consensus. In light of this, we have decided to start by gathering some information."

Dr. Siegel frowns. "We had hoped you would begin actual hearings as quickly as possible," he begins, but Erica interrupts him.

"Dr. Siegel, my colleague may have understated the depth of this rift. During lunch today, we came close to deciding it would be impossible for this group to reach any kind of consensus, ever. We need time to see if we can, in fact, function as a working council."

Dr. Siegel blanches. "Surely your divisions can't be that serious."

"I'm afraid they are," Daniel Massey says.

Monique Gaudet smiles. "At least we agree on something."

For people who can barely work together, they seem very civil.

"Very well, then," Dr. Siegel says. "And you've proposed to begin in the East End Detention Centre?"

"Yes. We want to start by taking statements from those who were important in the technocaust," Kenji Miyazaki says. "That is why we asked you to contact the prison officials. When we've heard from them—"

"We already have their response," Dr. Siegel interrupts. "It was swift and unequivocal."

"They said no?" Erica looks alarmed.

"Not exactly. You must understand security is their primary concern, and not only because prisoners might try to escape. Last year, they thwarted a group of terrorists who tried to infiltrate the prison staff. They planned to kill members of the former government by poisoning their food."

Kayko gasps, then covers her mouth as if to push the sound back in, but Dr. Siegel nods in sympathy. "It is shocking. We kept the story out of the press to discourage imitators. I can speak freely here because you are all bound by confidentiality.

"So, your access to these prisoners will be limited. You can present the prison officials with a list of the people you wish to see, but only actual councillors will be allowed access. If you require assistance, prison staff will be provided."

I don't know whether to feel relieved or disappointed. What would it be like, to meet these people and hear their stories? We're talking about the ones who ruined my life, who took my father and caused my mother to flee toward her death.

"These restrictions seem reasonable," Kenji Miyazaki says. "Can we agree to accept them?" While they talk, the message icon on my scribe begins to flash. I touch it.

"*This is awful,*" it reads. "*What will *we* do?*" It's from Kayko. I look across the table and shake my head. I have no idea what we'll do instead.

"We can accept these terms," Monique Gaudet says when the councillors finish.

Dr. Siegel looks relieved. "Prison officials can offer you access three days a week. They will provide transportation, picking you up and returning you here in one of their vehicles."

"And what about the archival materials we've requested?" Erica asks.

Kayko gives me a look so transparent, she might have spoken the words: Do you know what she's talking about? Again, I shake my head. Erica is fascinated by the past, of course, but I can't imagine she's asking for any trivial reason.

"We will contact the national archives of Australia and South Africa as soon as they open. It's still early morning on that side of the world, " Dr. Siegel replies. "I'm sure they will cooperate. The material will be digital, of course, so we'll have it in a matter of hours if our requests are approved."

"And viewing rooms?" Erica asks.

"We have media rooms in the basement that are fully equipped for holo-projection and -production. If we call a press conference, we'll require those rooms to be vacated, but that shouldn't happen often."

Erica looks pleased as she thanks him.

Dr. Siegel rises. "If there are no other questions, I'll leave you to your work. Feel free to call on me any time." He rises to go, then turns back. "I must stress how important it is for the Justice Council to succeed. Do whatever you must to bring closure for the victims of the previous government. This is your mandate. It's no exaggeration to say that the hopes of this entire society rest on your shoulders. We can't burden a newly elected government with the task of addressing the past. You must clear the way. " His voice rises. "If you resign, there would most certainly be rioting. The last time that happened, people died. We could be faced with the overthrow of the Transitional Council and a complete collapse of government. Chaos would ensue. You *must* find a way to work together."

As he leaves, a heavy silence falls. Finally, Daniel Massey speaks. "That kind of hyperbole is hardly helpful."

"I don't think he was exaggerating," Erica says in a quiet voice she uses only when she's furious. I realize much of their civility was for Dr. Siegel's sake.

Kenji intervenes. "I think that went well. We have an opportunity to see if we can work out our differences. If we can't, our investigations should be useful to those who replace us."

Before or after the chaos, I think, but of course, I say nothing.

"Erica, since it was your idea, perhaps you should explain to our aides what they can do while we interview the prisoners," Monique Gaudet says.

Erica smiles. "Yes, that works out very well. We want you to undertake some independent research, and now, it seems, you'll have time." She moves back from the table, beside me, to include us all. "We decided it would be helpful to have a complete picture of the technocaust, or at least as complete a picture as we can recreate. The official records were destroyed long ago, and the media were not allowed to report on what was happening after the technocaust started. Of course, Europe and Asia were under complete quarantine during that decade because of that terrible strain of antibiotic-resistant bubonic plague. But there should be good records in South Africa and Australia until the time foreign reporters were expelled. Both countries are stable democracies with freedom of speech, so the media reports will be honest. South Africa should be especially happy to cooperate. That country was our greatest ally in our struggle to overthrow the corrupt Protectors before the Uprising, organizing the boycott of North American goods that helped create an awareness of our problems around the world.

"So, while we are in the East End Detention Centre, you five aides can sort through the media reports to create a picture of the technocaust. We will provide you with the names and images of people of interest."

"Will you expect some kind of report?" Astral Robertson asks.

"Yes," Erica says. "We hope you will eventually present what you've found. In the meantime, feel free to ask us questions. So much of the history of these events has been suppressed or even distorted, we expect you to know very little."

"That sounds entirely fair," Astral says. I'm struck by the way he treats Erica, as if he were her equal. There's nothing disrespectful in his bearing but I'm taken aback by his confidence.

Griffin Stockwood speaks. "Some of you know I'm studying to be an historian. Would it be appropriate for me to brief the other aides on the history leading up to the technocaust? I've been trying to piece it together for a while now. I have some theories."

Erica beams at him. "What a good idea. I'd like the councillors to attend, too, if you don't mind, Griffin, so we can hear your ideas and maybe add some of our own."

"Of course, if you think it would be useful." Griffin looks overwhelmed.

"An excellent idea, Griffin," Monique says. "Now, I think we've had all the meetings we can tolerate for today. If everyone agrees, I suggest we adjourn."

The other council members seem grateful for this suggestion. As they relax, I notice how haggard they look. I'm just about to shut down my scribe when the mail icon flashes again. It's Kayko. "*We're going to die of boredom.*" I nod in agreement.

But Griffin Stockwood practically bounces across the room to grab Erica's hand. "I don't know how to thank you for this opportunity," he says. "I never imagined access to such great sources. Just to be in Ontario is amazing. I have roots here that go all the way back to the eighteenth century."

"Oh, your ancestors were United Empire Loyalists?" she asks. I can tell by her smile that she's charmed by his enthusiasm, by his use of the historic name for the province that once covered such a vast area.

Griffin beams. "Yes! Hardly anyone knows about them now. And one of my ancestors was a famous twentieth-century historian here in Toronto, Rodney Stockwood."

"The economic historian?" Erica says. "My master's thesis was based on his work."

"That's fantastic. I can't tell you what an honour it is to be working with you."

Erica, Griffin, and Monique Gaudet chat and smile, oblivious to the tensions around them as everyone else files silently from the room. I consider waiting for Erica, but Kayko grabs my arm and practically drags me with her. We're barely away from the others when she starts to grumble. "I can't believe this. I hate history." She turns on her uncle. "You get to do all the interesting stuff while we slave away."

I'm shocked by her rudeness, but he just smiles. "Kayko-chan, a journalist should have a good grounding in history. These reports were unavailable until now. Griffin's right. It's a great opportunity."

Kayko makes a sour face as we enter their offices. "If there's anything worse than boring work, it's doing it with someone who thinks it's fun. What a . . . keener."

Kenji laughs out loud. "Where did you pick up such an archaic expression?"

"In my twentieth-century media course. It fits, doesn't it?"

"Don't be too hard on Griffin, Kayko. An experienced historian will be useful in this work," Kenji says, and this silences Kayko because it's true.

"I think you'll find Griffin a real asset," Erica says. I didn't see her enter the room. "He's been struggling to educate himself about the history of the technocaust with the few sources available. Monique has done us a favour by bringing him here."

"What about Astral Robertson?" Kayko asks. "What's his background?"

"We don't know," Erica replies. "Daniel Massey is not the most forthcoming person."

"But he's got to be a Truth Seeker with a name like that," Kayko persists. "I wasn't expecting him to be so . . . so focussed."

"Kayko," Kenji says, "you shouldn't stereotype people by their religion. That's like someone assuming you'll love sushi. I expect better of you." He sounds unusually stern.

"Well, in my experience, Truth Seekers can be, shall we say, resistant to learning. There's a strong anti-intellectual streak in their culture."

I'm surprised to hear Erica come to Kayko's defence. She turns to me, adding, "Marrella came from a Truth Seeker family, although I gather they weren't very religious."

"Who's Marrella?" Kayko asks.

"She was—I mean, is—a bio-indicator in Kildevil," I tell her. "Before the Uprising, Erica's husband William was trying to train her to make UV readings, to help monitor the ozone layer. She was so reluctant to learn that they took me out of the work camp for homeless children to try to help her."

Erica smiles. "That was the best thing about Marrella's refusal to learn: it brought Blake to us."

"Is that why she was trying to contact what she called 'discarnate beings'?" I ask.

Erica looks shocked. "She did that? I never knew. She must have been more religious than we assumed."

"I don't think so," I say cautiously. Marrella and I are friends now, but the memory of her unkindness those first few weeks still stings. "She wanted them to give her the knowledge she needed without doing any work. I got the impression it was just a shortcut."

"Well, that's what Truth Seekers do, isn't it?" Kayko says. "They use their religion to get the answers they want and ignore reality."

"Kayko!" There's real anger in Kenji's voice now.

Erica quickly intervenes. "In fact, the point of the Truth Seeker religion was to gain knowledge by communicating with the dead. During the Dark Times, when so much was lost, the religion emerged as a desperate way of trying to recover knowledge. What Marrella was doing made perfect sense, given her background. But I don't get the impression Astral is going to behave that way, do you?"

The question is directed at Kayko. Although her uncle has said very little, she looks chastened. "No," she says, "I don't." Her tone is almost an apology.

Kenji only nods, but his nod implies forgiveness and Kayko relaxes. Their entire fight is over in two short sentences. That's how well they understand each other. And I have to hide a small smile, seeing how Erica came to Kayko's rescue. She must be warming up to her.

But I'm still troubled by this afternoon's meeting. "Did you really come close to quitting this morning?" I ask.

"Yes, we did. Paulo de Lucas and Daniel Massey want trials and punishment," Erica says. "They think that's the only solution people will accept."

"They might be right." The truth slips out before I can stop myself. Everyone stares at me.

Kenji recovers from his shock first. "They might be, but we hope not." Luckily, he seems to assume I'm talking about the way other people feel, not myself. I don't look at Erica.

"Kenji Miyazaki?" a disembodied voice says from the network console. "Is anyone there?"

"Yes, this is Ken Miyazaki."

"This is Security. We're trying to locate Erica Townsend. She isn't in her office."

"I'm here," Erica says.

"The archivist has a question for you. Could you go to his office?"

"I'll be right there," she says.

Before Erica goes, I can't resist asking one more question. "Do you think this Justice Council can work?"

Kenji and Erica answer at the same time. "We have to hope," Kenji says. "It had better," Erica replies.

8

Escaping from the Tribe was one of the most important things that ever happened to me.

—From the victim statement of Blake Raintree

Erica and I are both worn out by the stress of the day. We fall into a gloomy silence on the bus ride home that lasts into supper. As we eat, I think back to the beginning of my program of study in St. Pearl, two years ago. I was so excited. Even when the work got so difficult it scared me, I always felt the same. How could I have left that behind? Coming here seems like a big mistake. I feel more and more like I'm pretending to be something I'm not. Maybe I want to be part of the effort to put things back together. But maybe all I really want is to see the people who caused the technocaust pay for what they've done. If Erica knew that, if Kayko did, what would they think of me? Now, it seems, the aides will be doing something like history research. I feel the way Kayko does. The prospect bores me to death.

That night, I dream I'm back with the Tribe, lying on the floor of the big room in the abandoned building. We slept in the daytime because the Commission told everyone to be afraid of ultraviolet radiation, even though the ozone layer was recovering. The heat is suffocating, and reflections of the sun off the water of the harbour play on the ceiling, so bright I can see them even when my eyes are closed. I'm awake in the dream, and the familiar smell of unwashed bodies, the stench of the harbour, is vivid. I turn, and the little girl from the noodle stand is sleeping beside me. That's all, but the dream seems so real. When I wake, it takes a few moments to realize I'm no longer the slave of a Tribe.

But others still are. I try to shake the dream image of that little girl from my mind, but I can't. That's not why I'm here, I tell myself, but that doesn't help. By the time we reach work, I know I've got to do something for her.

There's a protest outside the legislature today, mostly women with babies and small children, a few men, carrying signs and chanting, "Daycare now! Daycare now!" They have my sympathy, but my stomach clenches involuntarily as we pass them.

Inside the building, a security officer stops me. "Aides for the Justice Council are requested to go directly to the media rooms today. Down those stairs and follow the signs."

In the basement, I follow the sound of conversation to find Luisa de Lucas and Astral Robertson sitting together in the conference room. I wish I'd gone to find Kayko first.

Before I can even sit down, Astral pins me with a look. "You're the homeless child, aren't you? I mean, you were." He sounds angry, as if my past were my fault.

I'm almost too shocked to reply. "Yes," I manage to say, ducking my head to avoid those eyes.

"You lost your mother in the technocaust," he continues. I can't imagine why he's doing this until he speaks again. "I did too."

My head comes up. "You? I thought Truth Seekers weren't harmed in the technocaust." I realize, too late, I've let him know we've been talking about him. I blush to remember what Kayko said yesterday.

But he ignores this, pressing on with his own questions. "How old were you? You couldn't have been every old."

"I was two."

"Two!" His voice is filled with scorn, as if he blames me for being so young. It's too much. Luisa looks too surprised to speak. I'm ready to turn and flee but Kayko and Griffin enter with a man I've never seen. They are laughing. Suddenly everything's normal again. I quickly sit as the newcomers seat themselves.

The stranger is a portly man in his thirties with long black hair and a beard. He seems pleasant and relaxed. "So this is everyone?" he asks, and Griffin nods. "Excellent. I'm Terry Raven, the archivist. I thought we'd better meet to discuss the materials you're getting."

Griffin leans forward in his seat. "How much is there?"

"I had a look at the indexes. Most of the material is holographic; it was shot for newscasts. But they didn't just send the finished product. This is raw, unedited footage of holoprojections. You have hours of material."

"Fantastic," Griffin says before anyone else can react.

Terry Raven smiles. "Once the technocaust actually starts, there's very little, but until then, the record should be quite complete. I need to know how much technical expertise we have here. Has anyone worked in an archive before?"

"I have," Griffin says quickly.

"So have I." We all turn to Luisa. Her voice is low and musical with a trace of an accent. "I spend one season—how do you say this?—semester, in the National Archives in Havana as part of my education." I'm surprised—and a little disappointed—by how serious she seems, how normal. I was hoping to learn something from her, something about feeling and love.

"Good," Terry says. "Then you'll both know how to use the indexes. Eventually, these materials will come to our archives. The micro-disks must be kept in order and not lost. It's too easy for those little things to disappear. Does anyone know how to run the holo-projectors?"

"I do," Kayko says.

Terry's dark eyebrows fly toward his hairline. "You surprise me. I knew about your holo-zine, of course, but I assumed you'd have, well, people to do the technical part."

"Servants, you mean," Kayko says. She sounds mildly annoyed and I gather she's used to this conversation. "In my family, if you want to do something, you have to learn to do it yourself."

Terry looks relieved. "Then you'll be able to work without extra staff. We need a few days to prepare our own indexes. You can get started on Monday."

We rise to leave. I try to get to Kayko as quickly as I can, but Astral is faster. He grabs me by the elbow. "Listen," he says in a low, urgent voice, "I'm sorry I attacked you like that. I didn't mean to. Sometimes, I get so angry I can hardly breathe. Do you understand?" I'm too surprised to reply. He looks at me for a long moment and then he says, "Of course you do." He lets go of my arm and leaves without saying another word.

"What was that about?" Kayko asks.

"Just a misunderstanding," I say. I can see she'd like to know more but I'm glad she doesn't press me.

9

Three Tribe members were killed last night in what was apparently a clash over territory at the old opera house. The dead appear to range in age from ten to fifteen.

—Newscast, *The Solar Flare,* September 6, 2370

On Friday, our aim is to finish organizing our offices and plan a weekly work schedule. The Council is still meeting "informally" over lunch, a process Erica says is starting to give her heartburn. Kayko is still taking me to exotic restaurants. Erica strongly suggests we eat in the cafeteria with the other aides, but after that encounter with Astral, I would rather keep my distance. All the while, I find I cannot get that little girl out of my mind. I have to see her again. It's hard to imagine Kayko at a vendor's cart, but I've got to try. I catch her in the hall outside our offices on Friday morning.

"What would you like today," she says, "Thai or Hungarian?"

"We can get really good noodles just behind the building here," I say. "How about that?"

She looks blank. "There's nothing back there but—Blake, you don't want to eat off a cart." It's not a question.

"Yes! The food is really good! Erica took me there!" I force the exclamation points into my voice.

"If you really want to. But my bodyguards will be, well, apparent. Everyone will see them."

I'd forgotten about them. I feel a wave of pure relief to know we won't be out there alone. "That's fine!" This time, the emphasis is not forced.

Kayko smiles. "You're acting funny today. What's going on?"

I wouldn't mind telling her, but Erica might overhear us here. "Just trust me, all right?" I whisper. Kayko leaves looking delighted by the promise of a mystery.

The morning goes slowly. I have to redo one directory index three times, but I keep at it, doggedly, so Erica won't notice how anxious I am. Finally, Kayko comes to the door.

"Where are you off to today?" Erica asks.

"Oh, Oriental food, you know," I wave my hand as if it's too much to keep track of.

Erica gives me a sharp look. She knows something isn't right. Then, to my relief, she lets it go. "Have a good lunch," she says.

"What are we doing?" Kayko asks as we leave the building.

I glance back to make sure her bodyguards are with us. They are. "Maybe nothing. I want to find a little girl. She hangs around the noodle cart."

"A homeless girl? Does she have a family?"

"No, she's with a Tribe. I'll tell you more later."

Kayko looks back, too. "For once, I'm glad they're with me," she says.

"So am I."

I've been wondering how the noodle vendor will react, but if she recognizes me, she gives no sign. The bodyguards seat themselves at a nearby cart, looking like two ordinary office workers. Office workers with audio implants who happen to be extremely athletic.

"These really are good noodles," Kayko says after awhile.

I'm glad she's happy, but as we eat, a heavy disappointment settles on my chest. There's no sign of the child. Maybe I'll never see her again. I scan beyond the park.

Across the street, some Tribe members are patrolling their territory. An old man crosses their path. He's pushing a battered turbo-pram crammed with cast-off, empty fuel cells. The food I've just eaten turns to stone. Empty fuel cells have a cash value.

"I wonder—" Kayko starts to say, then she sees my face. "Blake, what's wrong?"

"Across the street," I manage to whisper.

The kids from the Tribe have already swarmed the old man. Kayko waves her arm in the direction of the trouble. I don't understand, but, in response, her bodyguards rise. They don't hurry but there's no mistaking their intent. Even before they cross at the traffic light, the kids notice them and scatter, gone by the time Kayko's men reach the old man. The bodyguards help him load spilled fuel cells back into his turbo-pram, then they stay on that side of the street, conspicuously watching as he makes his way.

"That was amazing," I say.

Kayko grins. "I have to admit, they have their uses."

My appetite is ruined. I watch Kayko finish eating in silence.

"We can't sit here all afternoon," Kayko says gently.

"I know," I start to say. Then I see her, the girl. She slips out from behind a tree as if she's always been there, and sings for us, the song she sang before.

I kneel beside her when she finishes. "Hello, sweetheart. What's your name?"

Her eyes grow large with apprehension. The stranger who is too interested, too friendly, is always a danger. I remember. Her eyes flick toward the noodle cart. She's not sure what I want, but she's hungry enough to cooperate. "Sparrow," she whispers.

"That's such a pretty song, Sparrow. Where did you learn it?"

Her eyes go blank. "Time before," she says, her voice flat. I curse myself for forgetting. The Tribes don't let kids talk about the lives they had before. In St. Pearl, we were taught to call the past "last lifetime." Anything more, any detail about the past, would earn a beating.

"Do you live with a Tribe, honey?" I ask, already knowing the answer. She nods but says nothing. I'd hoped for more, but maybe that's enough for today. "Let me buy you some noodles."

The vendor hands them over, stone-faced but without complaint. "Take them somewhere where you can eat them yourself," I whisper to her. She looks up, amazed. Then she's gone.

"That's all," I tell Kayko. "We can go back."

"You just wanted to feed her?" Kayko sounds incredulous as she hops off her stool.

"I meant to find out all I could about her, but she was so frightened."

"Blake, what do you want to do, really?" Kayko asks as we walk back to work.

What I really want is to release her from the tight web of rules and punishments her Tribe has wound around her. To find the child inside that cocoon and set her free. I don't try to explain this to Kayko. I'm not sure I could. "I'd like to get her away from that Tribe," is what I say.

"Then what? You're going to adopt her?"

"I thought Prospero might take her."

"You thought. Have you asked him?" Under Kayko's scrutiny, the whole idea seems ridiculous.

"Not yet."

"Blake, you don't know how dangerous this is—" Kayko starts to say, but I cut her off.

"I think I do. I lived with a Tribe, you know." I don't try to hide my anger.

She softens. "They're not the only problem. People take kids like her for their organs, to work with toxic waste—you must know more about this than I do. If the authorities caught you taking a child like that, it wouldn't look good. You could get deported back to Terra Nova."

I stop walking. "They wouldn't do that, would they?"

"They might. They'd be more likely to if you already had a criminal past." She pauses. "You don't, do you?"

I laugh and start walking again. "I do, as a matter of fact, but I have no record. They never bothered to arrest us."

"Well that was lucky."

"Not really. When street kids were too bothersome, death squads took care of them."

Kayko stops, stunned. "You mean they were killed?"

"That's what happened to the homeless girl who cared for me. That's how I ended up with a Tribe." This isn't something I talk about easily, but I find I can tell Kayko.

She shakes her head. "I can't imagine. Was it awful, living with that Tribe?"

"The worst thing that ever happened to me. I lied, I stole—that isn't the half of it. I'd be dead by now if I hadn't given myself up to the Commission."

Kayko grabs my arm. "Look, Blake, this is probably crazy and dangerous, but if you want to rescue that little girl, I'll do whatever I can to help."

Kayko's eyes have lost their mischievous twinkle. I don't have to tell her this isn't some kind of game. "Thank you," I say. "I'll try to talk to Prospero over the weekend."

Until Kayko offered to help, rescuing Sparrow was just a dream. Now, it could be possible. But only if Prospero agrees to take her. Luckily, Erica already knows I plan to volunteer at the ghost library. For the rest of the day I think of little else.

I wake early Saturday morning, the sun barely up. Nervous

energy and the vague shadows of disturbing dreams propel me out of bed. I eat quickly, leave a note for Erica, and I'm gone before she wakes. But, when I reach the park, I realize how hard it will be to talk to Prospero. Even this early in the day, preparations for the ghost library have taken over his camp and everyone in it. I'm quickly handed over to other volunteers. They need help looking after the youngest children, who are kept a safe distance from the action, under some big oak trees.

When the work camp in Kildevil was abandoned by the Commission, after the Uprising, I spent months looking after the smallest children. I'd forgotten how happy they make me. The morning passes while I play with them, stop their fights, and help feed them. All the while, the ghost library unfolds nearby. It's wonderful, full of colour, sights, and sounds.

At lunchtime, Erica drops by to check on me. I realize I'm leaving her alone for the whole day. "Do you mind?" I ask.

"Not at all. I have so much reading to do, it's like a gift. We can shop for food tomorrow. That's all I need help with. It looks like you're needed here. Will you be home for supper?"

I remember why I'm here. "Volunteers can stay for supper."

"Try to be home by dark then," Erica says.

After lunch, we take the children out to see a puppet show, then bring them back under the trees for a nap. I sit on the ground beside their mats and rub their backs while they settle, and I remember my dream of Sparrow, sleeping beside me with the Tribe. She belongs in a place like this, where children are loved and cared for. My need to see her here is almost a physical ache.

Shadows grow longer, the crowds begin to thin out, and the puppet theatre is packed away. New cooking smells drift across to me. The children are cranky and exhausted from the excitement of the day. I pull one onto my lap. I know how they feel.

Will I ever get to talk to Prospero? I'll be surprised if I can get anywhere near him. But then, as if my thoughts have conjured him, he appears. Everyone else is dragging, but he seems energized. He looks as if he could keep going all night. "Well done, Blake," he says. "I hear you worked hard. Come and have some supper."

I rise and then sit down again. "The children—"

"Their regular caregivers are on their way," he says. He seems to know everything.

We are given wooden skewers with grilled meat and vegetables. Everyone just rips the food off with teeth and fingers. It tastes like the best meal I've ever eaten. Most of us sit in an exhausted stupor, but some of the performers are just as energized as Prospero. They regale us with stories of a sleeve set on fire while juggling flaming torches, of pickpockets exposed, mocked, and driven away, of the generous donations people have made.

The day is almost over. I've had fun and I've been useful, but I'm no nearer to getting Sparrow away from that Tribe. This place is perfect for her, but how will I get her here? It's time to leave. I've got to try.

"Prospero, can I talk to you before I go?"

"Of course. I'll walk you to the street." When we reach the park gates, he says, "What can I do for you?"

"What?" I'm stunned. How could he have guessed my secret?

He laughs. "Everyone wants something from me. What is it?"

"You know I lived with a Tribe for a while. I told you when I first came here." He nods. "It was bad. A lot worse than living with the homeless girl who took me from my mother." I take a deep breath. "There's a little girl in Queen's Park, she's only six or seven maybe," and I tell him about Sparrow. He doesn't stop me. He seems to know I've got to get all this out. "If I could just get her away from them," I add. "If Sparrow could come here—"

He shakes his head. "I don't like Tribes, Blake, but I can't afford to fight with them. If I started taking their kids, they'd take mine. It would be war."

"But this is just one child. They'd never know." I'm begging.

He tries to look stern but doesn't succeed. "All right. If you can get her here, I'll take her, no questions asked. But, if you get caught, you have to promise you won't mention our deal."

"I promise. Thank you."

"You're sure you know what you're getting into? You're in this without a net."

"That's all right. I understand." I'm not sure it is all right, but I won't back down now. And I do have Kayko.

He gives me a searching look. "I had a daughter," he tells me. "She would have been about your age. And a wife. I lost them both in the technocaust."

"Maybe you're my father!" I blurt the words without thinking, then fumble to explain myself. "We still don't know what happened to him. I don't even know his name."

He laughs. "My daughter had curly red hair, Blake, and blue eyes. Her name was Rosa." I feel so silly, I hardly know where to look, but he continues. "If she were still alive," he says, "I'd want her to be like you."

10

Until I came to Toronto, finding my father alive seemed like the best thing that could possibly happen to me. I used to lie awake and wonder what sort of person would think to plant a micro-dot inside my arm.

—From the victim statement of Blake Raintree

When Prospero agrees to help me with Sparrow, my dreams about the Tribe stop. By Monday, I feel rested and ready for whatever comes next.

"We're going to the East End Detention Centre today," Erica says at breakfast. "Maybe a field trip will make it easier for the Justice Council to work as a team." She smiles without humour at her own bitter joke. "Oh," she adds, "don't forget about your appointment with Code Scanning this morning."

I'm amazed. "I'd completely forgotten. Do you think I should bother?" Finding my father seems like such a childish idea now, like imagining he might be Prospero.

Erica stares at me. "What's gotten into you, Blake? This time last week you could hardly wait for that appointment."

"I know. Last winter, finding my father seemed so real, but now we're here, I realize how unlikely it is. Maybe I won't go."

Erica pats my hand. "Do what you think best. At least the ID codes building is near Queen's Park."

"That's right," I say, "it is." Which would give me a chance to scout around where Sparrow lives. "Maybe I'll keep that appointment."

When we arrive at work, a prison vehicle is already waiting for the Council members. It's unmarked, but somehow we know. It makes me shudder. "You'll have a much nicer time today," Erica says, "starting on those holo-projections. I'd love to be with you." I wish I could share her enthusiasm.

I find Kayko alone in the media conference room, looking as dismal as I feel. "So, today I begin my career as a holo-projectionist," she says.

"Won't you be able to work with us?"

"After I get things going I will. Griffin wants to run two holograms at a time, which makes sense. We'll divide into teams of two, and I'll join one when everything's set up."

"Sound like you've got it all worked out."

"Griffin and I met over the weekend. He insisted." She sounds mildly annoyed.

Mention of the weekend reminds me of Sparrow. Should I tell Kayko about my arrangement with Prospero? She'll need to know if she's going to help me. But while I hesitate, Griffin, Astral, and Luisa enter carrying boxes. Griffin practically bounces into the room.

"Please, everyone, have a seat," he says."Kayko and I developed a working plan over the weekend, but we welcome your input and questions." He holds up the box he carried in. "These micro-disks contain holo-projections of protest rallies, meetings, government press conferences, anything newsworthy in the years before the technocaust. We have the media reports that go with the raw footage. We're going to go through the material in chronological order, of course. The technocaust didn't start until 2353, but we're going back a little farther, to 2352."

"Why is that?" Luisa asks.

"The exact cause of the technocaust is still unclear," Griffin says. "We know that violence against people with technological skills began late in 2353, but we don't know exactly why. It may have started with ordinary people, but it's clear that the Protectors condoned it."

"Condoned it?" Astral says. "Who built the concentration camps those techies died in? The Protectors orchestrated the violence. They *created* it." He sounds furious, but Griffin only nods.

"So we've suspected for years. Now, we get to find out." Griffin leans forward. "Anything I've been able to piece together about the technocaust will pale in comparison to what we can discover here. This is very important work, no matter what becomes of the Justice Council. Think of yourselves as detectives, unravelling a huge mystery. But it isn't going to be easy.

"Luisa, give everyone their folders, please. The hard copy may seem a bit retro, but I find it's easy to work with. And, of course, you'll have identical text on your scribes if you need to search. This is information about the ones we're investigating, our persons of interest."

Astral interrupts Griffin again. "That's ridiculous. 'Persons of interest' is too awkward to keep repeating."

Griffin is not offended. "What would you suggest?"

"How about 'suspects'?" Astral says.

"'Suspects' is a nice, straightforward term," Griffin says. He sounds cautious.

"Suspect" makes this sound like a criminal investigation. Kayko leans forward to argue, then stops herself. I can guess what she's thinking. If Astral is going to be difficult, she can't afford to fight about something as trivial as wording.

Griffin seems determined to ignore our differences. "Identification of these suspects may be difficult if people aren't named in a projection. Some of the photos in our files are recent, and fifteen years is a long time. I suggest we spend the rest of the morning familiarizing ourselves with the contents of these files."

Griffin has managed to inspire us, in spite of Astral's hostility. I sense intense concentration in the room as we silently work through the files, trying to absorb all the information we can. These middle-aged men and women look so ordinary. But one of them might have signed the warrant for my father's arrest.

The alarm on my scribe beeps. I can't believe how quickly time has passed. "I've got an appointment," I tell the others. "I won't be gone long." I leave my bag, taking only the appointment card and my residency card.

I've given myself extra time. The ID codes building is just around the corner, but I walk away from it, into Queen's Park. I'm not sure what I'm looking for. The park is almost empty. I don't see Sparrow or any of her Tribe. I cross the road at the traffic light and enter a maze of tall buildings across the street. The road that circles Queen's Park is always busy, but there's little traffic on these side streets and the sidewalks are empty. Alleys run beside the buildings. Mid-block, I duck down one to see what's behind.

There's no sign of homeless people here, confirming to me that is the territory of a Tribe. The Tribes don't let stray homeless people squat on their turf. Children are absorbed and adults are beaten off. Or up, as the old man with the fuel cells almost was. The alley connects to a longer one running behind the buildings, the length of the block. I can see traffic on the busy streets in the distance at either end. I decide to walk farther west, then circle back to keep my appointment.

"You looking for something?" The voice is so near, I startle. A girl steps out of a doorway at the top of a concrete staircase under a fire escape just behind me. It's a good hiding place; I walked by without seeing her. She's young, about twelve, but she's done up like a fully initiated Tribe member. Her black jacket and pants are ripped in patterns. Her cheeks are ruddy with makeup, her eyes lined with black and highlighted with glitter. Tribes like makeup. Anything that makes them stand out. But underneath, this girl looks like a pinched, pale child. I know why she's here. She's a sentinel, on the lookout for anything that might threaten the Tribe, or be useful.

I should have said something by now, but I froze when she spoke. I thought I'd be braver. I was when I lived on the streets. The girl jumps down and gives me a quick look, head to toe, assessing, but there's nothing threatening in her manner. "You looking for something?" she asks again. "Because, if you are, I can find it for you."

"I—I don't know where I am," I say. Strictly speaking, this is true.

She smiles. "Where do you want to be?" I can't tell if she's mocking or friendly.

I dig the appointment card out of my pocket. "I'm looking for this building," I tell her. "I thought it was around here." As I hand her the card, I remember most street kids can't read. I'm making a complete mess of this. "See?" I say quickly, pointing to the words. "The ID codes building, on Grosvenor."

She peers at the card as if she could read it, then gives it back to me. "Sure. That's near here. I'll take you."

"That's all right. You can just point me in the right direction."

"I *said* I'll take you."

I know better than to argue with that tone. I can only hope she's not planning to lead me into some kind of ambush. At least she can see I'm not carrying anything valuable. But even if she's honest, she'll expect payment for this. I reach to the bottom of my pocket as I put the appointment card away. When my fingers touch a few cash tokens, I feel giddy with relief.

"How did you end up back here?" she asks as she leads me back to the street.

"I have a really bad sense of direction," I lie. "Do you live around here?"

She points ahead. "In the old subway station. We all crash there."

This makes sense. Tribes like everyone to sleep in the same place. It makes it harder for kids to run away. A subway station would probably be big enough.

"What's your name?" she asks. She sounds friendly and curious.

With my real name, her Tribe might be able to trace me after I get Sparrow away. "Blay," I tell her, my street name, from before we found out who I really am. It seems fitting, somehow.

"I'm Spyker," she tells me proudly. Most Tribe members never give their names to strangers. She should know that by now. I glance at her, sidelong, as we walk. Maybe I'm wrong about her age. By twelve, most street kids are hardened. There's an openness about Spyker that makes her seem younger.

"Here you are," she says. She's delivered me safely to the ID codes building. I'm sorry the walk went so quickly. I would have liked to learn more.

I pull the tokens from my pocket and give them to her. "Thanks," she says. She actually waves goodbye. She's the strangest Tribe member I've ever met.

My encounter with Spyker makes the visit to Code Scanning unreal, as if my past life has come back to distort the present. I wait twenty minutes for the thirty seconds it takes to scan my micro-dot, then wait another twenty minutes for a download of the number I already knew. In the Code Tracking office, I realize I should have brought my scribe with the forms I was supposed to submit with my number, so that takes twice as long as it should. Lunchtime is almost over when I finally leave the building.

Walking back to work, I pass an entrance to the old subway station, a stairway in the sidewalk leading down, the broken remains of a shelter around it. It's pitch-black down there. A gust of foul air sweeps up out of it, making me walk faster, my old life chasing me back to the new.

11

WE ARE NOT THE CONSUMERS

STOP TECHNOLOGY NOW

—Sign from a protest rally, July 2352

I find the other aides in the cafeteria, just finishing lunch. Now that we're all working together, Kayko seems content to eat here, and I'm happy, because that makes it easier for me to slip out to see Sparrow at lunchtime. The events of the morning have left me unsettled, though, not hungry. I gulp down a bowl of soup and I'm ready to leave with everyone else.

"You could stay and eat a proper lunch," Griffin says, but I shake my head.

"I don't want to miss anything," I tell him.

"We'll divide into teams of two, excluding Kayko," Griffin says when we return to the media conference room. "She can join one team when she's ready."

"Blake and I can work together." This is Astral, of all people. Luisa looks startled, probably remembering how he treated me last week. Astral notices. As he passes, he grasps her shoulders from behind and gently shakes her. "Don't worry, Luisa," he says, "I'll be nice to her." Somehow, he makes this sound like a threat.

"In that case, Luisa and I will work together." Griffin sounds uncertain, but no one can think of a reason to object to Astral's arrangement. Even I can't. "Ready, Kayko?" Griffin adds.

"I've got the first two disks," she says, holding them out on the palm of her hand. She consults the master index. "One's a protest rally held outside this building in July of 2352, the other's a public meeting held about a month later. The protest rally will be harder to sort out."

"Then that's what we'll take," Astral says. He seems determined to make things as difficult as possible. I give him a look of pure annoyance, but he ignores me.

"Off we go, then," Griffin says. He can hardly wait to get started.

I follow Astral into a projection room. It's large, so we can run the recording full scale. I pick up a remote, hoping Kayko will load the disk quickly, but nothing happens.

"So what was that appointment about this morning?" Astral asks.

I'd rather not tell him, but I don't have the energy to make up a story. "I have a micro-dot implanted in my arm," I tell him. "I went to get it scanned so the ID code can be traced. I'm hoping to find out who my father was."

"Don't you have any family at all?" He sounds incredulous, scornful. It's too much.

"No, I don't. It's not my fault, you know."

"I'm not blaming you. It just makes me so angry."

"You don't have to be angry on my behalf. I'm angry enough for myself." I've never actually said that out loud before. It feels good to speak the truth for once. I realize I've shouted, but somehow this calms him.

"Good," he says. "I thought you were all forgiveness."

"Well, I'm not."

Suddenly, the room is filled with people. The holo-projection has started. I have a hard time concentrating, though. Two minutes alone with Astral and I've somehow managed to spill my deepest secret. How did that happen?

The door opens and Kayko joins us. What we see in the

holo-projection helps me begin to put the early years of my life into context. The people at this protest are afraid of technology. They express the same fears, speaker after speaker. "We don't want another Dark Times," they say over and over. It's fascinating, but we don't identify anyone. After two hours, I feel frustrated and exhausted.

"Let's look at the last sequence," Kayko says. "That's the media report this footage was used to create." She pages through the menu and brings up the report.

A South African man stands in the foreground of the scene, with the rally behind him. He must have been superimposed, because we've seen this part of the scene before, without him. "At a protest rally at Queen's Park in Toronto Prefecture today, a coalition of environmental groups expressed concern about rapid technological advances . . ."

"Tell us something we don't know," Astral says impatiently.

"Noticeable by their absence were leaders of Save Earth Now," the reporter continues, "which seems to confirm rumours that the group has split from the coalition. Earlier today, I put this question to SEN spokesperson Swan Gil . . ."

The scene changes to an office interior and projection freezes. At first, I think it must be a glitch, but Kayko says, "I've seen that face." She has paused the disk. She goes to her file and starts leafing through. After a moment, she holds up a sheaf of papers. "See? Swan Gil. Here she is."

The woman in the picture is identical to the one frozen in the holo-projection before us, a small, delicate-looking woman with masses of curly black hair.

"Good work, Kayko," I say.

"At least we haven't wasted the afternoon," Astral says, but he sounds less than happy. I'm sure he'd rather have been the first to spot a suspect. "Let's see what she says."

"Anyone who says Save Earth Now has split with the protest coalition is spreading idle gossip. We weren't there today because of internal deadlines for annual reports. That's all." She finishes the interview without adding anything.

"That's great," Kayko says when the recording ends. "Let's take a break."

"You want to stop now?" Astral says.

"I'm exhausted," Kayko replies. "Just fifteen minutes, then we'll page back and find the raw footage of the interview."

I smell coffee as soon as we leave the projection room. We find Griffin and Luisa, talking excitedly over their mugs. "Who did you find?" Griffin asks. He seems to take success for granted.

"Just Swan Gil," Kayko replies. "Did you find anyone?"

"Six so far," Griffin says.

"Do you know how these protest groups relate to the technocaust?" I ask.

"I have some ideas," Griffin says, "but I'd rather save them for my briefing tomorrow. I'd hate to make you listen to everything twice." Griffin's modesty means I'll have to live with my curiosity for another day. "We could use some help," he continues. "Kayko, would you mind working with us for the rest of the day?"

"I'd love to." Kayko looks delighted to escape the tedium of our protest rally.

So I find myself alone with Astral again at the end of the break. This time, I'm determined not to let him get the better of me. He doesn't waste any time.

"Why don't you know your father's name?" he says as we walk back to the projection room. I'm getting used to his abruptness.

"I was taken from my mother by a homeless child on the street in St. Pearl," I tell him.

"You mean you were stolen?"

"Yes. I never saw my mother again. She died in a concentration camp. And I was too young to remember anything. We didn't know any of this until we found the micro-dot in arm." I'm tired of answering questions. It's time Astral answered some. "But what about you?" I say. "You have a Truth Seeker name, so why were your parents taken in the technocaust?"

I expect him to be defensive. To my surprise, he's not. "I don't know who my father was either. There was always just my mother," he says. "Not everyone raised in a religion grows up to believe. My mother lost her faith when she was young. She trained as a marine biologist. Instead of talking to the dead, she wanted to talk to whales. It wasn't that different, she used to say, except that whales exist." He smiles. "Her idea of a joke. Astral is actually my middle name. She gave it to me to please her parents."

"What's your real name?"

"Darwin."

"Darwin?"

"Don't laugh."

"I'm not laughing. I can understand why you didn't use it during the technocaust. So, do you believe? I mean, are you a Truth Seeker?"

"Yes, I am. My mother sent me to her parents before she disappeared. She knew there was a good chance she might be taken, and her parents lived in the interior, where it was safer. My grandparents are very religious."

"Yes, but . . ." I hesitate. We should be working now, but I'm too curious to let it go.

"You think the idea of communicating with the dead is wacky," Astral says.

"Basically, yes."

"I've taken a lot of comfort from the contact I've had with my mother over the years."

It takes me a second to process this. "You mean, you *talk* to her?"

He sighs. "It's not like making a voice-call. There are layers and layers of interference between her plane of existence and ours."

"But you have communicated with her?" I know I'm pushing, but I want to know what he believes. And he's been pretty hard on me.

"A few times, yes. When my life was in turmoil and I needed comfort, she was there. Now, we'd better get back to work."

"Wait, just one more question. How old were you when she disappeared?"

"I was ten."

"You must remember everything about her. You're so lucky."

"Am I?" Astral sounds angry. Then he looks at me and softens. "Maybe I am. I never thought of it that way." He presses the menu button and pages back to the raw footage of the interview with Swan Gil.

And there she is. She's beautiful, and she seems to know it. "Andrew, darling," she tells the reporter, "if you think you're going to get me to admit there's been some kind of split between SEN and the coalition—" she begins, but he cuts her off.

"Swan, darling," he says, "in my experience, people only talk about 'admitting' when they've got something to hide."

She looks furious, opens her mouth to speak, closes it again, then finally says, "Do your damned interview and get out of here." The rest is what we've already seen. I wonder how active she was in the technocaust. I hate her already.

At the end of the afternoon, I can hardly wait to tell Erica what we've been doing. We can't talk about our work on the bus home, of course, but over supper, I lay out my files. She frowns when I use the word "suspects."

"Persons of interest aren't suspects, Blake," she says.

I find myself using Astral's argument. "It's so awkward to say 'persons of interest' over and over." I pass Swan Gil's dossier to her. "We found this woman today. Did you meet her in the prison?"

"Swan Gil? No, Blake," she says after a moment's hesitation. "She's dead." She pages through the dossier. "See? Here's a summary of the media reports about her arrest. Not long after the technocaust began. I remember when it happened." The reports are dated 2354, the year my father disappeared. The other aides probably knew that. I didn't have as much time to read the dossiers.

I feel like I've been punched in the stomach. "Why is she in this file if she's dead?"

"She's a person of interest *because* she died. Quite a few of the people in your files are activists who died in the technocaust. We'd like to know what happened to them. That's why 'suspect' isn't the best word."

"But when I saw her on the holo-projection today, she seemed so, well, evil. I was almost looking forward to discovering all the bad things she did."

Erica sighs. "You're going to find there aren't many evil people in this story, Blake, or good ones either, for that matter. We're mostly looking at a lot of ordinary people who made bad decisions. I met a man today, very important in the technocaust. I'm sure he's in your dossier: Evan Morrow. When I asked him how he got involved, he said he was only trying to trace his wife and child. He was promised access to the tracking systems that might have let him find them if he cooperated. By the time permission was finally granted, his child was dead. He never found out what happened to his wife."

Another man who lost his wife and child. Like Prospero. Like my father. There must be hundreds of them.

"Are you all right?" Erica asks.

"Maybe. Erica, why are we doing this? We can't fix the past."

Erica thinks for a minute before she replies. "You're right. We can't change the past. I used to think everything would be better if we could only defeat the Protectors. Then, amazingly, that happened. The Uprising came, and I expected democracy would be restored, everywhere. Even if it took time, I was sure it would happen.

"But now it's stalled in so many places, and that seems to be because of the past. So many people are still hurting, the way you hurt, Blake. So many people have unanswered questions about the technocaust. It's as if the past is choking everything, leaving no room for a future. We have to put the ghosts to rest, to make room. That's what I came here to do. It's not about good and evil, it's about discovering the truth."

"But can't we just put everyone on trial?"

"Criminal trials aren't the best way to get to the truth. One crime is considered, a few at most, and it's in the best interests of those being tried to hide as much as possible. You learn less, not more. Look at you, Blake," Erica says. "Or me for that matter. Who's responsible for what happened to us? Which individuals?"

"I don't know."

"Neither do I. With trials, there would be no justice for people like us. No one would hear our stories, because we'd have nowhere to testify. I'm convinced that healing won't begin until victims can tell their stories. I believe healing is more important than vengeance. And we need all the stories. If we only hear from the victims, we'll never really understand what happened. We have to find a way to hear from the other side, too. Maybe that means we have to forgive anyone who agrees to participate in the process."

"That's what you want? Anyone who tells the truth will go free?" I'm stunned. "But, Erica, that can't be right."

"What's right is whatever brings the victims peace of mind. The truth is the only thing that will do that, and maybe the only way to get the truth is to offer freedom to those who are willing to provide it."

"I'm not sure I can accept this." My voice is shaky. I take a breath to calm myself, but it turns into a sob.

Erica looks distressed. "This isn't a new idea, Blake. It was used in the past, at the end of the Dark Times, for example, when generations of wrongs made it impossible to assign blame. I know it can work."

I've got to stop this conversation before I fall apart completely and tell her how I really feel. "I need time to think about this," I tell her. "Can we stop now?"

"Of course. Take all the time you need. Ask me anything when you're ready. I'm here." Erica looks as upset as I am.

I always knew our ideas were different, but suddenly, I feel as if we are standing on the brink of an abyss, with her on one side and me on the other. And I can't see any way across.

12

Deth to polutors

—Eco-terrorist graffito, November 2352

I leave Erica and go to my room. For a long moment, I gulp for breath. Gradually, I slow my breathing and my heart slows with it. I fall back onto my bed, exhausted.

Maybe the Justice Council won't do things the way Erica wants them to. Then, I'll be able to console her without having to consider what might have happened if they had. But what if she's right? What if the kind of punishment I want to see will only hide the truth and make it more difficult for everyone to put the past behind them? The idea is so much at odds with the way I want things to be, thinking about it gives me a headache.

So many wrongs in the world. How can I make anything right? Sparrow. In the excitement of the afternoon, I'd forgotten her. I've got to get her away from the Tribe, to do this one thing that I know is right.

In the night, for the first time since we came here, the nightmare about my mother returns.

At breakfast the next morning, Erica is cheerful, overly polite, cautiously skirting the divide between us, pretending it's not there. "Griffin's talk this afternoon should be very helpful," she says, and I agree. I'd agree with almost anything she said this morning, grateful for the pretense that everything is fine. Before we leave the house, I slip an apple into my bag with the file I abandoned on the table the night before. Street kids never see fruit.

At work, Griffin has a plan, as usual. "Luisa and I learned so much yesterday, we should split up this morning to spread the information around. Luisa will work with Astral, Blake, and you can work with me." I'm grateful I won't be working with Astral.

"What do we have today?" Kayko asks.

"A press conference by the coalition of protest groups that held the rally Astral and Blake saw yesterday, and a series of newscasts, about something called 'eco-terrorism.' They both date from November 2352, just a few months after the material we saw yesterday. The newscasts are longer," he says. "Frankly, I'm hoping for half an hour to go over my notes for my talk this afternoon. If no one minds, Blake and I could take the press conference. Kayko, maybe you could help Astral and Luisa. We can compare notes over lunch." We divide up.

As soon as our holo-projection starts, Griffin identifies two of the people at the table as suspects. "See, here they are." He shows me their dossiers from the file.

"How did you do that? You must have a photographic memory," I say.

He beams. "Well, actually, I do."

Working with Astral yesterday was like swimming against a strong current; working with Griffin is like drifting downstream. His enthusiasm cheers me in spite of everything.

The press conference we're viewing was held by a coalition of protest groups that came together to renounce eco-terrorism. "We cannot condone violence as a vehicle for change," the spokesman says. "The end does not justify the means."

I would have thought Swan Gil would be present. "Was Save Earth Now there?" I ask Griffin.

"No, they don't seem to be represented. Maybe that was the issue that made them split with the rest of the coalition."

"Who is that speaking?"

"Eric Wong. He was a spokesman for Pollution Watch."

"Where is he now?" I'm afraid to ask, but I have to.

"Dead," Griffin says. He pauses the disk, goes back to his file, and finds the dossier. "See? He died in 2354."

"How did he die?"

"It was an accident. He was hit by a car while crossing a street."

I'm stunned. "But that never happens. The sensors on the vehicle would stop it."

"It must have been some kind of system failure."

"What did he mean, about the end not justifying the means?" I ask.

"When people think they're absolutely right, they can believe that anything they do to accomplish their goal is right too. Let me give you an example: in the late twentieth century, there were people who believed it was wrong to let a woman terminate her own pregnancy. They felt it was taking a life. Some believed that gave them the right to bomb abortion clinics, and even assassinate doctors."

"They killed people to stop them from doing something they considered killing?"

Griffin gives me a grim smile. "Logic doesn't play a big part in this kind of thinking. I can't begin to tell you how much harm has been done to innocent people throughout history because members of some movements allowed themselves to believe their cause justified any action. No cause is so noble that it cancels ordinary human decency." Griffin glances at the clock. "I know we've got a shorter recording than the others, but I'd like to get back to work."

We're finished in just a few minutes. "Now, I want to go over my notes for this afternoon. Do you mind?" Griffin says.

"Not at all. I've got something to do myself. I'll be back in a while." I grab my bag with the apple in it and leave. I can't quite believe my luck.

Outside, rain clouds are gathering. The seasons are starting to change. Wind tugs faded leaves off the trees in Queen's Park. A few people sit on benches, soaking up the sun before it disappears. Sparrow doesn't seem to be anywhere, so I take an empty bench and rummage through my bag for the apple. It's golden, almost glowing in this yellow light. Looking at it, I remember a story Erica told me once, about people who were tempted out of a beautiful garden by an apple, the apple of knowledge, she called it, and then they could never return. Here I am, trying to reverse that story, using an apple to tempt Sparrow into a garden of sorts, and, if I succeed, she won't ever have to go back to the hell of her life with that Tribe.

I look up and there she is, watching me. She must have been nearby. "Hello, Sparrow," I say, softly. I hold up the apple. "Look what I brought you." She comes, drawn by the apple. For the first time, she smiles. She holds out her hand, but I pull the apple away, firmly but not too fast. "Come and sit with me while you eat," I say. She has to learn to trust me.

Sparrow perches on the edge of the bench like the small brown bird she is, ready to take flight at any hint of danger. The angry infection by her mouth has started to heal now. She eats the way I used to, cramming her mouth until it's almost too full for her to chew. There's no point in speaking to her while she eats. The food consumes her. But as soon as she's finished, I start to talk before she can slip away.

"Do you like it here, in the park?" I ask. "With all the grass and trees?" She nods. "It would be nice to live in a place like this, wouldn't it? To sleep under the trees, to walk on the grass."

"Yes," she whispers.

"There are bigger parks than this," I tell her, "places where people live." I want to say more, but I stop myself. The Tribes are predatory. If they knew I was trying to take a child away, Tribe members would follow me around, telling anyone who would listen until I paid them to keep quiet. I've seen it happen. I can't tell Sparrow what I want to do until I'm ready to do it.

"I'll bring you another apple. Would you like that?" Sparrow nods. "Good," I tell her. "I'll see you tomorrow."

The sun has disappeared behind the clouds now, the gold gone from the air, leaving the chill of winter-to-come behind. It's time to go back inside. Progress with Sparrow is slow, but it's progress. I have to school myself to be patient.

The other aides have finished with their holo-projections now. I find everyone in the media conference room. Kayko smiles at me. "Where did you go? We're just getting ready for lunch."

I dodge her question. "I need to get something from my office. Come with me?"

Kayko picks up on my tone. "Of course," she says. She calls out to the others, "We'll meet you in the cafeteria."

"What's going on?" she asks as soon as we're in the hall.

I look around quickly to make sure we're alone. "I was just talking to Sparrow, in Queen's Park. Prospero said he'd take her if I can get her to High Park. I need your help."

"Do you think she'll go with you?" Kayko asks.

"In awhile, I do." I hope I'm right.

"I can get a car to pick you up," Kayko says. "But Queen's Park will be tricky. The traffic's so hectic. Could you get her onto one of the side streets?"

"That wouldn't be a good idea. The Tribe has sentinels. We might be seen."

"Well, let me know when you're ready. We'll look at Queen's Park and plan the pickup." Kayko glances around.

"We really shouldn't talk in here. I'm not sure how closely Security monitors this place."

"That's fine," I tell her. "Let's eat. I'm starved."

Over lunch, Kayko, Astral, and Luisa talk about what they learned in the morning.

"These eco-terrorists must have been frustrating to deal with," Astral says."They attacked randomly. Maybe a generating station one month, or an airline office. Then they might torch a paper-making facility or a medical research lab. And they were almost impossible to infiltrate."

"Why is that?" I ask.

"They had very little structure," Astral says. "They did have a spokesperson who issued statements from time to time, but they didn't seem to have a leader. People who wanted to become eco-terrorists would act alone, or maybe with a close friend or two. They might imitate another group, or do something original. But they didn't seem to communicate with other cells."

"So there was no way to place agents inside," Kayko adds. "It must have driven the Protectors crazy."

Astral turns to Griffin. "Do you know anything about them?"

"They named themselves after a movement that was active in the twenty-first century," Griffin says, "with roots that go all the way back to the twentieth. They did a lot of damage. And, as far as I can tell, they provided the Protectors with an excuse to start arresting people."

"Really?" Everyone laughs because Kayko and I say this together in the same, incredulous tone.

"Well, I could be wrong—" Griffin begins, but Astral cuts him off.

"Don't be so bloody modest. You're not likely to be wrong." He's managed to make his compliment sound like an insult, but Griffin looks delighted anyway.

After lunch, we file into the same room where I saw all the members of the Justice Council for the first time, the day we discovered the depth of the divisions among its members. Griffin takes his place at the head of the ornate wooden table, looking excited and nervous.

Before he speaks, Monique Gaudet rises. "Since this meeting is more formal than most, I've been asked to say a few words about Griffin," she says. "I've encountered some gifted students over the years, but it's fair to say I've never had the privilege to teach anyone quite as talented as Griffin Stockwood. His ability to create new insights using materials gathered from the past is amazing. It gives me the greatest pleasure to introduce him." I'm surprised she's so brief. I suddenly realize I know virtually nothing about Griffin's past. He seems so open and honest, but he's actually more of a mystery than any other aide. Why is that?

"Thank you," Griffin says. "Monique, Erica, I find it intimidating to address an audience containing two such significant scholars. If either of you would like to comment at any time, please feel free. I'm sure we'll benefit from your insights. In fact, if anyone has questions, please ask.

"When I began this work, at the New Sorbonne in Port-au-Prince three years ago, I thought I'd always be struggling with fragments of information, looking through narrow peepholes, never getting anywhere close to a complete picture. The old, dictatorial governments in North America, collectively known as the Protectors, wanted to suppress information about the past. During the technocaust, freedom of speech was eliminated and whole libraries and archives were destroyed. I also thought I'd be working in exile in Haiti. But then the Uprisings came. Not even the most optimistic of us could have predicted what would happen in those historic months in late 2367 and early 2368. The Protectors fell all over North America, with minimal bloodshed, because they were already corrupt and crumbling, and because the military, which had been so active in the technocaust, refused to prop them up any longer.

"Since that time, I've been able to access new information, communications of the resistance movements that tried to find safe places for the targets of the technocaust, and now we have media reports from South Africa and Australia as well. I know I'm going to learn a great deal more about the technocaust as we prepare our report. This is just an overview of what I know now, with some of my ideas about why these events happened.

"What do we know about the technocaust today? In the early 2350s, thousands of people all over North America were imprisoned and many died. These were mainly people with specialized technological skills and information. The initial push to limit technology seems to have come from ordinary people. We've certainly seen that in the media reports we've been viewing over the past few days. But we know the Protectors took the lead when the technocaust began, issuing arrest warrants, conducting raids, imprisoning people in the concentration camps where so many died by design or neglect. All the Protectors participated, though some governments were more zealous than others.

"But why would the Protectors turn against technology? This question bothered me. Since the end of the Dark Times, North America society has been characterized by extreme contrasts between rich and poor. Before the Uprising, for example, debtors who couldn't support themselves went into forced labour camps in the industrial zones to manufacture goods the rest of us enjoyed. The medical system reveals the disparities in our society. The rich benefit from the best medicine while the poor get none. Those poor serve mainly as a supply of organs for the middle group, those who have some money but still can't afford the most advanced medicine. The poor might as well be living in the distant past for all the technology in their lives. Before the technocaust, the rich, including those who ran the governments, had all the privileges of advanced technology. Why turn against something that provided so many benefits?

"Looking at the years just before the technocaust, I've noticed this was a time of emerging freedom. Protest groups formed, meetings and rallies were held. The media reported these events and could even comment on them with no restrictions. If this had been allowed to continue, democratic forms of government might have followed. The technocaust eliminated all those freedoms. That doesn't seem like a coincidence to me.

"I began my studies assuming that the technocaust was designed to stop the rampant growth of technology. But I think it may be possible that the real target of the technocaust was not technology at all. The real goal was to stop the re-emergence of democracy."

"Bravo, Griffin," Erica says beside me, but softly, so most people don't hear.

"But—" Kayko says, then stops herself. "Sorry for interrupting."

"No, go ahead, Kayko," Griffin urges.

"Well, technology *was* restricted during the technocaust. Only industries and occupations classified as 'ancient' were allowed to continue. If my parents had been making, I don't know, say, nanotech construction kits instead of bread, they would have been shut down."

"That's true," Griffin says. "But did the government change the way the bread was made?"

"No, the bakeries used the same technology. They were even able to upgrade at one point. That's always puzzled my parents. It made things harder for them, too. People assumed they must have been collaborating with the government because we were left untouched by the technocaust."

Erica speaks. "If the technocaust were about control rather than ideology, as Griffin suggests, a steady supply of staple foods, like bread, would be necessary to prevent shortages that might lead to chaos." She looks to Griffin and nods, encouraging him to continue.

"Exactly. If the technocaust had been driven by ideology, no one would have cared about political stability. People would have been forced to revert to older ways of doing things, making their own bread, for example, or building community ovens, even if that resulted in chaos or starvation," Griffin says. "But, as far as I can tell, nothing like that happened."

"But in the media reports from before the technocaust, we can see how hostile ordinary people were toward technology," I say. "It certainly looks like technology was the target." My head is almost spinning with these new ideas.

"I agree completely. Those people were afraid of technology," Griffin replies. "Some were so frightened, their fear turned to hate. I believe the Protectors channelled those emotions to create an enemy, a scapegoat. Then they took the energy that had been pushing for political freedoms and directed it toward destroying this phony enemy. In the process, they were able to bolster their power, which had become weaker."

"If any of this is true, the people who created the technocaust are even more evil than we supposed." Even though I secretly agree, the finely controlled fury in Daniel Massey's voice is chilling. Across the table, Astral traps my gaze. His eyes seem to probe all the feelings I'm trying to hide. I manage to look away.

Monique deftly steers the conversation back to safer waters. "Whether this theory is true or not," she says, "popular fear of technology was vital to the creation of the technocaust. Have you thought about where that fear came from, Griffin?"

"I have." He looks uncertain, then he plunges on. "I believe the fear of technology is rooted in the Dark Times."

"How could people be influenced by things that happened two hundred years before they were born? That's ridiculous!" To my horror, I realize I've blurted out my thoughts. "Isn't it?" I add, trying to sound less aggressive.

"It sounds ridiculous," Erica says, "and if we were talking about a small event, you'd be right. But large historical events—the fall of the Roman Empire, the Reformation of the Christian Church, the Renaissance—these events can and do affect the way people think for centuries. The Dark Times was a similarly huge event. Civilization collapsed. Centuries of knowledge were lost.

"In North America, the three ancient countries—Mexico, Canada, and the United States of America—disappeared. For years, there was no real government at all. Gradually, the old countries were replaced by a patchwork of fragmented protectorship governments. In the process, democracy was lost. This is basic, first-year history. Now what caused the Dark Times?"

"Even I can answer that," Kayko says. "The environmental disasters of the twenty-first century. Climate change—what did they used to call it? global warming?—and the destruction of the ozone layer created an endless series of natural disasters. Floods, mega-hurricanes, ice storms in colder parts of the world, destructive levels of UV radiation, droughts, forest fires, diseases turning up in new places, mass extinctions. It must have seemed, you know, biblical."

"But why did that eliminate democracy?" I ask.

"Luisa, what do we say in Cuba?" Paulo de Lucas seems anxious for his daughter to join in the conversation.

Luisa recites, "'Democracy is like the gardenia. Unless everything is exactly right, it will not bloom.' Which means," she adds, "that democracy requires many conditions, stability being one of the most important. The almost endless environmental disasters destabilized the ancient countries of North America. During the Dark Times, in the twenty-second century, anarchy reigned in most places. The Dark Times ended when the Protectors emerged during the twenty-third century, which we call the Recovery."

"Because we began to recover lost knowledge, but democracy was not restored." Griffin eagerly takes up the narrative. "For a century and a half, we have lived with governments that provided stability. This should have allowed democracy to return, but it hasn't."

"Because those who have power will never share it unless they are forced to." Astral speaks for the first time. His voice is bitter. I cannot look at him again.

"History would tend to support that assertion," Erica agrees. Her voice is soothing. Like Monique, she gently keeps the discussion on topic. "We're not finished with the Dark Times, though. Griffin, the Dark Times were caused by the endless chain of environmental disasters, but what caused those disasters?"

Griffin frowns. "That's a complex question, isn't it? Greed, maybe, or the sin of pride, the feeling we could control everything, our inability to think about the future . . ."

"They *knew,*" Astral says. "The Consumers knew they were changing the planet, and they didn't stop. They consumed everything, including the future."

"It's true," Erica says. "We have nothing to thank our ancestors for. But the tool that caused all this to happen, I mean. What was it?"

Griffin blinks. "Why, technology, of course."

"That's why those people in the holograms were afraid?" I ask.

"Exactly," Griffin says. "They didn't want history to repeat itself."

"And the Protectors played on that fear and created the technocaust, just to prevent democracy from being restored?" Kayko says.

"That's what I believe," Griffin replies.

"It worked, didn't it?" This is Astral.

Griffin looks Astral in the eye. He's younger, he's smaller, he's not the sort of person anyone would take for a hero, but he doesn't back down. "The story isn't over yet. The Protectors are gone now. Maybe *because* of the technocaust. Maybe they fell so easily because people remembered what happened before and didn't want another bloodbath. The Protectors stalled democracy, that's certain. But did they prevent its return? I'd say that's up to us."

13

The homeless girl's eyes
blue as the sky above her
and as empty too

—Kayko Miyazaki

Griffin's talk makes us even more eager to unravel the history of the technocaust, but it's still unclear whether the Justice Council will work. That brief glimpse of Daniel Massey's hostility gives me some idea of the tensions within the Council. Three days of each week the councillors go to the prison. I wonder what Erica's learning there, but don't ask. I know I'll have to confront those people and what they did eventually, but not yet. Meanwhile, we aides help organize mountains of documents and watch the Justice Council's painfully slow progress. I look forward to the days we spend with the archived holograms, smiling when I remember how Kayko and I expected to be bored to death.

A few weeks pass this way. Almost every day, I bring an apple for Sparrow. Kayko's prepared to cover for me if anyone asks where I am, but it only takes a few minutes. I'm usually back before we sit down to lunch. Spyker has noticed us by now. I look up and catch her watching us sometimes. I hold my breath, waiting for her to do her job and report what she's seen to her Tribe. Waiting for the enforcers to show up. For some reason, this never happens. Every day, Sparrow sits a little farther back on the bench, and a little closer to me, until one day, she rests her head on my arm. That's how I know it's time.

"She's ready," I tell Kayko as we return to our offices after lunch. I don't have to tell her who I'm talking about.

"Meet me in Queen's Park after work," she says. "This will take planning."

"I know," I say, but I can't stop smiling. In our office that afternoon, while Erica and I sort through her correspondence, I can hardly sit still.

"What's going on, Blake? You look like the cat who swallowed the canary," Erica finally says.

I've always found it difficult to hide my feelings from Erica. I can't tell the whole truth, but I don't want to lie. "I just feel as if something good is about to happen," I tell her.

"You may be right. The Justice Council has agreed to begin accepting victim statements."

"Really? Does that mean you're starting to work together?"

"Maybe. See if you notice a difference in the climate when you attend our meeting this week. I'd be interested to know what you think."

The hope that I might be able to make my victim statement grounds me for the rest of the afternoon.

At four-thirty, I excuse myself. "Kayko and I have to plan some work for tomorrow," I tell Erica. Again, this isn't exactly a lie.

Kayko is already waiting in Queen's Park, her bodyguards at a discreet distance. The heavy traffic that flows around the circular park goes one way on either side, southbound on the west, northbound on the east. "We'll have to pick you and Sparrow up on the northbound side. That's where the only traffic light is, it's the only possible place to stop now," Kayko says, frowning. "The light on the west side was ripped out during the riots last spring and it's never been replaced."

We walk through the park to the traffic light at the eastern edge. A sidewalk leads toward the crossing, but there's no sidewalk right by the road. Instead, the base of a statue blocks the street where the cars stop. It must be ten metres long and taller than I am. "You'll have to leave the park," Kayko says. "We'll try to pick you up on the red light on the other side of the street, but if we miss you, we won't be able to wait."

Unlike the treed park, the opposite corner is exposed, visible from blocks away. This is where I often see Spyker. "How long will it take you to come back?"

"Only a few minutes if we can change lanes quickly enough to circle around. We'll be in the outside lane to pick you up. We'd need to be in the inside lane to go south, and there's only about a block between the traffic light and the turn. If we have to go north, we'll be longer, maybe ten minutes." The idea of being out in the open with Sparrow for that long makes me want to run away. I take a few steps away from the road in pure panic. "Will you be all right?" Kayko asks.

"I'll have to be."

"Look, Blake, if you're worried, one of my bodyguards could come with you."

I glance nervously at the beefy men pretending not to hover in the background, then I picture Sparrow facing one of them. "That wouldn't work. A stranger would scare Sparrow off. Especially those strangers. Besides, we don't want them to know what I'm doing until it's over. It has to be me, alone."

Kayko agrees. I almost wish she hadn't. "What if she won't come with you?" she asks. "I can order the car anyway, and tell the driver I need to do some shopping if Sparrow won't come, but I really do need to know. If we don't see you the first time, I have to know whether to try again. You don't carry a com.D for voice-calls do you?"

"I never have. Just a scribe for text messages. The weavers don't use frivolous technology."

Kayko smiles. "They must be the last people on the planet who'd call that frivolous technology. Most of the girls I know have implants. I'll give you a spare com.D tomorrow. We'll set the auto-call to my address. Just press it and disconnect. When I see my name displayed, I'll know it's you. That can be our signal."

I shudder with excitement, or maybe fear. "So this is really going to happen?"

"I hope so," Kayko says.

That night, I dream Sparrow is playing with other children somewhere I've never been. I wake with the sound of her laughter in my ears, a sound I've never heard. I hope this is a prophecy, but I'm afraid it's just a wish.

Somehow, I make it through the morning. At least the councillors are at the prison today, so Kayko and I have more freedom of movement. At lunchtime, Kayko says, "Blake and I are eating out today," and we leave before anyone can react.

In the hall, she hands me the com.D, which is about the size of my baby finger.

"How do you keep track of these things? I'd be afraid of losing it," I tell her.

"That's why people get implants," she says. "I'll call the car now. You have about twenty minutes. When you're sure she'll come with you, call me and take her to the pickup point. I'll be there as soon as I can." She starts for her office, but I call her back.

"Kayko, no matter how this turns out, thank you."

Kayko smiles, then she's gone.

During the short walk to the park, I'm almost overwhelmed by what-ifs. What if Sparrow doesn't show up? It happens. What if she won't come with me? What if I miss Kayko? I have to stop myself, literally. When I reach the park, I stop walking and take a deep breath. For the next hour or so, I have to focus. I push the doubts from my mind to make space, and silently call on the street kid who I hope is still somewhere deep inside of me. She took risks. She'll know what to do.

At the bench where I always meet Sparrow, I scan the park. The trees are looking bare now. A few men stand at a distance, muscular and alert like bodyguards. Someone important enough to warrant that kind of protection must be out here today. But I don't see Sparrow. I force myself to sit down. Act normal, I tell myself. Act like this is any other day.

Ten minutes pass, then fifteen. I'm beginning to think Sparrow won't show when I see her, darting across the street through a gap in the traffic. Someone should teach her not to do that, I think, and then I smile. If I succeed today, someone will. As she sits on the bench beside me, I realize I've forgotten the apple. I never forget. I almost panic, then I realize I can use this.

"Sparrow," I say, "I forgot your apple. We can go and get one together. Would you like that?" She agrees, looking a little worried. "You know the garden I've been telling you about? The park, I mean? We could go there. Would you like to?"

"Yes," she says. Then she looks around. "Will you bring me back again?"

"You could stay there. The people who live there look after children. Not a Tribe, they're grown-ups. They'll feed you, every day." I remember how food was used to reward and punish when I was with the Tribe.

"Do you live there?" she asks me.

"I live very near. I could come and visit you."

"How will we get there?" Sparrow asks.

"My friend Kayko has a vehicle—a car, I mean," I correct myself to use the word she'll understand. "She can give us a ride. How does that sound?"

"It sounds good," Sparrow says. She's warming to the idea now. "Will there be apples?"

"Yes. If we can't find an apple there, I'll buy you one. Let me call Kayko." But I'm too nervous to function properly. I rummage through my bag until it seems I've lost the com. D. Finally, there it is. I press auto-call, then disconnect. Now Kayko knows we're coming.

I make myself sit still for a few minutes, then I take Sparrow's hand. "We have to go over there," I tell her, pointing across the street.

We're about to step off the curb at the traffic light when I look down the side street ahead and there's Spyker. I'm not surprised. It's the same street I met her behind. She hasn't seen us though. I drag Sparrow back, behind the base of the statue, jerking her arm. She cries out in fright. "Sorry," I say. "Sorry, sweetheart, I didn't mean to scare you. Let's just wait here for a few minutes, in the shade." It's a good thing Sparrow is used to doing exactly what she's told, because I sound crazy. The air is chilly, the sun's not out; there's no shade and no reason to want it.

When I look again, Spyker is walking away from us. It's safe to cross. But as I reach the curb again, the walk light turns red. Kayko sees us from the window of her car as it pulls away. I curse myself for being such a coward. When the light changes again, I take Sparrow's hand and march across the street. I don't care who sees me now, I can't risk missing Kayko again.

I have no idea how long we stand there. It seems like months. The lunchtime people try not to stare, but I know how strange we look. I'm well dressed, neatly groomed, normal by their standards. Sparrow is filthy and dishevelled.

I stare down the street, willing Kayko's car to appear. And there's Spyker, on the street ahead. She must be patrolling. She sees me with Sparrow and her stride becomes purposeful. She's going to confront me. My heart starts to race. What should I do?

Suddenly, on the road in front of us, a door flies open. "Get in, get in," someone says. I look up. It's Hanif. "Hurry, the light is changing." I look back at Spyker, who has broken into a run, and I obey, pulling Sparrow with me. "Sit down," Hanif says. The smiling minibus driver is gone. The bus is otherwise empty. What have I done? If he means to kidnap me, he already has. "What do you think you're doing?" Hanif continues. "Taking risks like this. What if someone from that Tribe had caught you?" I'm too stunned to reply, but at least this doesn't sound like something a kidnapper would say.

After a long silence, he pulls a com.D from the dashboard of his bus. "I have the passengers," he says. That's all.

"Where are you taking me?" I ask.

"You tell me," he says. He's still furious.

"You could leave us at the corner of Keele and Bloor." I'm so tentative, it sounds like a question. I'm afraid of him now.

We stop for a red light and he looks at me. He's still angry, but there's nothing cruel or violent in his face. "I will take you to the main entrance of High Park."

"How could you know that? Who are you?" I ask.

The light changes and he turns his attention to driving. I notice we're not stopping to pick up passengers. When he speaks again, his voice is calmer. "You cannot be allowed to wander around by yourself. Do you know what would happen if anyone kidnapped you? This is a risk the Transitional Council was not prepared to take, even before anyone knew you could be so reckless."

It takes a minute for this to sink in. "Are you my bodyguard?" I ask.

"I'm a minibus driver. I happened to come along and see you in a moment of need. I helped you out. That's all we need to say."

I remember how he "happened" to be at the entrance to High Park the night I met Prospero, and the men in Queen's Park today who looked like bodyguards. How much of that was planned? I wonder, but there's no point in asking now. Suddenly I picture Kayko, circling Queen's Park endlessly. I'm reluctant to expose her involvement, but she has to know I'm safe. "Kayko Miyazaki will be looking for me," I tell Hanif.

"Her people have been notified." His voice is still curt with anger.

"But I can take Sparrow to High Park?" I can't believe they'll let me do this.

"Don't make a habit of picking up stray children," he says. He pauses for a moment, then continues. "We managed to contain this episode. Next time, there will be repercussions."

"What does that mean?"

"It means this event was dealt with at the ground level." I can tell he's not accustomed to speaking about his work with someone like me. He's struggling to explain without giving too much away and I can hardly understand him."Your actions were deemed to be ill-considered, but harmless. So no one in authority will speak to you about this, because no report will be filed."

"You aren't going to tell them?"

"No one will be told." He's deliberately making his statements impersonal. "But, if it were ever to be known that this happened, well, you would never see me again."

I begin to understand the risk he's taking for my sake. "Thank you," I say.

"You can thank me best by being more careful."

Sparrow hasn't spoken since we left Queen's Park. She looks terrified. I put my arm around her and give her a little hug. "Don't worry. Everything's fine. We're going to the park."

I'm afraid Hanif might confront Prospero, but he stops the bus and opens the door as soon as he turns through the gates. "I will pick you up at the corner of Keele and Bloor in exactly thirty minutes," he says as we leave the minibus. "Promise me you won't take another risk like this." His concern is genuine, not professional.

Somehow, his sincerity undoes me. The tension of the day wells up, filling my eyes with tears. I can only nod as we leave the bus.

I look down at Sparrow as Hanif drives away. She's picked up on my distress and looks as if she might cry as well. If I were alone, I'd be useless now, but I have to pull myself together for her sake. I sniff and square my shoulders. "See over there, under the trees? That's where you'll be living." I give her hand a little tug. "Come on," I say. "Let's meet everyone."

I've been worried that Prospero wouldn't be here, but he must have seen us right away, because he's walking toward us, smiling. His charm is like the warmth of the sun. Even Sparrow seems to feel it, for she doesn't lag back as she might with another stranger.

"So, this is Sparrow," he says, smiling at both of us.

"Do you have an apple for me?" Sparrow asks.

"Hold out your hands," Prospero says. He reaches behind her ear and a perfect apple drops into her hands, so quickly Sparrow gasps. "You had it yourself, all this time," he tells her. "Now come and sit with Blake and me."

Prospero walks us through the encampment, saying nothing, letting Sparrow see the happy, busy children. Her eyes grow large as she takes everything in. He takes us to a bench, just a few metres from a playground swarming with raucous children. Sparrow clings to me at first, but Prospero steadfastly ignores her, making small talk with me about nothing. After a few minutes Sparrow says, "Could I go over there and play?"

Prospero smiles. "I think you could. Blake will be leaving soon. Would you like to stay here with us?"

"Yes, I would."

"Off you go then. After you play, someone will clean you up and then you can pick out some new clothes."

Sparrow runs to the edge of the playground, but stops, suddenly shy. An older girl comes over and squats down, talking to her and pointing to the monkey bars. After a moment, Sparrow takes her hand and off they go. She doesn't look back at me.

"She'll be fine," Prospero says. "We take in new children all the time. The other kids are very good with them. We teach them to welcome newcomers." He pauses, then says, "This may be hard for you, but it's best to give her time to settle in."

I hadn't imagined this. "I was planning to help out with the ghost library."

Prospero is gentle, but firm. "The weekend after next you can." I stand up, feeling empty. He seems to understand. "We know what we're doing, Blake. She'll be settled by then, you'll see."

Sparrow is climbing the monkey bars now, laughing just as she did in my dream. She doesn't need me. I take a deep breath. "All right," I say. "I'll see you in a while."

14

My micro-dot has shaped my life, sometimes in ways I barely understand.

—From the victim statement of Blake Raintree

I'm afraid to face Hanif when Erica and I board the minibus the next day.

"Good morning, ladies," he greets us. "You look particularly fetching today."

There's no crack in the facade. He's an ambitious minibus driver with a quaint way of talking. Harmless, trivial. His disguise is perfect. But he doesn't meet my eyes.

Erica and I talk about anything but the day ahead of us while we travel, because the aides are sitting in on another Justice Council meeting today.

"Have you heard from Marrella?" I ask. Unlike me, Erica is in contact with people from home daily. I've used the confusion of relocating and the demands of the work to explain my silence. If Erica sees through these flimsy excuses, she says nothing. It would be cruel to talk to everyone but Fraser. Even if he's mostly in St. Pearl, he'd be sure to hear if anyone had news of me. But Marrella is pregnant, and she has auto-immune problems that are causing complications. I should be paying more attention to her.

"I haven't heard from her since she went to the hospital in Corner Brook," Erica replies. "But Donna says everything is stable. Donna can't wait to be a grandmother."

I smile. Donna's had a hard time accepting wilful Marrella as her daughter-in-law. This baby seems to be changing everything. People do change.

"I'm hoping the holo-conference line will be connected this weekend, so we can see William," Erica adds. I nod and smile, but my heart lurches. Fraser is working with William.

At work, when I see Kayko, I long to tell her what happened with Sparrow, to find out what happened to her. But I know we'll have to wait, not just until we're alone, but until we're out of the building. Even then, we may not have privacy. Maybe privacy doesn't exist. We fall in together behind Kenji and Erica on our way to the conference room.

"This should be interesting," Kayko says, "working out the details of accepting victim statements."

"That's a breakthrough, isn't it?"

Kayko smiles as we enter the room. "It means the Justice Council will accomplish at least part of its mandate," she whispers quickly.

"Who's chairing today?" Daniel Massey asks when everyone is settled.

"I am," Kenji replies. "You'll find the agenda on your scribes. I took the liberty of sending it to the aides as well. The first item is carried over from yesterday: Who will be allowed to file a victim statement?" That sounds like an easy question, but when I call up the agenda, I see how complex it is. At least ten topics are listed under this heading.

Kenji seems to want every possible opinion to be heard before decisions are made. Over the next few hours, the conversation goes back and forth. Sometimes it goes around in circles. That's one thing I've learned since the Uprising: democracy has many appealing features, but it's tedious. After an hour or so, I stop listening. Even Griffin appears to be doodling.

"Next item: Will people living outside the prefecture be allowed to submit a victim statement?" This catches my attention.

"Why would anyone living outside the greater Toronto area want to make a statement?" Daniel asks.

"Maybe they were relocated during the technocaust, as I was," Erica says. "We have the opposite question to deal with as well. What if someone living here wants to make a statement about events that happened because of the technocaust in some other protectorship?"

"We can only deal with things that happened because of Queen's Park," Monique says. "If people want to submit statements about events that happened elsewhere, we could pass those along to Justice Councils in those places."

"But Justice Councils aren't being established everywhere," Erica says. "Take my case, for example. I was forced to flee from Toronto, and I ended up in a concentration camp in Terra Nova. They've already held elections in Terra Nova. There may not be a Justice Council there."

"Yes, but your problems began here," Paulo de Lucas says. "So you should be able to submit a victim statement here."

"So everyone in those circumstances will be able to?" Erica asks.

As everyone agrees, I realize I've been holding my breath. What would I do if I couldn't present my victim statement?

The councillors work out the fine points of victim statements and geography, then move on. "Should immediate family of those who perpetrated the technocaust be allowed to make victim statements?" Kenji reads. "This question is complicated, of course, by the fact that we don't know how we're going to deal with perpetrators."

"Let's not whack that hornets' nest today," Daniel growls.

"Hornets' nest?" Paulo says. Monique quickly explains in what sounds to me like perfect Spanish.

Kenji smiles. "I wasn't planning to, but you can see how this muddies the waters. People applying for amnesty will seem very different from people facing trial."

"No matter how you look at them, why would their immediate family members qualify as victims?" Daniel asks. "These are the people who caused the suffering." His voice is tight with the effort to control his anger.

"We'll need time to discuss this," Monique says, "and it's almost noon. I move we break for lunch."

Leaving the room, I can barely contain my fury. Those people and their family members shouldn't have rights.

We go back to our offices before lunch. Reflexively, I think of an apple for Sparrow, then I smile. Sparrow won't need little scraps of help from me any more.

"So, what did you think of that?" Erica cuts into my thoughts, jolting me back to reality.

"I thought it was interesting," I say, trying to keep my voice as neutral as possible. It doesn't work.

"Won't you tell me what you really think?"

"Erica, how can anyone even think about letting the relatives of those monsters make victim statements?" The words rip themselves from my throat. I sound like I'm choking.

Erica looks shocked. "Does it mean that much to you?"

I try to collect myself before I speak again. "Yes, it does."

"Blake, can't you imagine how someone close to those running the technocaust could have been a victim of the events that unfolded?"

I shake my head. I'm not even willing to consider the possibility. Anyone who lived with those criminals is guilty in my mind. Even they deserve to be punished.

Erica comes over and takes my hand. "I understand this

is hard for you," she says. "I admire the way you've been able to deal with it."

I turn away quickly, tearing my hand from Erica's, too ashamed to meet her eyes. I am not the person she thinks I am. I don't even come close.

I feel her hand on my shoulder. "Please don't be angry with me, Blake." She's misunderstood my reaction, but how can I explain?

"I'm not angry with you. I'm really not." I turn back to her and wipe the tears that have started against my will. I've got to get away before I tell her the truth. "I've got to meet the others for lunch now," I say. Erica looks disappointed, but she lets me go.

When I came to work this morning, I hoped Kayko and I might go out for lunch so we could talk about yesterday, but she's already gone when I look for her. By the time I reach the cafeteria, Kayko and Astral have faced off over their food. I can't hear the words, but their angry voices carry over to me while I get my meal. The Transitional Council employees who sit at the other tables throw worried glances their way as I approach.

Kayko's words come into range. "That's guilt by association. You can't say someone is guilty of crimes committed by their parents or a spouse."

"Why not?" Astral shoots back.

"They might not even have known. How can you be guilty of something you didn't know about?"

"They benefited, didn't they? Didn't they live comfortable lives while the rest of us suffered?"

"Astral, not sharing in the suffering of others is not the same as being guilty," Griffin says. These are harsh words, but his tone is mild.

Astral looks like he wants to hit somebody. I know how it feels, that overwhelming anger, with nowhere to aim it. I sit down beside him. "What do any of you know about it?" he finally says, his voice bitter. Kayko looks down quickly, shamed because he's right, she knows nothing of the kind of suffering he's living with. Griffin does not look away, but he doesn't answer either.

What *does* Griffin know about it? I wish I knew. But now's not the time to ask.

Griffin looks at me. "What do you think, Blake?"

I freeze. I'd rather not side with Astral against Kayko and Griffin, but my heart's with him.

Astral picks up on my distress. "Leave her alone." His voice is quiet, but the intensity of it literally makes the others draw back. He sounds like he's ready to kill.

"Griffin isn't trying to hurt her, Astral," Luisa says quietly.

"A lot of the people who harmed us weren't trying to, Luisa. They didn't even know we existed. They ruined our lives anyway." Astral stands. His lunch is barely touched. "I've got to check about . . . something." He leaves.

Before I know what I'm doing, I've pushed my chair from the table to follow him.

"Astral," I call just before he disappears around a corner. The sound of my voice stops him.

"You're the only one who understands," he says when I reach him.

"I'm not sure that's true," I say. I intend to share what I wonder about Griffin's past, but he cuts me off.

"Blake, you'd be a lot happier if you didn't always try to be so bloody good." He makes the word "good" sound like a disease. I'm speechless, because I've often suspected the same thing about myself.

"I'm sorry," he says, but he doesn't sound sorry, he sounds furious. Then he says, "It's always the same. Every time I care about someone, I drive them away." He's gone before I can respond.

I'm not sure I believe what I just heard. Did he say he cared for me? The shock is almost physical. Any other girl would follow him, I suppose. Not me. I flee back to the cafeteria.

"We shouldn't have pushed him," Griffin says as I sit down. He sounds contrite.

"What's pushing Astral is inside him," I say. "You just poked at it." My voice is shaky.

Luisa and Kayko look puzzled, but Griffin nods. I wasn't expecting anyone to understand, but he seems to.

There's a long silence, then Kayko speaks. "What's coming up in the holograms next week, Griffin?" There's a forced brightness in her tone.

He looks puzzled. "We went over the indexes this morning. You know as well as I do."

"I think Kayko is trying to change the subject," I say. "Thank you, Kayko."

"You're welcome, Blake." We exaggerate our politeness, making it a joke, but Kayko is doing me a real favour. I need to escape these overwhelming emotions.

Griffin blushes. "Oh. Sorry. We're into the reports from 2353 now so things should be heating up. We have some newscasts, and then there was a major protest rally at the Hippodrome that summer, the last event the outside press was allowed to cover. There were holo-cameras attached to all the poles in the stadium, of course, to get the action of sports events from all angles, so the projection should be quite detailed. It might take a while to mine that one for information, but it's the last we have. We should take our time, give it serious scrutiny."

"There's always the option of breaking the projection into smaller sections," Kayko says.

"How do you do that?" I ask.

"You scale the projection down to get an overview, then

impose a grid and break it into identifiable fractiles. I can do that in the master projection room."

She's about to tell us more, but Luisa interrupts. "The meeting starts again soon."

Astral catches up with us in the hall. I'm afraid of what he might do or say, but he just puts his hand on my shoulder, squeezes lightly, then lets go. He's saying we're in this together. Astral's at ease with physical contact, I know that by now, but I have to wonder what else his touch might mean. What would life be like with Astral? He would protect me from the world. *Yes, but who would protect me from Astral?* The thought comes from nowhere, as if a stranger has spoken inside my head, but I have to admit the truth in it.

By now, I'm almost glad of the distraction provided by the Justice Council. The councillors take up where they left off, discussing the relatives of those who carried out the technocaust, considering their rights from every possible angle. Voices are raised. Finally, Kenji says, "It's clear there's no consensus on this. We'll have to vote. Does someone want to make a motion?"

Daniel volunteers. After a few minutes of furious keyboarding, he reads, "I move the Justice Council refuse to accept victim statements from immediate family members of those being held for crimes in the technocaust."

"I'll second the motion," Paulo says.

"We've already talked this to death. Call the question," Daniel says.

"Those in favour?" Kenji says. Daniel and Paulo raise a hand. Then, so does Erica. The other councillors look shocked. I have to stop myself from gasping.

With only Monique and Kenji to vote against, the motion is carried.

When the session finally ends, Astral looks grimly satisfied. He leaves without speaking.

"Did you know she was going to do that?" Kayko whispers in the hall. I shake my head.

Erica is waiting for me in our main office. "I broke ranks with Kenji and Monique," she says. She sounds stricken, surprised.

"Why did you?"

"I couldn't bear to see you so unhappy."

"Oh, Erica, you shouldn't have done that for me." I feel I've pushed her to act against her better judgment.

"We'll talk later," she says. "I've got to catch Kenji and Monique before they leave for the day. We've got a press conference tomorrow and I want to make sure they aren't upset. This may take awhile. Wait for me?"

This is the chance I've been looking for. "I'll come with you and find Kayko."

Kayko and her uncle are just about to leave. As Erica takes Kenji with her to find Monique, Kayko says, "Do you mind if Blake and I go out?"

"Half an hour, maximum," Kenji says, and they're gone.

When they leave, Kayko takes off her security badge and mine. "Oops," she says. "We forgot these." She puts them into a desk drawer. "Let's go," she whispers.

"How will we get back in?"

She laughs. "I guess they'll have to rely on our retinal scans."

Her bodyguards see us at the front entrance and follow at a distance. "I would have called you last night," Kayko says, "but I was pretty sure our communication would be monitored. Besides, I was in big trouble."

I'm surprised. "I thought this wasn't going to be reported."

"Who told you that?" she says, and I explain about Hanif.

"Well, your bodyguard reports to the Transitional Council, apparently. Mine report to my parents. And they're very loyal. I spent hours defending what I did."

"Kayko, I'm so sorry," I start to say, but she waves this away with a grin.

"Once or twice a year I do something that sends my parents into meltdown. They'll recover. Tell me what happened."

Kayko listens silently, but smiles when I describe Sparrow on the playground. "So Security let us have a happy ending."

"But how did they know?"

"I wondered about that. It seemed unlikely the building would be so carefully monitored, so I ran some scans. The security badge was the culprit. They're completely plugged in."

"And we wore them every day. When I went into the park to look for Sparrow."

"Yes, and the afternoon we worked out how to pick you up. It all fits. But that Hanif must be special." Kayko glances back at her bodyguards and lowers her voice. "Most don't think for themselves."

Then I remember a piece that doesn't fit. "Weeks ago, the night I met Prospero, I ran into Hanif at the main entrance to High Park. But I didn't have a security badge then. It wasn't ready."

Kayko frowns. "They must have planted a tracker on you. It's lucky you come from such a low-tech culture. If you had an implant, they could track you constantly."

I stop walking. "What kind of implant?"

"You know, a micro-chip."

"But I do," I say, and I quickly explain about my microdot. "You mean they could use that to track me?"

"Sure," Kayko says. "With satellite tracking, they'd

always know where you were, give or take a few centimetres. But they'd have to scan it first."

I remember the unexplained blue light. "I think they did, when I had my retinal scan. Oh, and that was the same day I met Prospero."

Kayko nods. "It all fits. I never could believe they'd just let you wander around without bodyguards. So they knew about your plan to rescue Sparrow. They could have turned us in. Instead, they created a backup in case we fouled up. Which we did."

"But why did they let us go ahead with it?"

"I thought a lot about that last night, too. It's just a theory, but I think they were protecting the Justice Council. If we'd been caught, it would have been hard to explain what we were doing. If it got into the media, the Justice Council would have been discredited. We'd probably have lost our jobs at least. Security must have decided it was safer to let us follow through."

"That's what Hanif said. 'Ill-considered, but harmless.'"

"A fair assessment. We were lucky, but, you know, this whole thing scares me."

Her words chill me. I didn't think Kayko was afraid of anything. "Why?"

"Security knows how stable the society is. There was so much unrest until the Transitional Council set up the Justice Council. Things have been fairly quiet since, but Security must have reason to believe it's a fragile peace." She turns to me, looking deadly serious. "From now on, we'd better behave."

15

I grew up without a family, without a home. I'm not sure I can ever love anyone in the way someone who has had those things can.

—From the victim statement of Blake Raintree

On Friday, the Justice Councillors hold their press conference, announcing that they will accept victim statements. Celebration is in the air, but I can't share it. Erica compromised her principles to make me feel better, but I have kept everything about Sparrow from her. This nags at my conscience.

On Saturday morning, Erica says, "The holo-conference line is finally connected. We can talk with William when you're free."

"Great," I say. "Any time today is fine with me."

She looks puzzled. "Aren't you helping with the ghost library?"

This is the opening I need. "Erica," I say, "do you remember that little girl who sang in Queen's Park?" And I tell her the whole story. She listens without interrupting.

"It's lucky you have such good security," she says when I finally finish. "Otherwise, you might have gotten into a lot of trouble." I'm surprised she isn't angry.

"Did you know about Hanif, about them using my microchip to track me?" I can't believe she'd keep something like that from me.

"No, but just after we arrived I went to the Transitional Council and Dr. Siegel told me not to worry, that you'd be safe even when you weren't with me. I was so grateful, I didn't ask how." She hesitates, giving me a chance to respond, but I only nod. I can hardly object to her keeping that one secret from me. "I'll call William now," she adds, "to set up a time for the holo-conference." Her eyes shine with the thought of seeing him.

A few minutes later, she's back. "The call will come through any moment now," she says. "I'm glad William is working in St. Pearl. We couldn't make this kind of connection to Kildevil." Then she frowns. "William said Fraser would like to see you. If you'd rather not—"

I cut her off. "It's all right. I can't avoid him forever." That encounter with Astral made me realize I have to start facing my emotions.

Erica and I wait in front of the holo-display unit in the living room. At first, there's nothing but the high-pitched whine of an idle HD unit, then suddenly, the air around us seems to crackle with static electricity and William appears, sitting in some kind of formal chair. He must be at the House of Assembly where he's working in St. Pearl. William is a tall, balding man who always reminds me of an ancient warrior. Even his hologram fills the room with a commanding presence. He and Erica eagerly exchange news. I've known them for three years now, but the depth of their feeling for each other always fills me with wonder. Their marriage seems like a kind of garden that I will never enter.

The time for the holo-conference is limited. After a few minutes, William turns his attention to me. "Have you been using that holo-lab I gave you?" he asks. I blush and admit it's unopened. "Soon," I tell him.

"Make sure you do," William replies, my stern science teacher again for a moment. Then he glances off camera and says, "Someone else here wants to talk to you." He leaves the chair and Fraser appears. He's small for his age and slight, with silky dark hair and gentle brown eyes.

The way I feel about Fraser is always a mess of tangled emotions until the moment I see him, and then my confusion disappears. Every fibre of me yearns for him. I tried to explain this to Erica once. She said it was called "chemistry," I guess because that's the way molecules bond. I don't like having feelings that think for themselves. It terrifies me.

Fraser smiles when he sees me. "How you getting on then, Blake?" he says.

I tell him about Prospero and Sparrow, quickly because time is running out. Then he tells me about the work he's doing, helping to draft new child protection legislation. We quickly catch up on news from home. But the words hardly matter. Our real conversation needs no words. And then, so soon, it's time to say goodbye.

The virtual visit leaves me with a glow. For a few hours, my feelings about Fraser are perfectly clear and focussed. But I know that won't last. It never does. Soon my fears and doubts will overwhelm these feelings. They always do.

Erica and I spend the rest of the weekend catching up on her correspondence. This isn't part of my job, but I want to show my gratitude to her for siding against Kenji and Monique. These letters, simply addressed to the Justice Council, are divided equally among the councillors, who are expected to reply personally to each one. Most are from people pleading for the right to make victim statements. Many are victim statements in themselves. It's heartbreaking work, but we keep at it, stopping only to eat and sleep.

"There," Erica says on Sunday night. "That's the last one. Thank you, Blake. I couldn't have done this much without you. Come on, I'll make some tea."

"At least they have good news," I say as I follow her to the kitchen.

She smiles. "Yes, and now that everyone knows we're going to accept victim statements, these letters should stop."

"But there will be hundreds of victim statements. How will we cope?"

"That's what all those empty offices are for. We'll be hiring a full staff soon. We're almost finished our interviews at the prison. It's going to be a whole new phase."

I've controlled my curiosity about the prisoners for weeks to keep myself from falling too far into the pit of my own anger, but now, I have to ask. "What are you learning in there?"

She frowns. "Not enough. I'm sure Griffin is right. The Protectors must have orchestrated the technocaust to stall democracy, but we're not finding the evidence to prove that. We've learned a lot about the technocaust once it was fully established, but the details of exactly how and why it started are just, well, missing."

"Is that important?"

"I think so. So many people still cling to the idea that science and technology must be evil. Otherwise, the technocaust would be totally irrational. The guilt of allowing such a thing to happen for no reason is just too much for them to bear. If we can provide a logical explanation for the technocaust, the political reason, it might help to eliminate that stigma." She hands me a cup of tea and sits down. "I'm not saying this will happen overnight, or even that people will realize why they feel differently, but I do think it will help. It could be an important part of the healing process. I'm just not sure we'll be able to do it." Her voice is tinged with frustration, and I understand why.

We may be so close to the truth, only to find it out of reach.

I wake the next morning feeling more content. I'm not hiding anything from Erica now and we got a lot of unpleasant work out of the way. I've finally talked to Fraser. My feelings about him aren't any clearer, but I don't have to feel guilty about avoiding him. The Justice Council is moving forward. Soon, I'll be able to see Sparrow again, and some day, I'll make my own victim statement. Maybe I'll even hear from Code Tracking. All reasons to feel happy.

At work, Griffin pairs me with Astral. I don't know what to say to him, but he takes the lead. "Did you have a good weekend?" he asks as we walk into the projection room. Small talk from Astral? Maybe he's trying to keep things light.

"We had a great weekend," I say with honest enthusiasm. "We cleared up all Erica's correspondence."

He gives me an odd smile. "Don't you people ever stop working? What do you do for fun?"

I find myself blushing. Kayko asked the same question the night I met her, and I couldn't really answer. "Sometimes I volunteer at the ghost library," I say. "It's a protest, but it's more like a circus, really."

"That's as close as you get to fun? Volunteering at a protest?" He laughs. I've never seen him do that before. When the scowl leaves his face, I can appreciate just how handsome he is. He should laugh more often, I think, then I wish I hadn't.

"Life is hard in Terra Nova," I say, forcing myself to keep the conversation impersonal. "People spend more time working. It's what I'm used to. I can't share this enthusiasm for fun that everyone has here." Then I startle myself by adding, "You're in a good mood this morning." I don't seem to be able to resist the urge to know Astral better. Playing with fire.

He smiles. "I am. We're making progress. It's encouraging. And I had a great weekend. Maybe one day you'll come clubbing with me." Is he asking me out? Before I can react, we're facing a wall of roaring fire. I panic, throwing my arm up to shield my face from the intense heat—that isn't there. It's just today's hologram, of course. I'm unnerved by the coincidence. I could almost believe I called this fire down upon myself, and I'm embarrassed to have imagined such a thing. Astral sees my distress, but he doesn't tease me.

"That was rough. Are you all right?" he asks when he's muted the audio.

I nod. Now that I look, there's something wrong with the projection. "It's two-dimensional," I say.

"It would have been impossible to situate cameras around this. They went for two. Even at that, it must have been pretty dangerous."

"What is this? It looks like a forest fire." As I speak, the scene changes. Now we see burning houses with firemen and hoses all around. "All the people who must have been trapped inside," I say, feeling sick.

"I don't think those houses were finished," Astral says. "Look up the street. Some were just being framed up."

Then the scene switches again, and we see the reporter standing in front of smouldering ruins in grey morning light. "Once again, eco-terrorists have left their grim mark on greater Toronto," he says. "The Oak Moraine development was highly controversial because of its proximity to sensitive forests. These half-finished houses were torched last night in a well-orchestrated act of wilful destruction. But, ironically, high winds carried the fire beyond the development, destroying a part of the surrounding forest as well. At a press conference earlier today, the chief of Internal Protection at Queen's Park made this statement."

The scene shifts once again, this time to a room I recognize. "That's one of these media rooms. Right here in this building."

A man sits at a desk, facing us over the heads of seated reporters. He has a large head with a flat-looking face and hard blue eyes. He scowls with fury. Suddenly, the projection freezes. "I've seen him," Astral cries. We leaf through our folders. "There," he says with grim satisfaction. "Falcon Edwards. One of the architects of the technocaust. We've finally netted a big fish."

It seems silly, but my heart starts to pound, as if we'd really captured him. "Turn it on. I want to hear what he has to say."

The projection resumes. "I'm here today to tell you, to tell everyone, that the Protectors will not tolerate these acts of violence. The Oak Ridges Moraine housing development was situated to blend peacefully with the surrounding forests. Now, the very people who professed to be most concerned about the area have destroyed a part of it, and millions in investment funds have been lost." He puts most of his anger into this last fact. "We call upon all environmental groups to come forward with information that will help us remove these disruptive elements from our society. They threaten the peace that the Protectors have provided for more than a century. They threaten our way of life. They must be stopped." He rises. "No questions," he says to the reporters, and he leaves.

Come back, I want to yell after him, get back in here and explain yourself. But he's gone. I have to remind myself that he was never really here. Not today.

"That looks like progress," Astral says.

The remaining newscasts show a sharp increase in ecoterrorist attacks, but nothing as spectacular as the Oak Moraine fire. Before lunch, we tell the other aides about Falcon Edwards. I can't contain my excitement. "Erica was saying the councillors aren't even close to finding out how the technocaust began. But he must know a lot."

Griffin looks nonplussed. "Blake, he's been dead for years. It's right there in his dossier."

I'm outraged. "He was busy killing everyone else. Who killed him?"

"Pancreatic cancer," Griffin says. "It's one of the few types that's still fatal."

I can't believe this man got away from us. His death gives me no satisfaction at all. "What about transplants? What about regeneration?"

"My father had a friend with pancreatic cancer," Kayko says. "There's no hope unless it's caught in the early stages."

Griffin has been flipping through his folder. "Here it is. He died in 2356."

"We're never going to get to the bottom of this, are we?" I feel like crying.

"Don't give up yet," Griffin says. "I have a lot of hope for this last projection. We'll start on it tomorrow."

Later that afternoon, walking home from Bloor Street, I tell Erica all about our day. "It's so discouraging. It seems as if *anyone* who could fill in the blanks is dead."

Usually, Erica would try to console me, but this time, she agrees. "We have to brace for disappointment."

When we get home, Erica says, "I'm going to start supper now, Blake. Why don't you check the mail? A message from home might cheer you up."

I log in at the computer console in the kitchen. In mail, the Code Tracking address flashes onto the screen. Erica rushes over in response to the cry that I hear before I realize it came from me. My hands start to shake. "Open it for me, please," I say, standing aside.

She takes over. Then she looks up, confused.

"What does it say?" I ask.

"You'd better sit down, Blake. According to Code Tracking, you died in 2355."

16

Those who cannot learn from history are doomed to repeat it.

—Twentieth-century philosopher George Santayana

When Erica and I enter the Queen's Park building the next day, we march into the main office of the Transitional Council. Erica demands to see Dr. Siegel so forcefully that the young receptionist is too intimidated to refuse.

Dr. Siegel appears moments later, smiling. "Erica Townsend, what a pleasure," he begins, then stops abruptly. "Is something wrong?"

We must look terrible. I spent most of the night crying while Erica tried to comfort me. How did this happen? Could it somehow be related to what my parents suffered during the technocaust? Neither of us slept much.

Erica points to me. "Does this girl look dead to you?" she demands.

"Why no, of course not."

"Then why would Code Tracking tell us she died in 2355?"

Dr. Siegel glances around. "We should discuss this privately. Please follow me." Inside his office, he closes the door and asks us to sit down. "Suppose you tell me the whole story." He listens attentively while we tell him what we know. "That's quite a mystery," he says when we finish.

"How is a person declared dead?" I ask.

"The codes that allow the tracking implant to be used are removed from the system. Anomalies like this do occur from time to time. In most cases, it's some kind of bureaucratic accident, but, given Blake's story, I think we should investigate further. Would you agree to meet with your Security officer?"

"Yes, of course," Erica says.

"Excellent. You can see him early tomorrow morning. Hanif Abu-Muhsin is one of our best men." I wonder what he would say if he knew just how true that is.

Erica seems cheered, but, when we're back in the hall, a wave of despair washes over me. "I don't think this is going to get us anywhere," I say.

She gives me a searching look. "That doesn't sound like you, Blake. This is a nasty shock. Get a good night's sleep before you take your feelings seriously." She gives me a quick kiss on the cheek. "You'd better get down to the media rooms. The others will be waiting."

Not exactly waiting, I discover. They've left me a note, telling me to meet them in the master control room. Kayko's normally the only one who works there, but I know where it is. I follow a long corridor to a spiral staircase that opens onto a room with small widows on every wall. It's full of control panels for holo-projection equipment and cameras. Everyone is there.

"There you are," Kayko says. "Just in time." She stands at the main control panel, looking totally in command, like the captain of a ship.

"What are you doing?" I ask.

"We're calibrating the fractiles on that huge rally that was held in 2353."

"Come and have a look," Griffin calls to me. He's with the other aides by a bank of windows. I find they face the largest projection room, which is huge. Suddenly, the room is filled with little people, thousands of them. It's as if we're watching everything from a great height. "I don't see the outside edges of the stadium," Griffin says, "Take it down another ten percent. That's good," he adds when she does.

"Here we go." Kayko hits a few keys and the whole image is suddenly overlaid with neat squares of red light. "Let me have a look," she says, joining us. "What do you think? Do those fractiles look manageable?" She seems to love this work.

"In terms of viewing, they look fine," Griffin replies, "but how many are there?"

"One hundred."

"One hundred?" Astral sounds incredulous. "And each will be a separate projection? That would take months to work through."

"We'll focus on areas that look important." Griffin points to a big stage at one end of the stadium."There's the speakers' platform. Some of us will need to monitor that fractile."

"What's that tent to the side?" Kayko asks.

"I don't know," Griffin says. "Could we have a look?"

"As soon as I code the fractiles and save this, I'll have a master copy in the server. We can run any section we want. I'll have to ask the archivist to dub some copies onto micro-disks. Then we can run different parts of the rally at the same time in different projection rooms."

"You can't dub copies from the server yourself?" Griffin asks.

"I seem to be locked out of that function. It must be a security feature. I'll save this now." Kayko goes back to the panel and hits another key. Suddenly, every glowing fractile is marked with a code. "Which one do we want, Griffin?"

"B-10."

Kayko pushes a few more keys and brings that section of the hologram up, full scale.

"We can't see from here. Too much in the way," Griffin says. "Let's go down."

Kayko hands us all remotes and we follow her to the big projection room. Most of the holograms we've seen were shot to be viewed in someone's living space. They don't cover much area. But this is different. It's like walking through the actual place. It must have been a hot day; the people around us wear light summer clothes. For one long, surreal moment, we pass through them. The projection simply flows around us, undisturbed. It's too disconcerting.

Luisa feels it too. "Can we pause this?" she asks. "It's like walking through spirits." The projection freezes as Kayko silently complies.

I'm relieved. "That's better."

"I didn't like it either," Astral says.

We can see the tent ahead now, though the crowd still blocks our view. "It looks like a rest area, probably where people went when they weren't on the speakers' platform," Kayko says.

"Just imagine what we'd learn if that had been recorded." Astral sounds wistful.

We pass through the last of the people. Kayko gasps. "It was." The door of the tent has been pinned open, maybe to let the air in, and we can see inside part of it, a big wedge of light where a woman sits frozen in conversation.

"How can that be?" Luisa asks, incredulous.

"Whoa," Griffin says. "This is unbelievable."

"What does it mean?" I ask. We've all spoken at once. Everyone laughs.

Kayko answers. "Anywhere the cameras reached was recorded. Look at that image, though. Doesn't it look odd?" She points inside the tent.

"It's one-dimensional, isn't it?" Astral replies, "I used to have friends who played around with ancient media. It looks like an old cinematic projection."

Kayko smiles. "That's right. Only one camera hit the right angle to reach inside the tent. It was outside this fractile, but we'd be able to see it in the full projection," she points directly behind us, "probably fixed to a light post over there."

"So it's just a fluke," Griffin says, "but such a lucky one."

"Where there's light, there's sound. That's the first rule of holography," Kayko replies.

"You mean we'll be able to *hear* what went on inside that tent?" Astral asks.

"Sort of. It's going to be weird. Allow me to demonstrate," Kayko says with mock formality, pointing her remote at the tent. The people around us come to life again. The ones who walk through me are incredibly distracting. I tense involuntarily every time it happens, bracing for an impact that doesn't come. "Listen," Kayko says. With so much noise around us, it's an effort to tune in the voice of the woman inside the tent. When I do, I realize we're hearing only parts of a conversation.

I listen for long moment before I realize this woman is Swan Gil. She's aged so much since I saw her in that first hologram, even though they were taken only about a year apart. She looks careworn. "Who's going to look after that?" she says, sitting on a folding chair, facing someone in the tent who's out of the frame. After a silence, she adds, "Oh, he's a good person." She rises and walks toward the inside of the tent. "I've been meaning to—" she disappears from the frame and her voice does too. Kayko pauses the holo-projection, her point made.

"We might learn a lot from this, even if parts are missing," Griffin says.

"When can we get started, Kayko?" Astral asks.

"We need to spend more time analyzing the big picture before we plunge in. This tent is an obvious area of interest, but there may be others. We can't study the whole projection, but I don't want to overlook something important." She goes to a control panel on the wall. "Why don't we take a break? I have to ask the archivist if he'll dub copies of this new master file for us."

She speaks to him briefly, then says, "He's on his way down. He says he's got a document of interest to us, something about the technocaust."

"But how?" Griffin asks. "The official records were destroyed years ago."

Kayko shrugs. "We'll find out."

Moments later, Terry Raven joins us in the main conference room. When we first met him, he seemed like a calm, deliberate man, but today he's flushed and excited. "I've already captured your file from the server," he tells Kayko. "You'll have copies by the end of the day. But I wanted to talk to you anyway. Sit down, everyone."

When we sit, he places a micro-disk on the desk. It's larger than the ones we've been using. "This arrived a few weeks ago. Anonymously. The return address doesn't exist. Security thought the package might be a bomb or a bio-toxin, but it was harmless. They finally released it yesterday. I couldn't resist listening, of course. The equipment it runs on is generations out of date, but we have some in the archives."

"What is it?" Kayko asks.

"Radio broadcasts from the year 2353. A station called RTLM. I did a search and found it was something called a pirate radio station. It managed to stay on the air by illegally patching into existing communications systems for short periods, moving from one to another. The authorities shut it down when they could, raiding the offices when they were located and arresting everyone, but mostly it stayed on the air."

Astral gives a snort of disbelief. "Who listens to radio?"

Griffin replies, "The poorest of the poor. You need a home to run a holo-display. Radio receivers are cheap and small. They run on solar power and you can use them anywhere. Radio can be an important source of information for the poor."

Kayko's eyes shine as she looks around the room. "We need a plan. Griffin and I and one more person should explore the Hippodrome rally to identify the fractiles most likely to yield information. In the meantime, the two who aren't working with us can listen to the radio broadcasts." She turns to Terry. "I don't know how to thank you. We're especially interested in 2353. If we're ever going to learn the truth about the technocaust, that's where we need to look."

"I hope this helps. Come to me when you're ready and I'll set you up in media booths."

"I'd like to hear the broadcasts," I say quickly. "I have no technical skills to help with the hologram."

Kayko nods. "We need someone who's done indexing."

"I know how to index," Luisa says.

"And I'll work with Blake," Astral says. "It sounds intriguing."

"Give me time to make working copies," Terry says. "You can start tomorrow. And please make notes—dates, type of programming, names of people on air, that sort of thing."

"I am not the only one to index, then," Luisa says, and everyone laughs.

There's a feeling of elation in the room. This might be a crack in the solid wall that stands between us and the truth about the beginnings of the technocaust.

I look at the old disk on the table and a shiver goes right down my spine. What will it tell us?

17

To cut through all the red tape and give people the truth about our society and the WEAPONS *to create real change.*

—Mission Statement of Radio RTLM

Early the next morning Erica and I follow directions to Hanif's office, tracing a maze of tunnels through increasingly serious-looking security checks. When we finally reach the right reception area, we're told to wait. Erica doesn't like to waste time. After fifteen minutes, she says, "Maybe we should come back later . . ." but the main door opens and in walks Hanif.

"Ah, ladies," he says. "Good morning again. Sorry for the delay. Another driver takes over after I deliver you to work, but I have to complete the run to protect my cover. Please, follow me."

Meeting Hanif in this setting throws me off balance, but he's perfectly at home. His office is large and comfortable, the office of someone important. I don't know whether to feel flattered or frightened by the fact that he was assigned to us.

Hanif motions for us to sit before he takes his chair. "Why did you wait so long after the Uprising to submit your ID code?" he asks.

I quickly explain what I learned about my mother when we found my micro-dot. "For a long time I wasn't ready to know more," I tell him, "but when we came here, I couldn't resist trying to find out. Do you have any idea why my code was removed?"

He shakes his head. "I had a look at the records. It's a mystery. But it doesn't look like an accident."

"But why would anyone do this deliberately?" I ask.

Hanif looks at me for a long moment before replying, his dark eyes filled with compassion. "I'm not supposed to indulge in speculation," he begins. My heart sinks, but then he adds, "I find it impossible not to wonder, though. If you had been taken for organs or murdered, it would make sense, but it doesn't seem as if anyone was trying to hide a crime. I can only conclude this was an act of malice."

"You think someone wanted to harm Blake?" Erica asks.

"I don't think Blake was the target. It might have been aimed at one of her parents."

"But my mother was probably dead by then," I say.

Hanif nods. "Yes, and you were both thousands of kilometres away, out of range of Queen's Park. That leaves your father."

"My father? You think he was still alive in 2355?"

Hanif holds up his hand. "Let's not get ahead of ourselves. I don't want to give you false hope. If someone in power was trying to harm him, there's a good chance he didn't survive."

I look down to hide my disappointment.

"A lot of data was removed from your file when the ID code was disabled, but don't give up. If you know your mother's name, there's a chance I can trace her through the system."

"Her name was Emily Monax." Even now, speaking my mother's name causes a rush of powerful longing.

"Monax is an unusual name," Hanif says. "I can work with that. If I can locate your mother in the files, I'll learn a great deal. Once I have her ID code, I'll be able to trace her marriage. Then we should discover your father's name and ID code."

I'm too stunned to speak, but Erica says, "We'll know who he was?"

"His name, whether he's still alive, everything Blake wishes to know about her father's fate should be in those files. I'll be in touch when I've finished my search." He's completely polite, but there's something so final in this last sentence that Erica and I rise as if on cue. "I'm sure I don't have to remind you that it's vital for me to maintain my cover," Hanif adds, opening the door for us. "We mustn't talk about these things outside these buildings. Just make an appointment through Dr. Siegel's office if you want to talk again. Do you have any questions before you go?"

"I do," I say. It's silly, but I want to know anyway. "That night just after we got here, when I met you at High Park, was that really your wife and child?"

For the first time in his professional persona, Hanif grins. "Yes. I had assumed you'd stay close to home for the first few days. When Security realized you were out, we had to scramble to cover you. I knew you might recognize me, but I didn't want you to feel threatened, so I brought my family. Shauna was not amused to be drawn into my work."

So at least that mystery is solved.

As we walk back to our office, I try to process everything we've learned. "If my father had enemies inside the government, he must have been special, Erica, don't you think? Maybe he was a leader of the resistance, like you and William were in Terra Nova."

"Try not to get your hopes up, Blake." I hear the caution in Erica's voice, but I'm already beyond that.

In our office, I find a message from Kayko, directing me to the archives for the morning. Terry Raven is waiting with a copy of the radio broadcasts for me. "You can work anywhere, of course, but I'd be happy to have you work here. That way, I can download your content notes before you leave." He waves toward a cubicle. "Astral has already set up in there."

Inside the media booth, he hands me earbuds and loads the disk while I patch my scribe into the system. Then he leaves me alone with the past.

"Good morning, human animals!" a voice yells into my ears. "You're listening to RTLM, Toronto, Radio to Liberate Your Mind! Here's last week's number-one hit, 'We Bin Robbed, We Bin Robbed,' by the Silent Spring Tribe." The music throbs. As I listen, it occurs to me I might have heard this broadcast, or one just like it, as a baby passing some radio receiver on the street in my mother's arms. Or my father's. I'm powerfully drawn to that vision of the past. I have to force my attention back to the music. The singer is chanting against a rhythmic backup. The song is about the toxins in the atmosphere. The final verse gets to the heart of the message:

Tell me who took away our ecology?
Well it must'a been all that technology.
The time is coming to show some might,
To blast away the techies and get back what's right.
We bin robbed.

That's just the start. As the morning passes, I realize RTLM existed to whip up hatred against science and technology. And they were very creative. Like "We Bin Robbed," all the music decried the destruction of the environment, or urged people to revolt against technology, or both. I listen to an episode of "All the Earth's Children," a serial play about a girl with environmental diseases. She seems to have three or four, all fatal, and her parents rage helplessly against technology, while her friends try to trace the toxins back to their sources. It's dramatic, wildly unrealistic, and very effective, I'm sure, in making people hate technology and science.

My father was a scientist. At least, I know he worked in a lab. What would it have been like to be the target of such intense hatred? By lunchtime, I feel sick. Astral looks grim when he comes out of his cubicle. I remember his mother was a scientist too.

"Are you all right?" he asks.

"I'm fine," I say automatically, then I stop and shake my head. "Not really. It's awful, isn't it?"

"I always wondered how my mother knew she had to send me away. I guess it was like that everywhere. It must have been a nightmare. At least we're finished for the day. I never thought I'd be happy to sit through a Council meeting."

"Neither did I." But I'm almost giddy with relief. I'd forgotten about the meeting.

At lunch, Kayko, Griffin, and Luisa ask about RTLM, but Astral and I don't say much. The feelings those broadcasts have provoked are too intense to discuss. The others are so excited about their hologram, they don't notice. This enthusiasm helps wash away the residue of hatred that seems to cling to me like a fine layer of filth.

We spend all afternoon watching the Justice Council debate the finer points of accepting victim statements, but I barely listen. Instead, I spin daydreams about my father, the brave resistance leader. But I can only create my dream father for a few moments at a time. RTLM keeps intruding. There's something horribly contaminating about those radio broadcasts.

I don't talk to Erica about RTLM after work. I'm too confused by the unaccountable shame of knowing that someone related to me incited such hatred. The hate was wrong, evil even, but it floods my system like a toxin. By nightfall, I feel like I'm crawling out of my skin. I wish I could go to

High Park, to see how Sparrow is, to talk to Prospero, but I've promised to stay away. I've got to distract myself.

Then I remember William, during the holo-conference, reminding me to use the portable holo-lab. I still haven't touched it. I've almost forgotten about science since we came here, about what I'm supposed to be. Now, I feel the need to reclaim that part of myself. I open the case, set up the rods that run the tiny holo-projectors, and patch my scribe into it. The lab can be used for original experiments, but I'm too involved with the Justice Council to think creatively, so I call up the menu of classic experiments and disappear into the world where I feel most at home.

I choose something basic, a twentieth-century experiment that creates organic compounds from inorganic materials. This might just be a cute trick, or it might help explain how life began on earth. Nobody knows. This experiment would be dangerous to run in my bedroom real life, because a flame is needed to keep water boiling inside glass tubes and a power source sends an electric charge through the artificial atmosphere, so it's perfect for the holo-lab. I call up the glass tubes and configure them into a closed circuit with a chamber for boiling water, a spark chamber, and a cooling area. It takes time to work out the best configuration. Then I insert the virtual sterile water and select the amounts of hydrogen, methane, and ammonia to create the reducing atmosphere. I set up a virtual fuel cell to provide the spark that charges the gases, simulating lightning. I work with intense concentration, loving every moment. Finally, after a few hours, I light the virtual burner that will keep the water boiling. It's a simple experiment, but the holo-lab won't produce results unless I've done everything properly, just as in real life.

When I'm finished, I shut off my lights and lie back on the bed so I can admire the skymaker's stars on the ceiling, but I leave the holo-lab open, so the blue flame lights my night as well. Science is not evil. Technology harmed the earth, but only because people weren't good enough to use it better. The Consumers could have stopped the destruction of the planet. Instead, they went on consuming.

The next few days are going to be difficult, but I've got to get through. Some lost truth about the start of the technocaust might be hiding in those broadcasts. If it is, I've got to be strong enough to find it.

18

Violence is justified when the future of the planet is at stake. Take out the techies.

—Radio RTLM, July 2353

When I meet Astral in the archives the next morning, dark circles smudge the skin under his eyes. "I can't take a whole day of this," he says before I can ask him what's wrong. "I barely slept last night, thinking about those broadcasts. I'm going to ask the others if you and I can spend afternoons working on the hologram of that rally. I know Kayko wanted to study the fractiles more first, but we've already identified that tent as an area of interest. Are you with me?"

He's taken me by surprise; I was steeled to carry on. "If we only listen in the mornings, those broadcasts will just take longer to get through."

"But I'd probably be able to sleep at night. Blake, you're a lot stronger than I am—" he starts to say, but I interrupt him.

"Oh, I don't think so. It upset me too, you know. I felt contaminated."

"But you found a way to overcome that, didn't you?"

"Well, yes."

"I knew you would. You can endure anything. Probably because you've been through so much." He spreads his hands and lets them fall in a gesture of helplessness. "I just don't have your resilience. This is eating me alive."

"All right," I say, "we'll talk to the others at lunchtime."

But I back away from Astral. In spite of my loathing for RTLM, I can't get into the media booth fast enough. I knew his anger was protecting something. These caustic radio broadcasts have stripped away his shell. He's so vulnerable, it scares me. I patch my scribe into the system, but before I load the disk, I stop, suddenly ashamed of myself. Everybody's afraid of something. Astral's fear of this hatred from the past is honest, at least. What am *I* afraid of? His weakness or his honesty? The intensity of his emotion? The thought that he might want me to feel something for him? When it comes to feelings, I'm the coward.

Maybe because I'm braced for RTLM today, it doesn't hit me quite as hard. I still have to listen to hate-filled songs, but there's a new feature: "Creatures from the Lost Ark," profiles of animals that disappeared during the mass extinctions of the twenty-first century. Today, it features the great apes, the gorilla and the orangutan, not-so-distant cousins of humans, now gone forever.

"They were like us in some ways," the broadcaster says. "In the twentieth century, we taught them sign language and learned they were capable of creative thought and deep emotion. But their native habitats were already threatened. Our greed for land and timber destroyed the orangutan even before the planet was plunged into chaos." Somehow, this is easier to listen to. The broadcaster sounds sad rather than bitter.

So the morning isn't nearly as bad as I expected. By lunchtime, I wonder if I could possibly persuade Astral to continue. But when I see his face, I know there's no point in trying. "As bad as yesterday?" I ask.

"Worse, if possible," he says. "The shows that invite listeners to express their opinions really get to me. You hear the hate in their voices. They managed to blame science for just about everything." He looks like he can't take much more.

"We'll ask about the hologram," I say.

The other aides are sympathetic when we explain. "Why didn't you tell us yesterday?" Kayko asks.

"I think we were too shocked to talk about it," I tell her. "Mine wasn't bad this morning, but Astral is right, it's very hard to listen to. Can you give us something else to do in the afternoons?"

"You can start to work on the fractile with the tent, but it won't be what you expect," Kayko says. "We're going to have a hard time with that projection because of the gaps that will appear as people move out of camera range. I'd like you to fast-forward all the way through the projection and identify as many of the people as possible. Keep track of when people leave the tent. Map their movements so we know which fractiles they disappear into and record the counter numbers at those points."

"So we won't actually have to hear anything today?" Astral says. "That's a relief."

"Why do you want us to record where people disappear?" I ask.

"So we can follow them," Griffin says. "We're hoping people will talk about things that went on inside the tent after they leave."

I shudder. "Eavesdropping on the past. It's a bit creepy, isn't it?"

"This whole exercise is eavesdropping on the past," Griffin replies.

"But today, you'll just be watching," Kayko says as she stands. "I'll get you started now. I'll put the counter on the wall. Record the numbers when you make notes. Fast-forward with your remotes and pause when you need to. Go to the main projection room now and I'll load the disk." As we start to leave, she says, "This will really be helpful. I didn't think we'd have time to do it."

"Are you all right?" I ask Astral as we go into the projection room. We ask each other this a lot now.

"No. I feel like I'm living the last year of my mother's life. She wasn't here, but things must have been about the same in British Columbia. If this keeps up, I'll have to try to talk to her."

The idea startles me, but I try not to show it. His ability to believe gives him strength. Who am I to argue with that?

"It's not as bad for you, is it?" he continues.

"No, I don't think it is. But there's a reason. I haven't told anyone else yet, but I might be about to find out more about my father." As I speak, I realize I've been afraid to tell anyone, as if talking about him might make me less likely to learn about my father's past.

The projection suddenly fills the room and freezes. Large red numbers glow against a wall. Kayko's voice floats over to us. "There's the counter. If you run into problems, we're here."

We should start work, but Astral ignores the projection around us. "Tell me about your father," he says.

So I do. "And I guess living in 2353 seems somehow fitting to me at the moment," I say when I finish. "But we may not find out much about him."

"Sounds like there's a good chance you will," Astral says. "I envy you. I don't know a thing about my father."

"Nothing at all?"

"Nothing. 'He checked out before you checked in.' That was all my mother would say when I asked." He points his remote at the control panel on the wall. "I'm going to mute this. It will be weird enough without the sound."

He's right. A full-scale hologram in fast-forward is completely bizarre. People rush around and through us in fast, jerky motion. At first, we only see Swan Gil inside the tent talking to someone who never comes into view. Then a crowd of people arrives. Astral freezes the projection. "Those faces look familiar."

We find every one in our files. "Let's keep going," Astral says. He sounds more like himself now. After an hour or so, there are about twenty people in the tent, and almost all of them are persons of interest. I can't think of them as suspects any more.

A tall blond woman carrying a baby enters the tent. She sits down, puts the baby to her breast, and begins talking to the people around her. The baby has curly red hair, and white, white skin. One hand waves like a little floating starfish while she nurses. I'm fascinated. "Do we know who that woman is?" I ask.

Astral pauses the projection. "Maybe."

It takes us awhile to find her. "Here she is," he says at last. "Dido Anders."

I hate to ask, but I can't stop myself. "Where is she now?"

Astral sighs. "She died in 2354."

Suddenly, this is just as grim as RTLM. I look at the baby, frozen in her mother's arms. Another orphan. "Keep going."

More people enter the tent. "This is incredible," I say. "These are all people we want to know about." A few minutes later, a man approaches the tent. I feel a shock of recognition. "I know him," I say before I can stop myself. He's clean-shaven and much younger, but I recognize his face and the way he carries himself. He stops at the door of the tent. Dido Anders comes out and gives him the baby. It can't be, I think. "Do you mind if we play this part?" I ask, and Astral complies.

The man stands at the opening of the tent and calls to Dido. She comes out and gives him the baby. "She's fed," she says, "so she'll be fine until this afternoon. Bring her back around two. And Gary, try not to do anything stupid, will you?"

He laughs. "You know me."

She lowers her voice to a furious whisper. "I mean it. Get yourself arrested today and you're on your own. What's going on here is too big for me to be distracted. Understand?"

"Got it." He grins. "Without a net." But she's still angry as he leaves.

Astral pauses again. "Is he in our files?"

I shake my head. "He looks exactly like someone I know. But I must be wrong."

I find it difficult to concentrate after that. Luckily, Astral is engaged enough for both of us. He barely notices how distracted I am. I must be mistaken, I tell myself while the rest of the projection whizzes by around us. No one would speak to Prospero that way. It seems unthinkable. But there's the red-haired baby. Rosa, he said she was called. The wife who died in the technocaust, that would be Dido Anders. Even his phrasing. "Without a net." That's what he said to me when I told him about Sparrow. But why was she worried he'd get arrested?

"Look at that!" Astral jolts me out of my thoughts. I look up to see a man surrounded by bodyguards approach the tent. Falcon Edwards.

He enters with someone who looks like an aide, and the bodyguards arrange themselves around the tent. "He's sitting right in the middle of camera range," Astral says. "We should be able to hear everything he says."

"Should we listen?"

"I'd love to, but that isn't what we said we'd do. We should wait until everyone can watch." For a long time after, we simply fast-forward. No one goes in or out.

"Maybe they wanted to shut the rally down," I say.

"But we know they didn't," Astral replies. "We have a full day of recordings."

"What's going on then?"

"I can't imagine. But it looks important."

Edwards finally leaves the tent after what must have been several hours, followed by his entourage. We map his course out of the fractile, then fast-forward again. No one else leaves for a long time after. The man named Gary comes back with the baby and Dido Anders leaves with him, looking upset. Soon after, a number of important people leave too, Eric Wong among them.

Kayko, Griffin, and Luisa finish for the day, but Astral and I send messages to our offices and stay on. Just before the projection ends, everyone leaves the tent. We spend a few frantic minutes viewing and rewinding until we get everyone's coordinates mapped as they disappear. Then the projection ends.

"That was a good afternoon's work," Astral says.

I'm still trying to process everything. "That wasn't really a speakers' rest area. Nobody went in or out for such a long time, but the speeches on the platform must have continued."

"You're right. We should meet with the others tomorrow morning to tell them about this."

"You're just trying to avoid RTLM." I'm surprised to find I can tease him.

He smiles. "Avoiding RTLM is a bonus, but the others really do need to know what we've found." He sighs. "And it won't take long to tell them. We'll still have plenty of time for hate radio."

That evening, at home, I'm pleased to see my experiment is already showing results. The water has turned pink, a sign that amino acids are collecting. Everything is falling into place.

19

I wanted to know my father died an honourable death. That would have been enough.

—From the victim statement of Blake Raintree

On Thursday morning when we tell the others what we've found, Griffin can hardly contain his excitement. "This could be what we've been waiting for," he says. "A real breakthrough." He pages through our notes on his scribe. "Look at this. Virtually everyone who was important in the environmental movement was in that tent. Maybe we should start on this projection right away."

Kayko frowns. "We need to work methodically, Griffin. We'll be ready to start next week."

He struggles to control his disappointment. "You're right. Next week it is."

"Griffin, what do you think was happening?" I ask. I'm as curious as he is.

"My guess is that Internal Protection offered the leaders of the protest movement some kind of deal. But it doesn't seem likely they accepted."

"Why?"

"Because every single person in that tent who we know anything about was dead within a year," Griffin says. "Except Falcon Edwards, of course. Look at the names. Swan Gil, Eric Wong, everyone. Most of them were arrested in the spring of 2354, all within a few weeks."

We fall silent while the horror of this settles.

"We'd better get back to work," Kayko says gently. "The faster we go, the sooner we'll find out what happened."

"Are you going to be all right with RTLM today?" I ask Astral as we walk to the archives.

"I'll have to be. We're onto something now. We've got to see this through." He sounds determined. I'm glad he's found a way to face this.

But when we arrive in the archives, Terry is waiting. "Blake," he says, "Erica Townsend wants to see you right away."

Astral pulls a face. "Lucky you," he says as I leave.

I can't imagine what's so urgent that it can't wait until lunch, but when I find Hanif waiting with Erica, I know why I'm here. I also know, from the way they look, there isn't going to be a happy ending. It's just like the day I found out about my mother. Well, I wasn't expecting him to be alive. Goodbye, daddy, I say silently.

"Sit down, Blake," Erica says. She looks stricken. I wish she wouldn't. I'll be fine.

"You found out about my father," I say, trying to make it easier for them.

Hanif plunges right in. "You were right about the name Monax. It's uncommon, so it didn't take me long to trace your mother. After I found her ID code, it was easy to locate your parents' marriage record. And that was how I found your father's name."

"And he's not alive," I say. "You don't have to be upset for me. I didn't think he would be. How did he die?"

Hanif shifts uncomfortably in his chair. Erica speaks. "He's not dead, Blake."

"My father's alive?" I laugh with sheer joy. "I can't believe it. Alive." Then why do they look so miserable? "What's wrong?"

"Your father's name is Evan Morrow, Blake," Erica says. "He's a person of interest. I talked to you about him once."

"I don't remember. A person of interest? So he *was* he an environmental leader?" I allow myself to hope.

"No, he wasn't. He was a scientist, working on satellite surveillance. He had nothing to do with the environmental movement."

"Well, that explains the implant in my arm. But why is he a person of interest?"

"Blake, this is going to be hard on you. But he only wanted to find you and your mother. Internal Protection offered him the opportunity to track you, in exchange—" she falters.

"In exchange for what?" I ask.

"In exchange for helping to track down others. People they wanted to capture." Hanif says this. Erica can't.

Everything fades around me. "That can't be true. How do you know? Did you talk to him without me?"

"Blake, I spoke to him before I knew he was your father," Erica says.

"How?" I feel overwhelmingly stupid. They are trying to explain, but I don't seem to be able to understand.

"In prison." Erica almost whispers the words. I look at her without comprehension.

"Your father is in the East End Detention Centre," Hanif adds.

I struggle with the idea. And then I understand. My father was a collaborator. My world implodes. "No!" I yell, as if noise could drive the idea from my mind. I stand up and back away. "You've made some kind of mistake. It's not true. It can't be true." I turn and run from the office. As I leave, I hear Erica say, "Let her go."

In the hall, part of me disconnects. I feel as if I'm watching myself from a great distance. That distant part takes control. Keep walking, it says. I'm relieved to see I walk past the archives. I can't possibly face Astral.

I don't realize I'm going to leave the building until I go through the main doors. Just keep walking, I tell myself. Outside, I notice something odd has happened to my senses. Passing a flower bed, I see every leaf and every petal on the asters. In the lawn, each blade of grass is separate. I just let myself run on autopilot, walking past the government buildings in front of Queen's Park, heading south. I only know I need to go somewhere I've never been. I don't care where. I stop at the stoplights and walk with the other pedestrians. I'm surprised I would bother to protect myself from the traffic, but, as quickly as I register that emotion, I push it away. There is no room for feeling inside me now. I am swollen and hollow and empty.

"Hey," a voice calls. "Hey, stop!"

I don't know if this is directed at me and I don't care. I keep walking. Someone grabs me by the shoulder and spins me around. It's Spyker. "Don't try to pretend you don't hear me," she says. "I know you. You took Sparrow. What did you do with her?"

"Go away," I say, but she won't. I try to leave her behind, but she follows, yelling, "Where is she? What have you done to her? I know you took her."

She's giving me a headache. I've got to find the magic words that will make her go away. I stop walking. "Sparrow went to a better place," I say.

Under all that makeup, Spyker pales. "You killed her, didn't you?" She doesn't shout the words, she whispers them. Somehow, the terror in her eyes makes me feel something—pity for her. I shake my head. "I didn't kill her. She's safe." I hope this will be enough to send Spyker away.

I walk for what seems like a long time, blocks and blocks. Sometimes I think I'm alone again, but then I see Spyker, still trailing me. We're far from the territory of her Tribe now. I wish she'd go back.

Suddenly, the street ends. I'm facing a huge stone building, grey, fronted by a bank of stone steps that runs the length of the facade. The steps are covered with homeless people. No children, I notice that right away. Only adults. I register all this while crossing the street. But now, if I want to keep walking, I've got to figure out how to get around this building. My brain is barely functioning. The problem stops me.

Spyker has caught up with me. "We shouldn't be here," she says. "Those debtors are squatting in Union Station. It isn't safe."

"Leave if you're worried." My voice is dead. I'll stay here if that's what it takes to get Spyker away from me.

She bites her lip. "Look," she says, "couldn't you take me where you took Sparrow? I hate my life. I really need to get away."

So that's why she's been following me. Life with a Tribe is awful for a girl Spyker's age. I remember. But I don't see what I can do. "I can't," I tell her. I don't elaborate.

Tears spring to Spyker's eyes. "Come on," she says. "You did it for Sparrow." She's begging.

"It's not that easy," I start to say, when I suddenly feel a tap on my shoulder.

"Hey, girlies," a voice says behind me, "what are you doing down here all by yourselves?"

I turn to find a man in filthy rags. Worse is his skin, which is also in rags. Long strips have peeled off his face and hands to reveal a pink, cracked, tender surface beneath that cannot rightly be called skin. I've seen this before. It's a reaction to toxins. Spyker and I are both speechless. "Well, come on," he says, finally. "You must be here for something."

A crowd collects around us. The sharp odour of unwashed bodies stabs my nostrils.

"The young one's from a Tribe," I hear a woman say. "What's she doing off her turf?"

"Yeah, what are you doing here, darling?" The first man speaks again. "And who's your friend? You girls buying or selling?" More people have gathered. I feel trapped. The man puts his hand on my shoulder, and this time he leaves it there.

"Get your hand off her!" Spyker is so forceful, the man's hand flies off my shoulder, and people back away. From nowhere, a makeshift knife appears in Spyker's hand. "Don't you dare touch her," she whispers. Her voice is filled with fury. I have a feeling that this isn't about me.

The man holds his hands up as he backs off. "Hey, I didn't mean anything," he says, but as he speaks, a man behind Spyker lunges. Her small knife clatters to the stone.

"Everyone stand away from the girl in blue." A magnified voice, calm and authoritative, comes from the street. When the crowd parts, I find a group of armed security men pointing weapons in our direction. Then I spot Hanif.

"Come here," he orders. He doesn't sound angry.

I grab Spyker's hand. "She was trying to protect me."

Hanif wavers for only a nanosecond. "Bring her, too."

We are whisked into an armoured vehicle. I can't believe it. "How did you find me?" I ask.

Hanif looks surprised. "Your micro-chip, of course. We can always find you. You knew that," he reminds me. "Remember how we tracked you to High Park?"

"I forgot."

He nods. "You've had a shock. We were just going to track you, but when I realized where you were headed, I thought we'd better intervene. Union Station is a dangerous place."

"I tried to tell her," Spyker says. "She wouldn't listen. I had to use my shiv to try to protect her. I lost it." She sounds devastated.

Hanif looks at Spyker with interest. "And who are you?" he asks. Spyker is only too happy to tell him. While they chat, I slump into my seat. In those brief moments of danger, I'd forgotten about my father. Now, I sink into despondency again.

Our vehicle goes into some kind of tunnel under the Queen's Park complex that I hadn't even suspected was there. The doors open and everyone gets out. "I'll take you back to your office in a moment," Hanif says to me, then he turns to Spyker. "If you ever want to get off the streets, we need people like you," he says.

Spyker's eyes widen. "Really?"

"Really. It's not an easy life, but I have a feeling you'd take to it." He hands her something. "Come to the address on this card. My name's on it. Tell them I asked to see you."

"Can I do that today? Now?" she asks.

Hanif laughs. "If you want." He turns to one of his men. "Take her up with you," he says. "I'll be there shortly."

"That's good," I say when we leave the others. "She needs to get off the streets. You can't imagine what it's like."

"Actually, I can," he replies. "You aren't the only one who's escaped that life, you know."

"You?"

Hanif nods, but he doesn't elaborate.

Erica is waiting in our office with Kayko. "I don't think I can work any more today," I say.

"Nobody expects you to," Erica says gently. "Kayko has a suggestion for you."

"I'd like to take you to our house in the Muskokas, north of here," Kayko says. "We could come back on Monday."

"But what about work?"

"We'll only miss a day and a half. We can leave right now, Blake. I have a car waiting. We have everything you'll need there.

My vision blurs with tears. "Did she tell you?" I whisper. Kayko nods. I let her take my hand and lead me away.

20

The morning mist weaves
a shawl of consolation
through autumn-bright trees

—Kayko Miyazaki

When I wake in the morning, I don't know where I am or how I got here. I see long planes of dark, polished wood that gradually resolve themselves into walls. The ceiling, high above, is criss-crossed with thick, lovely wooden beams. I'm lying on a mattress on the floor in a room that seems otherwise empty. Lying on the floor would normally remind me of rats and my time with the Tribe, but the mattress is soft, the bedding clean and warm. I snuggle into it. I never want to leave. But I feel heavy, as if an unbearable weight of grief has settled on me. Did someone die? I wonder. Then I remember. No. Someone who should have died didn't. My father.

The full force of yesterday washes over me like a wave of dizziness. I close my eyes. Everything I knew and valued about myself is gone. I want out of my life. I wish I were the sort of person who could just shuck off reality and disappear into my own mind, but I know that isn't going to happen. What was it Astral said? "You can endure anything." He said that the day before yesterday, a million years ago, or neither, or both. And now, I have to find out if that's true.

Behind me, the house sighs, as if it's whispering a secret, but I don't move. Kayko appears in my field of vision, carrying a tray. She's wearing a kimono, as she did the night I met her. She kneels beside my bed and pours green tea from a cast-iron teapot into a delicate porcelain cup. The scent of it tickles my nose. She offers me the steaming cup. "Sit up," she says. Her voice is gentle, but it's an order. I obey before I have a chance to reconsider.

Kayko pours a cup of tea for herself.

"Where's all the furniture?" I ask. I didn't know I was going to say this until the words leave my mouth.

Kayko laughs. "This is a traditional Japanese house. The rooms are almost empty, so they can be used for anything. When the bed's not being used, it goes away in there." She points to a wall of cupboards I haven't even noticed. "It's a nice day," she adds.

"Do I have to get up?"

"I think you'd better."

"Is anyone else here?"

"Not in this house. There's another house out of sight up the hill. The help lives there. They'll look after us, but they won't intrude. My grandparents wanted to create the illusion of a traditional Japanese house. But it's just that. The floors and walls are heated. I even have an office in the basement. I used to do a lot of my holo-zine work here."

"Work," I say. "They'll start on that hologram without us—"

Kayko interrupts. "No they won't. I spoke with Griffin this morning. He and Luisa will help Astral with the radio broadcasts. They won't touch the holograms until that's done. Anyway, today's Friday. Don't worry about it. Why don't you get dressed?"

"I don't think I can handle a kimono."

Kayko laughs. "Neither can I, not for outside. This is just a dressing gown. You'll find regular clothes in the cupboards. My clothes should fit you."

Kayko leaves, closing what looks like a sliding paper wall behind her. When I stand, I see that the front of the room gives out onto a glassed-in porch. The view beyond is mostly water. I cross a floor covered in mats of tightly woven straw, warm to the touch. The land in front of the house slopes down to the water. The lake looks large, but it folds into smaller bays dotted with little rock islands. The one directly in front of me has a pavilion with an elaborate peaked roof in a graceful little garden.

I want to wear something that mirrors my turmoil. I remember Erica once told me about people in the Middle Ages smearing their faces with soot and wearing coarse, uncomfortable clothes to express sorrow and regret. "Sackcloth and ashes," it was called. I would do that now, but Kayko's cupboards hold nothing even remotely like sackcloth and ashes. I settle for black pants in some kind of velvety microfibre, and a charcoal-grey sweater of incredibly soft wool. If I want to punish myself, I've come to the wrong place.

I slide the paper wall open and walk through large empty rooms to find Kayko sitting on the floor at a low table by a wall of windows. She is also wearing pants and a sweater. She smiles. "Fruit and croissants for breakfast. Are you all right with no chairs?"

"I think so." I fold my legs awkwardly and sit facing her. As I do, the view beyond her comes into focus. "It looks like something out of a book," I say.

Kayko glaces over her shoulder. "My mother's garden? It is, mostly. Books and paintings. That's what she used to create the design. I'll show it to you after."

As we eat, I begin to realize Kayko is willing to let me spend the next few days talking about nothing. If she said anything, I would probably retreat into myself. Knowing she won't makes it possible for me to face what's happened, somehow. When I finish eating, I say, "Will the others hate me?" I intended to speak in a normal voice, but my words come out in a whisper.

"You're the same person you were yesterday, Blake," Kayko says. "We know that."

"But I'm not who I thought I was."

"You are so. Nothing about your past has changed. You had to struggle through that impossible childhood alone, and you came out a fine person. I am so proud to be your friend."

Kayko's kindness makes it impossible for me to reply. She seems to understand. "Come on," she says, rising, "I'll show you the garden."

Kayko leads me to a small, closet-like entrance hall where we find our shoes. We go outside. The fall air is damp and cool. It smells of pine.

The house is built into the side of a hill of grey rock and lichen. A stream flows from one pool to another with little waterfalls and bridges between. The low, rambling house is roofed with wooden shingles and dead pine needles and moss. "The house looks as if it grew here," I say.

"It never ceases to amaze me," Kayko says. "The idea came from the other side of the world, but this house *belongs* here."

"Does it always feel so peaceful?"

"Yes. Even with other people around. The house was designed to create a sense of inner harmony, of course, but there's something about this place as well. My grandmother used to say being here is like being cradled in the hands of a god. Come on."

We follow the stream along a bare dirt path winding up the hill. The garden looks sparse at first. A single tree or shrub, sometimes just a few rocks are displayed here and there, with space composed of water or grass or moss, or white gravel between. But it doesn't seem barren. Instead, it seems clear-headed, somehow. As if I'm seeing the gardener's thoughts about peace and beauty. Even at this time of year, when nothing is blooming, it's perfect.

We reach a plateau at the top, and I see the smaller, more usual-looking house. Kayko points to a bench. "I love this view. Sit and have a look." From here, the Japanese house is part of the landscape. The hills around the lake glow, even in this subdued light. Rare splashes of crimson and scarlet are woven into the orange and yellow maples and birches against the evergreen trees, the darker backdrop of fir and pine and spruce that will not change. The colours are mirrored in the calm waters of the lake.

"I wish I could stay here forever," I say. For a few moments, I've felt all right. Then, suddenly and without warning, the weight of my grief presses down. I feel as if I can hardly stand. "I think I need to lie down." Kayko doesn't argue. She leads me back to my room. The bed has been made, but it's still waiting for me. "I thought you said it went into the cupboard," I say.

"I told them to leave it out, in case you needed it."

I'm so tired. Kayko fetches a padded quilt from the cupboard and places it over me. I don't even hear her leave the room.

When I wake again, it's late afternoon. I wander around the house until I find Kayko, sitting at a kind of low desk built into a window box. She smiles when she sees me. "You missed lunch. Are you hungry?"

"Not really, but I'll eat."

She rises. "Good. Wait here. I'll order something."

I look down at the papers when she leaves, expecting to see reports about work, something official. Instead, I find pages of short, three-line poems, handwritten. I remember Kayko once talked about writing a Japanese form of poetry.

I probably shouldn't, but I glance at one. "The homeless girl's eyes . . ." I read.

"I asked for soup and a sandwich." Kayko's voice is unexpectedly close behind me.

I jump away from the papers. "I'm sorry," I say, "I shouldn't have been so nosy."

"The haiku? I don't mind. I'm not very good at it. It's more of a writing exercise than anything. Let's get your lunch," she says, "then we should talk." The serious note in her voice makes my heart misgive.

The food looks wonderful in an abstract way, but I eat without tasting. When I finish, Kayko says, "We can stay here as long as you need to. I spoke to Erica while you were sleeping. She'll come too, if you want."

I shake my head. "We can't stay here. They need us at work. And I want to find out what happened, now more than ever. If I can make sense of the technocaust, maybe it will be easier to accept the news about my father."

"We'll go back early on Monday, then. I'll tell Erica."

"I should tell her myself."

"Good," Kayko says. "We'll call her later." But she still looks troubled. "There's something else—" Kayko starts to say. I cut her off.

"Whatever it is, can't it wait until next week? I'm still pretty shaky."

"I know, but we should talk about this, because I might be able to do something about it."

"Something about what?"

"Your father is in prison because he helped the Protectors during the technocaust. That means you won't be allowed to make a victim statement."

I go numb. "That decision was made because of me. Erica would never have voted in favour if I hadn't been so upset by the idea that those people might make victim statements.

And now, I'm one of those people. How's that for justice?"

"It's not justice at all. I didn't think so then and I don't now. Blake, I'm not willing to let this go."

I laugh. "What can you do about it? Ask the Justice Council to make an exception for me? Because they know me and I'm not like everyone else who's related to people who ran the technocaust? They'd totally discredit themselves before their real work has even started. I'm not that important. I did this to myself, and I'm stuck with it."

But when I look at Kayko, there's that gleam of mischief in her eyes. "That wasn't what I had in mind," she says. "We're not asking the Justice Council for anything. Do you have your victim statement with you?"

"Yes, it's almost finished. I carry it everywhere. It's in the bag I brought from the office. Why?"

"I want to record you, reading your victim statement. Then I'll interview you about your life and post it all on my holo-zine, so everyone can hear your story."

"Wouldn't that violate our confidentiality agreement?"

"I don't think so," Kayko says. "We didn't learn any of this because of the work we're doing with the Justice Council. Will you do it?"

I bite my lip. "I can hardly bear to think my story might never be heard. But this seems, well, self-serving, as if my story were more important than anyone else's."

"But don't you see? Your story *is* important, especially now. People have got to realize that things are more complex than they want them to be. This isn't as simple as guilt and innocence. Until everyone realizes that, we'll never get over the technocaust. But most people don't think in concepts, Blake, it's too abstract. They understand stories. Whether they realize it or not, your story will help them understand why we need to be able to forgive."

"But I can't say that. Kayko, I can't even begin to forgive.

I hate the people who did this to me, to everyone who suffered." Hot tears spill down my cheeks. "I hate . . ." I pause, gulp a deep breath, and go on. "I hate my father for betraying everything that matters to me. I've never been as good as you and your uncle and Erica, as Griffin and Monique. I was only pretending because I thought you'd lose respect for me if you knew."

There. Now Kayko finally knows. I stare at my hands, waiting for her judgment. Pity is the best I can hope for now that I have shown myself to be so inadequate.

"It doesn't matter," she says softly.

I look up at her. "What?"

"You always ask so much of yourself, Blake. Anyone in your position would feel the way you do. Let me ask you something. Do you like hating?"

"No. I hate it," I say. When I realize what I've said, I laugh. "When we first came here, I thought hate gave me the energy I needed to keep going. But when I met Astral, I started to realize what hate could do to someone. Kayko, I'm tired of hating."

"Good," she says. "I think, one day, you'll be able to let your hate go. Tell your story. That might be the beginning. And maybe not just for you. That's what I'm hoping."

"I'm not sure—" I start to say, but she won't let me finish.

"I know you're not, but I am. Just trust me, all right?"

"All right," I say, because I'm too confused to trust myself.

21

At dawn the crows call
the moon beyond the water.
We must leave this peace.

—Kayko Miyazaki

We work hard the next day Kayko helps me finish my victim statement. Then we record it in her holo-zine lab and she interviews me. Her questions are tactful. She sticks to my story, never asking me to reveal more about my feelings than I want to. I find I can even talk about my father. I begin to realize the work Kayko's been doing with us at Queen's Park must seem terribly limited to her. On Sunday, we edit and format the holograms, getting everything ready to post on her holo-zine site. As always, work has a therapeutic effect on me. It lifts me out of the lethargy that was sapping my strength, makes me feel maybe I'll be all right.

"We're done," Kayko says on Sunday afternoon. "Everything's posted."

Will anyone even notice? I wonder. Maybe Kayko and I have just been talking to ourselves. But it would be ungrateful to say that.

We rise before the sun on Monday and Kayko's driver delivers us to Queen's Park before work begins. When I see Erica, she hugs me, then studies my face. "You look good," she says, "better than I expected. I told William over the weekend. He'll come for a few days, if that would help. Fraser too."

I shake my head. "Disrupting everyone else's life won't make things better. I want to get back into my normal routine." I wish I could leave it at that, but I can't. "Erica, what do you know about him?" The question just spills out.

She doesn't have to ask who I'm talking about. "I tried to tell you about him once. Do you remember? When you started working on the holograms. He never cared about politics, Blake. He was just plucked out of a group of techies who were arrested early in the technocaust." She hesitates.

"But . . . ?" I prompt.

"But he made himself useful, tracking down techies, and he rose though the ranks until he was very high in Internal Protection."

Falcon Edwards's portfolio. I wince. "How high?"

"Until the Uprising, he was Assistant Deputy of Tracking."

"He must have caught a lot of people who might have gone free otherwise." My bitterness comes out in my voice. "Does he know I'm alive?"

"Not yet, but he will. Hanif told me, when someone who has been declared dead is discovered alive, their relatives are informed. It's official policy."

"What if he wants to meet me? I don't think I can."

"Nobody's going to force you."

This is all I can handle right now. "I'd better get to work."

"Are you sure? We've started hiring extra staff. The building is full of strangers. If you wanted to take a few more days off—" Erica begins, but I interrupt her.

"What we're doing now is important." This sounds harsher than I intended. "Besides," I add, "I need the distraction."

"If you're sure. I checked the work schedule. You're all in the archives today."

I'm worried about facing the other aides, but they're already at work in media booths when I reach the archives.

Terry Raven looks worried. "You really want to work?" he asks. He obviously knows what's happened to me. I don't have the energy to explain how important this work is to me now. I just nod and let him load the disk.

The others made real progress with the RTLM recordings while Kayko and I were away. The programming has changed dramatically. I seem to be listening to an official announcement. "Anyone engaged in research or production in the following areas must report to the nearest office of Internal Protection immediately to obtain a technology registration number: any form of nanotechnology, biotechnology, satellite tracking, genetic modification of any type including gene therapy, tissue, nerve, and bone regeneration research, any artificial intelligence research or application, any form of subatomic modification . . ." The list goes on and on. The technocaust has started. The announcement ends by saying, "Failure to report to Internal Protection is a crime. Failure to report anyone who does not obtain a technology registration number will result in arrest. Harbouring anyone who has been ordered to report will result in arrest. Citizens are urged to cooperate in this effort to register those involved in advanced science and technology for the sake of stability within our society."

Between the propaganda music and a call-in show that invites people to name friends and neighbours who should report to Internal Protection, this announcement is repeated every half hour. The change is hard to understand. RTLM used to taunt the government and demand changes. Now, they're broadcasting official government policy. How did that happen? Nothing in the broadcast helps to explain.

The recording ends just before lunchtime. I find the other aides already gathered outside the media booths. "I'm ready for a new recording," I say.

"There aren't any," Griffin replies. "That was the last of them."

"Thank goodness for that," Kayko says. She looks pale and shaken, and I realize she is the only one of us who was hearing RTLM for the first time. Everyone else looks grim but satisfied. I situate myself beside Kayko, out of Astral's line of vision. I have no idea how he'll treat me now, and I'm not ready to find out.

"You did an amazing job while we were away," Kayko says. "Does this mean we can start on the hologram this afternoon?"

Griffin nods. "Just as soon as we put our notes about RTLM together to see what we've learned. That won't take long. Let's break for lunch first."

While we were working, the hallway outside the archives filled with people. A long line snakes all the way back to the main lobby. I remember what Erica said about hiring, but it's still surprising.

"How did all those people get past Security?" I ask as we enter the stairwell.

"They've all been cleared for interviews," Griffin says. "It was crazy around here on Friday. Just as well you were . . ." he stops and turns bright red.

"It's all right," I say quickly. "I know what you meant." Behind us, I feel as if Astral's eyes are burning a hole in me.

Conversation at lunch is forced. There are too many strangers in the cafeteria to talk freely about our work, and my friends skirt around the discovery of my father as if it were an unexploded bomb. I meet Astral's eyes only once, by chance, and we both look away quickly. We were friends, at least. Now, it seems, we're something worse than strangers.

It's a relief to find ourselves in the quiet media rooms again. I'm not the only one who thinks so. "At least this area is still off limits to most people," Kayko says when we all sit down.

"So," Griffin says, smiling, "let's find out what we've learned about RTLM." His energy takes some of the grimness out of the task. "These recordings covered a few months in 2353, the time period we're especially interested in."

"How do these broadcasts relate to the big rally on the hologram?" Kayko asks. "Didn't that happen around the same time?"

"Yes, they overlap," Astral says. "I heard announcements urging people to attend that rally on some of the broadcasts I listened to."

"And RTLM's purpose was?" Griffin throws the question out at us.

"To promote hatred for science and technology," I reply. "That seems to have been the reason for its existence."

"And who do you think the audience was?" Griffin asks.

Astral answers. "That's an interesting question. From what you said about radio before we started, I expected the target audience would be disadvantaged people. 'The poorest of the poor,' you said. But that's not the impression I got from listening. Some of the people calling in were quite articulate. They didn't sound disadvantaged."

"So the audience was wider than you expected," Kayko says.

"It's not surprising RTLM gained a broader audience," Griffin says, "given the climate of hostility."

"Yes, but I noticed something odd today," I say. "This was a pirate radio station. Why would they broadcast an official government announcement?" I explain what I heard.

"That's interesting," Griffin says. "Could you date those broadcasts?"

I check the notes on my scribe. "October 2353."

"How could a station like RTLM become an instrument of the government?" Astral asks.

"They began as enemies, but suddenly they were—how do you say this?—on the same page," Luisa says.

Griffin shakes his head. "And we may never know how. A lot of questions about the past just go unanswered. Well, if that's all we know about RTLM we can start on the hologram. Blake, why don't we work on the speakers' platform?"

"When Falcon Edwards goes into that tent, I'd really like to see what goes on," I say.

"We'll all watch that projection," Griffin agrees. "It would be cruel to leave anyone out."

As soon as we're alone, Griffin speaks. As always, he's very direct. "I don't know what to say to you, Blake. It doesn't seem right to express regret at the discovery that your father is alive, but congratulations are hardly in order."

"Regret is closer to what I feel," I say. "That's selfish, isn't it? To wish my father dead because it would make my life easier? But everything is more complicated now."

"I think everything was just as complicated before, really. Now, it's just impossible for you to ignore that."

Until now, Griffin's breathtaking bluntness has always been directed at Astral. His honesty hurts, but I know it's not malicious. Luckily, the recording starts before I think of a reply.

We're back in the same hot day in August 2353, inside the Hippodrome, facing the stage at the rally. Some of the faces on the stage are familiar, but most are not. "These are just minor players," Griffin says to me after awhile.

"Everyone important was in that tent," I reply.

Speaker after speaker rails against technology, against science, against the government for not slowing the pace of technological advance. There is one new twist. Near the end of the day, a man with long blond hair and flowing robes comes onto the stage. He raises his arms, and the crowd falls completely silent. "What man can enter paradise with two hearts?" he says. "When a heart is replaced, that's natural, but when a new heart is grown from a man's own tissue and placed within his breast, he will find himself, on the day of resurrection, with not one heart, but two." His voice rises and the crowd's energy seems to rise with him. "This is an abomination. We must call upon the Protectors to live up to their name and stop regeneration therapy, and stop the research that feeds this loathsome practice." The crowd roars as if he's given them what they've been waiting for.

"That not like anything we've seen before," I say.

"No, and it doesn't belong here," Griffin replies. "Finding regeneration therapy morally offensive is not an environmental issue."

"Who is he?"

"Fern Logos is his name."

"I suppose he's dead too?" I ask.

Griffin consults his scribe. "Yes. Around the same time as everyone else. This is odd, though. He was killed in an eco-terrorist attack. He seems to have been the target." Griffin looks puzzled. "That doesn't make sense, does it? The eco-terrorists didn't kill people, and he wasn't involved in anything they'd attack."

"Well, there's another mystery. It's odd. I know I've heard something about regeneration therapy recently, but I can't place it."

Soon after Logos speaks, everyone who has spoken over the last few hours comes back out onto the stage as Eric Wong comes forward to stand before the prompter. I've seen him often enough now to recognize uneasiness in his manner. Something was troubling him.

"We call upon all governments to restrict the following types of technology," he reads. "Any form of nanotechnology, biotechnology, genetic modification of any type including gene therapy, tissue, nerve, and bone regeneration research, any artificial intelligence research . . ."

"Stop," I yell. "Stop the recording."

"What's wrong?"

"That's why I remembered regeneration therapy. I've heard that list before. This morning, on RTLM, in the government announcement about registering people at the beginning of the technocaust."

"Is that so surprising?"

"Yes! Griffin, the lists are identical. Come to the archives with me. Wait." I get out my scribe. "Back it up, will you? I want to record this speech."

In the archives, Griffin listens to both recordings. "You're right. They're identical."

"But why?"

"I don't know. The day's just about over. Why don't we see if the others have learned anything that can help us make sense of this?"

Leaving the archives, I almost walk into Hanif. I'm genuinely pleased. I haven't seen him since the day he rescued me. I'm not even sure I thanked him.

"I was coming to get you," he says. "We need to talk." He looks around. Job-seekers still line the hall. There's no privacy here.

"We can finish up without you," Griffin says. "I'll send my notes to you immediately. You won't miss a thing."

I find myself walking toward my office with Hanif, trying not to wonder what unpleasant surprise he might have for me now. I suddenly remember something. "Can I ask where Spyker is?" I say as we turn into an empty hallway.

"Not specifically. She's being educated. I hear she's fine. Eventually, she can apply for a job in Security. We find homeless children are often adaptable and fearless. They're good at the work if we catch them young enough. I'm always on the lookout for kids like that. It gives me some satisfaction to do for them what was once done for me." We enter my office and close the door. "I came looking for you because someone wants to talk to you."

"If it's my father, I'm not ready." I've been expecting this, maybe even waiting for it.

"Not your father," he replies.

A surge of emotion catches me unawares. To my dismay, it's disappointment. "Oh, who then?" I try to keep my feelings out of my voice.

"A reporter from *The Solar Flare.* She says she saw something about you." Hanif raises one eyebrow. "On a holozine? She wants to interview you."

This is the last thing I want. "But that's not allowed, is it?"

"We've learned from experience that it's unwise to refuse a specific request like this. If we do, *The Solar Flare* will accuse the Transitional Council of curtailing freedom of speech. People get very upset. We can't afford that kind of attention. So, you have permission to give an interview, from Dr. Siegel himself."

"I have permission to give an interview. Do I have permission to *not* give an interview?"

Hanif smiles. "No, Blake, you do not. We have to honour this request."

"Will you come with me?"

He shakes his head. "My identity has to be protected from the media. In fact, if you were accompanied by anyone, the interviewer might portray that as an attempt to control what you could say."

"So no one can come with me? Not even Erica?"

"Not even Erica. You'll be briefed by a media officer tomorrow morning, to make sure you understand which areas of your work are confidential. Other than that, I'm afraid, you're on your own."

22

Love those who seek the truth; fear those who find it.

—An old Truth Seeker saying

The next morning, while my hair and face are styled into someone I barely resemble, I'm briefed by a brusque government media officer. She does not hide her disapproval of the unwanted attention I've attracted as she reminds me not to talk about the internal workings of the Justice Council. Then she takes me to a media room.

The reporter she introduces me to is a shock. She's much younger than I was expecting, around my own age. At first glance, her hair, makeup, and clothes make her look like a Tribe member. Then I realize the ripped clothes are new, the skin under the makeup is flawless, and her hair is only styled to resemble a Tribal Mohawk. This is artifice. She introduces herself as Zoe Nova. I wonder if the name is also her creation. We are left alone, cameras running all around us. I can't believe I'm forced to deal with someone who thinks being part of a Tribe is a fashion statement.

But, as we talk, I start to like her. She's focussed and articulate. She quickly explains it won't be necessary for me to discuss my life in detail. "I'll summarize in my intro to this interview," she says, "and I'll ask you to sign a release, so we can put the whole of your victim statement up as supplementary viewing for those who want more in-depth coverage." When I agree, she continues for the cameras. "I saw your victim statement and the interview you did with

Kayko Miyazaki. Stories like yours must be everywhere, but we can't get anyone to talk."

I wouldn't be talking either if I hadn't trapped myself like this. I wish, one last time, that I could hide my feelings by talking about my work, and then I begin. It feels like jumping off a cliff. "I wasn't expecting this to happen," I say.

"You mean this interview, or what you found out about your father?"

I shrug. "Any of it. When I came here, I thought everything was black and white. I thought it would be a simple matter of punishing the bad people." I take a deep breath. "I know people who feel we'll never make things right without forgiveness, but I wasn't one of them. I wanted to see the ones who had ruined my life suffer. My hate sustained me, it gave me a reason to carry on, an excuse to avoid looking at the complexity of the situation."

Zoe Nova looks shocked. I guess she wasn't expecting this kind of honesty. But honesty is the only thing about myself that I can be sure of now. Everything else is in a state of flux.

"You said in your interview with Kayko Miyazaki that you won't be allowed to formally present your victim statement because of a ruling by the Justice Council. This is because you are closely related to someone imprisoned for playing a major role in the technocaust, your father. But you haven't seen your father for years, isn't that right?"

"Yes. I didn't even know he was alive until last week."

"Is it fair that his activities are going to keep you from making your victim statement?"

"I thought it was fair when the decision was made. I still do." I'm glad I'm not allowed to talk about how that happened.

Now she looks confused. "But, surely your experience must cause you to have more compassion for people in your situation."

I find myself smiling. "You're asking me to have compassion for myself?"

She looks totally bewildered now. "Well, basically, yes," she falters.

"Look, I was willing to think people deserved to be punished because of their family circumstances." I search back to that heated conversation in the cafeteria the day the decision was made. "That's called guilt by association, isn't it? It sounded like a good idea to me. And now, I find I'm one of those people. I can't very well say, 'Oh, this changes everything, I deserve to be treated differently,' can I?" I don't wait for Zoe to reply. "If you're asking me if I've reconsidered my ideas about guilt and innocence, well, then yes, I have. I used to think I was a victim of the technocaust, so that made me innocent. I'd played a small role in the Uprising, so that made me good. Everyone who wasn't on my side was bad. Then, there was this whole category of people who were guilty. They deserved to be punished, and I wasn't very careful about who I put into that category. So it turns out I put myself in there.

"I don't know exactly what I've learned from this experience yet. I haven't had time to sort it out. But there is one thing I think I have learned. There aren't just guilty people and innocent people, just good and evil. All of us are innocent, and all of us are guilty to some degree."

"So you *are* more likely to forgive others?" she insists.

"At this point, I'm less likely to forgive myself. Maybe, eventually, I can work toward being more likely to forgive others. It's a goal." I shake my head. "I don't know if I'll make it."

This isn't so bad, I think. Maybe I even feel better, getting my feeling out into the open. But then, I hear the next question.

"Are you going to see your father?"

The word "no" comes to my lips, but I stop myself. "I don't know," I say. "I really don't."

Suddenly, Zoe Nova relaxes. "All right, I think that covers everything. This is going to make a big splash."

Just what I need, I think, but I don't say it.

The morning is almost over. I wonder if the other aides have been working on the holograms. Then suddenly, it hits me. Falcon Edwards and the tent. Have they watched that recording without me? The media rooms all have red lights above the doors. When a room is in use, the light is lit. I pop my head into an occupied room and find Astral with Luisa.

Luisa smiles and waves me in.

"Did you look at the tent yet?" I ask.

"Griffin promised we'd all do it together," Astral reminds me. "We haven't even started on that recording."

There's an uncomfortable silence. "It's almost lunch-time, I think I'll take a break," Luisa says, and suddenly I'm alone with Astral.

I'm not prepared for this. Neither is Astral, apparently. "I've never met anyone like Luisa," he says. His voice is filled with admiration and I feel a stab of something like jealousy, but he continues. "When this is over, she's going back to the man she loves. Her parents disapprove, but that doesn't matter to her. She knows exactly what she wants, how she feels." He sighs. "Which is more than I can say. Listen, Blake, I'm sorry this happened to you."

I remember Griffin's ambivalence yesterday when we talked about my father. No such complexity of emotion for Astral. Here it comes, I think. "We don't have to talk about it. I understand how you feel."

He shakes his head. "Then you're doing better than I am. If I'd known about your father when I met you, I'd never have had anything to do with you, I admit that. Because knowing you would contaminate me."

This hurts so much, I draw a breath in sharply. I start toward the door, but he grabs my arm. "Wait," he says. "I didn't get that right. I don't mean I'd be contaminated by your guilt. I mean I'd be contaminated by confusion. Because you aren't guilty. And you aren't bad. I wanted everyone who was bad to be bad. That sounds so childish now, but it's true."

"I wanted the same thing," I say. That's practically what I said in the interview a few minutes ago.

Astral searches my face. "But it isn't possible, is it? Reality has this way of asserting itself."

"Not for everyone," I tell him. "Only for people who let themselves think. I was afraid you'd see everything the way you did before, and lump me in with the people you hate." Until I speak, I haven't realized just how afraid of that I've been. "But you haven't. Why not?"

"I have a father too. For all I know, he's Attila the Hun."

"Who?"

"Pol Pot, Joseph Stalin, the Mississauga Butcher, some awful tyrant. When I found out about your father, it made me wonder if there was a reason why my mother never told me who my father is. A serious reason. So, who am I to judge you?" He puts his hands on my shoulders and stoops so he can look me squarely in the eyes. "How are you doing?"

I sigh. "I don't know. This is so confusing. I wish I could sort my feelings out."

"Would it help to talk to your mother?"

It takes me a nanosecond to understand what he's asking, but then my heart leaps at the idea. "Do you think I could?"

"Of course," he says. "There are some great divining parlours here."

But when I try to picture myself communicating with the spirit of my dead mother, I draw a complete blank. I shake my head. "It wouldn't work, Astral." For the first time, I see the huge gap that lies between us. I could never believe as he does.

He looks so disappointed. "You won't even try?"

"Belief isn't something you can force. You must know that. Even if I'd like to believe, I can't make myself."

He gives me a wistful smile. "My mother used to say something just like that."

And now you talk with her spirit? I think, but I say nothing. Astral's faith gives him comfort. I have no right to interfere with that.

And maybe he understands, because he doesn't press me. "Come on, let's find the others."

When Kayko sees me, her eyes widen in surprise. "You look amazing. Who did the interview?" I tell her, and she says, "They must think this story is important. She's one of the anchors."

"Why does she dress like that?" I ask.

"Faux Tribe, you mean? It's very stylish in some circles."

"Well, I think it's perverse."

"That is the desired intention," Luisa says. "How do you say this? The point, I think."

Kayko agrees, and I shake my head. "Some things about your culture escape me."

On the way to the cafeteria, the halls are still crowded with strangers, but not as many today. "Does anyone know how the hiring is going?" I ask.

"It should be done by the end of the week," Kayko replies. "So the hearings will start soon."

Through lunch, while the others chat, I can't help feeling jealous of the people who will make victim statements before the Justice Council. Publishing my statement isn't the same. Their words will become part of the official record, of history. I thought I'd be one of them. And I'm going to have to listen to them, day after day.

We normally take an hour for lunch, but as soon as we've all finished eating, Kayko says, "We could get back to work, you know."

Griffin grins. "What are we waiting for?"

In the projection room, Kayko goes to load the disk, and soon the tent appears. This summer day in 2353 is so familiar to me now, it's starting to feel like part of my own past. We pass through the holographic people, closer to the doorway of the tent.

And there is Swan Gil again, looking worried and somehow diminished. For the first half hour or so, we see only her, talking to the person inside the tent we never see. Sometimes she goes toward the interior and disappears completely. We fast-forward when that happens. When we can hear her, she talks only about organizational details, the schedule for the speakers' stage, problems with travel arrangements, that sort of thing. Then she says, "I'm not sure about bringing these anti-regenerationists into the coalition." There's a long pause while she listens to the off-camera person. "I know, but this whole idea of broadening our base of support bothers me," she replies. "Do we want that kind of supporter? Are you opposed to regeneration therapy?" The person off camera says something and she laughs. "Well, I didn't think so. It's disingenuous to be cozying up to a cause we can't support.

"Lately, I feel everything is getting out of hand. I used to think I knew my causes, I understood our base of support, and I could, well, manage things. If there were conflicts, I knew how to reconcile the different factions, or at least keep them all under the same roof. I don't feel that way any more." She runs both hands through her thick, dark hair in a gesture of frustration. "Who's looking after the cleanup?"

Nothing of interest happens for a while until a group of people arrives. "How many did you identify when you went through the recording earlier?" Kayko asks.

Astral brings up the notes on his scribe. "All five are persons of interest," he says. I notice even he has stopped saying "suspects."

I recognize Eric Wong, the spokesman from Pollution Watch. Fortunately, he stands in the middle of our wedge of recording. "Listen up, everyone," he says. "Something really large is happening. We don't know why, but Internal Protection has requested a meeting with the leaders of all the coalition groups right here this afternoon. The request came from Falcon Edwards."

This causes a sensation, but Swan looks alarmed. "What if this is some kind of a trap?"

Eric laughs. "You think they'd ask to meet us here if they wanted to harm us? We're surrounded by supporters."

Another man speaks. "Eric's right. It seems the request to meet here was intended to build trust. We'll be safe." They debate until they finally agree to meet with Falcon Edwards.

"We'll have to contact everyone. We can use this tent as a meeting place if we can rig up another rest area for the speakers," Eric says. "Swan, can you handle that?"

"I don't know. Maybe, if we squeeze all the food concessions together and use the eating area for speakers. But that would create real problems with lines for food."

Others offer suggestions until the problem is solved.

"They were good at organizing," Kayko says. "See how adaptable they are." There's a note of regret in her voice.

I put my hand on her arm. "They would have been with us now if they'd survived."

She nods. "And everything would have gone back together more smoothly."

For the next hour or so, everyone in the tent is busy with

organizational details, rearranging the rally, making up a list of people who need to be contacted. "What about the anti-regenerationists?" someone asks.

"They're with us now," Eric Wong replies, "so they have to be represented."

"Then we'll have to ask Fern Logos," Swan says. She consults her scribe. "Oh, too bad. He's scheduled to speak at 3:30. I guess he won't be able to join us." Her voice drips with false regret. A few people laugh.

"I know you don't like him, Swan," Eric says, "but I'd guess about half of the people at this rally today wouldn't be here without the anti-regenerationists on our side. And suddenly, Falcon Edwards wants to talk to us. Do you supposed that's coincidence?" There's no anger in Eric's voice. He's trying to convince Swan, not antagonize her. She seems mollified

"If it gets us somewhere with the Protectors, I suppose it's worthwhile," she says. "I can rearrange the speaking schedule, put him on closer to the end."

Eric nods. "He's a good speaker. He'll leave the crowd with something to remember."

Even though I know everything is going to end so badly, I'm caught up in the excitement inside the tent. It's as if I've entered their world. Dido Anders arrives and nurses her baby while Swan sits beside her.

The tent starts to fill up. Suddenly, the projection freezes. "This is getting complicated," Griffin says. "We should each choose a different conversation to listen to."

"I'll listen to Swan Gil," I say quickly. We divide the work and resume.

At first, Dido is absorbed by her baby, but then she speaks. "So, everything Eric predicted is coming true. A lot faster than any of us expected, too. Congratulations, Eric," she calls to him, but there's an edge in her voice.

Swan's reply is almost too low to hear against the din inside the tent. "I don't like this new alliance either, you know that, but it does seem to be getting results. More than other tactics we've tried, eco-terrorism for example." She puts stress on the last phrase.

Dido replies in a furious whisper. "It's not as if I can control him, Swan. You've never been married, you don't understand. He just doesn't listen to me."

"So Dido Anders was married to an eco-terrorist," Kayko says beside me. I jump. I'd forgotten the present for a moment.

"How many conversations can you follow at once?" I ask Kayko.

She grins. "Only three."

Dido lapses into silence after that and Swan is called away. Soon after Dido leaves the tent to give the baby to Prospero, the projection freezes.

"We've almost reached the point where Falcon Edwards comes in," Griffin says. "I'd like to stop now and pick up here tomorrow morning."

Everyone groans. I try to stand up. My foot's asleep.

23

Power tends to corrupt and absolute power corrupts absolutely.

—Lord Acton, nineteenth-century historian

I would rather not watch the interview on the HD in the evening, but Erica insists. After supper, I linger in my bedroom as long as possible. The experiment I started in the holo-lab a week ago is complete now. I download the data into my scribe. At least, when *The Solar Flare* is over, I'll have a better use for the holo-display.

"Blake, it's starting," Erica's voice calls from the control panel on the wall. I scoop up my scribe and go downstairs. Most people seem to watch the holo-display networks every day, but Erica and I never got into the habit. In Kildevil, there was only one holo-display for the whole community. It was used rarely, when something important happened, during the Uprising, for example. Since we've been here, we've been too absorbed in our work to pay attention to the HD. Like so many other things about this culture, the need for entertainment strikes me as trivial.

I settle on a couch beside Erica. Zoe Nova introduces the item, briefly telling how I lost my mother and my identity, and how I only discovered my name and some details about my past a few years ago. Then she describes what's happened to me since I came here, how I was working with the Justice Council and hoping to make my own victim statement until I got the news from Code Tracking. At this point, I tuck my feet under me as if I fear getting sucked into the display. But, in fact, I have been, because there I am, facing Zoe Nova. It's odd to see me sitting before us in the room like this. I feel as if I've stepped out of my body. I'd hoped my feelings might be hidden, but they aren't. I look scared and vulnerable. Fortunately, the interview is short.

Erica pats my foot on the couch beside her when it's over. "You were exactly yourself, Blake. Perfectly honest. I do wish you could be a little easier on yourself, though. I knew how angry you were—anybody who went through everything you have would be." She sighs. "I thought you'd get over that on your own. It probably wasn't fair. I wish I'd made it easier for you to talk about."

"I couldn't talk about it because I was trying to be better than I am. It doesn't work that way, though, does it? You don't get better by pretending you don't have feelings."

Erica laughs. "I think it works the other way. You get over feelings by letting them out."

"But I wouldn't have known how. And look at Astral. He lets his feelings out all the time. It just seems to make him more bitter."

Erica looks worried. "How has Astral been with you?"

"He's fine. We had time to become friends before this happened, so he's being kind. Maybe this has helped him in the same way it's helped me. He's not so likely to judge people now."

"I'm so glad. Blake," Erica says, then she hesitates. "You told that interviewer you didn't know what you were going to do about your father. Have you given it any more thought?"

I shake my head. "Not yet."

Erica must sense the turmoil her question creates in me, because she backs off immediately. "You have time to think," she says. "No one will rush you."

I pick up my scribe. "I'm going to load the results of my experiment into the holo-display to see which molecules were produced. Do you want to watch?"

She shakes her head. "We're hoping to make final decisions about hiring tomorrow, and I want to go over the lists again so I know who I want and who I'm willing to accept. Anyway, science is lost on me. You know that."

She leaves and I patch my scribe into the holo-display, recalibrating the magnification so the molecules will be visible. Then I load the results of the experiment. The room around me suddenly swims with glowing globes, representing atoms. They move in sets, held together by the invisible forces of attraction that create molecules. Some look like chains; some have forked attachments at one end or both; a few have extra atoms tagged on the sides. Chemistry isn't my strongest subject. I recognize lactic acid and urea, but that's all. There are at least ten more compounds in the soup created by the experiment. I bring up the holo-lab program on my scribe and go to the identification unit. The hydrogen, methane, and ammonia I put into the tubes recombined with the air and water to create virtual amino acids and other organic compounds. The results are predictable, but they thrill me anyway. I play with my pet molecules until bedtime.

In my room, I change and turn out the lights, flopping onto the bed to watch the skymaker projection, and that hot summer day in 2353 comes back in vivid detail. Prospero was an eco-terrorist. Is that why Dido and their daughter died? But so many people who were in the tent that day died, maybe she would have in any case. I'm going to see him again, of course, to see how Sparrow is, if for no other reason. I don't know how I'll react. A few weeks ago I would have condemned him. It's that easy now. It may never be again. At least, tomorrow we will find out what

Falcon Edwards wanted with the activists. Maybe that will give me some clues about Dido's death.

The stars have traversed my virtual sky before I finally drift off. I dream I'm in the living room, molecules swimming around as I try to identify them. "Come on, Blake," a man's voice says. "You can do better. What's that one?" The voice is friendly, enthusiastic. I see no pointing hand, but I know which compound he's asking about.

"Glycine?" I say.

"That's right! Good. Simple because it's so short. What about this one?"

The next compound is much longer. "Beta alanine?" I guess.

"Look at the position of the ammonia," he coaches.

"Alpha alanine."

"That's my girl." His voice is filled with satisfaction and pride. I turn to look at him. The man I see is nothing like the friendly voice. He's hunched over, as if in pain. His face is pale, thin, and haunted. I've never seen him before, but I know who he is.

I force myself out of the dream, struggling toward consciousness as a drowning person would struggle toward air, and I wake up gasping, already upright in my bed. No, I tell myself. Stop it. No dreams about my father. I fall back onto my pillow, exhausted and dismayed. I feel as if my dream-self has betrayed me.

I don't tell Erica about my dream in the morning. When we reach Queen's Park, a small group of women has gathered in front of the steps. They aren't doing anything, just standing there.

"I thought you'd finished interviewing," I say to Erica.

"We have. This must be a demonstration." The women seem to watch us intently as we pass them on the way into the building.

The other aides are waiting in the conference room downstairs. "Good, you're here," Kayko says when she sees me. "We can get started." She picks up the holo-disk and disappears.

"I saw you on *The Solar Flare* last night," Luisa says as we enter the largest media room. "I think you are very brave."

I remember how I woke up, panicked by the thought of seeing my father. "I don't feel brave."

"Courage isn't the absence of fear," Griffin says. "It's doing the right thing, even in the presence of fear."

"You sound like a fortune cookie," Astral says. We all laugh, even Griffin, and I realize how far we've come from those early, tense days. We are friends now.

But how can you do the right thing when you don't even know what's right? I'm still wondering when Kayko starts the recording.

We begin where we left off yesterday, with Falcon Edwards approaching the tent, flanked by security men. Inside, he wastes no time. "I'm glad so many of you were able to join me today," he says. "Rest assured that your movement is gaining legitimacy with the government. The Queen's Park Protectors acknowledge the impressive base of support you have assembled." This creates an agreeable stir. "The Protectors have considered the situation carefully, and I'm here to tell you we are willing to curb the pace of technological research in some areas, and stop it altogether in others." He pauses as people burst into applause, then continues. "This represents a significant shift in government policy. In addition, if you agree to work with us, we will offer some of you positions of responsibility within the government. Let me be clear, we're talking about real power." He pauses to let the idea sink in. There's complete silence; everyone is absorbed by his words. "Of course, nothing in this world is free. In exchange, we expect your organizations to cooperate fully in rounding up eco-terrorists."

I look at Dido when he says this. Her face is still frozen in a smile from the previous news, but she pales.

"What if we don't know anything about eco-terrorist activities?"

"Swan Gil," Edwards chides, "that's disingenuous. We know which groups have been aiding and abetting these criminals. Do you really think you can hide these things from us?" But he's not angry. The smile he gives Swan chills my heart.

"What if we were able to get the eco-terrorists on side?" Eric Wong asks. "If you make these concessions, they'll have nothing left to protest."

"Before the Oak Moraine fire, forgiveness might have been possible," Edwards replies, "but eco-terrorism has gone too far. These people are criminals. They must be removed. That's our offer, take it or leave it. You have twenty-four hours to respond. I'll leave you to reach a consensus shortly, but before I do, we'd like to make a list of all your groups, which kinds of technology you want banned, which research you'd like to see slowed or stopped altogether. I'll give you a few minutes to sort yourselves out." Edwards goes farther into the tent, out of our view, and the meeting dissolves into chaos as people scramble to organize themselves.

"That was clever," Griffin says. "Allowing people to present their wish lists before they even had a chance to discuss whether they wanted to cooperate."

"Yes," Kayko says. "It would have made their goals seem just within reach."

"All for the price of betrayal," Astral says. That old, unforgiving tone is back in his voice, but it's understandable. How could they?

"Do we need to listen to these discussions?" I ask.

"They'd be difficult to hear and there's no point," Griffin says. "The results will be presented to Edwards in a few minutes. We can just let this part play through. The conversation after he leaves the tent is what I really want to hear."

After about half an hour, people line up. They speak directly to Edwards while an aide at his side records their lists of objectionable technologies. There's no new information here. We've already heard the end result on RTLM.

Edwards is impassive until Fern Logos approaches. "All types of regeneration therapy and research," he says.

"That's it?" Edwards asks, and Logos nods. Falcon Edwards raises one eyebrow. "People will suffer if regeneration therapy is suspended," he says.

Logos draws himself up to his full height. "What is earthly suffering compared with the loss of eternal life?"

"That's not a question I can answer," Edwards replies. "Next."

An idea occurs to me. "Do you suppose that's why he died?" I ask. "Falcon Edwards, I mean. Because regeneration therapy might have saved him, but he agreed to suspend it?" This grim irony would somehow balance the one in my own life, but Griffin shakes his head.

"I doubt it. I don't think the Protectors ever really suspended any kind of research or therapy they found useful."

"No, they'd just make it impossible for ordinary people to access," Astral adds.

When they're finished, Edwards says, "I'll give you a copy of the list we've compiled before we leave. At the end of the rally today, read it out. Make sure everyone knows you're demanding the government restrict these technologies. That way, we can be seen to concede to your demands.

And, of course, any agreement we reach will be completely confidential. Use the next twenty-four hours wisely."

"What, exactly, will happen if we agree?" Eric Wong asks.

Edwards flashes that chilling smile again. "First, we'll require an expression of good faith from your side. Once we are convinced we're getting good intelligence about eco-terrorists, we'll announce sweeping new policy changes to meet your demands. The exact details can be worked out after you decide whether to accept or reject this proposal."

"What if you take our information, arrest the eco-terrorists, and renege on your part of the deal?" Swan asks.

"We're prepared to appoint your people to key government positions as soon as the first arrests are made. That's our expression of good faith. But this requires trust on both sides. You decide if you can make the leap. Contact us when you're ready to reply."And then he leaves.

A stunned silence follows his departure. "This is everything we've been working for," Eric says.

"At what price?" Dido asks. Her voice is almost a whisper.

"Look, Dido, everyone knows Save Earth Now has eco-terrorist sympathies," Eric says. "That's why we almost split with your group last year. But Edwards is right, we're talking about criminals. They're far too extreme. If they have to go to jail for the crimes they've committed, what's that to us?"

People in the tent agree. It's clear that Eric has no idea of Dido's situation. Swan seems to be the only one who shares her secret. Now, she comes to her friend's defence. "Eric, this is such a huge betrayal. I remember what you said at a press conference last November. I wasn't there, of course. We weren't invited. But I watched. You said, 'The end does not justify the means.' There's nothing moral about betraying people who trusted you. This is so wrong."

"We need to purge our movement of violent elements and go forward, cleansed, into the brave new world the Protectors offer us," Fern Logos says. His eyes shine. Everyone in tent seems to get caught up in his fervour, everyone except Dido and Swan.

Shortly after, Prospero returns with the baby. I lean forward so I can catch what Dido whispers to Swan before she leaves.

"A lot of the files in the office are encrypted," she says. "I'll send you my passwords tonight. Goodbye, Swan." They hug and she goes. That goodbye sounds very final. I wonder if they ever saw each other again.

For the rest of the recording, the people inside the tent envision the world they've always wanted. It's clear they are going to make the deal. They're elated. Swan Gil leaves before most of the others do. Eric Wong is elected to represent them in further talks. Then they all go out to participate in the end of the rally, which Griffin and I watched a few days ago. The recording ends, and we're abruptly alone in the present. It's a strangely empty feeling, as if we've been catapulted forward in time.

"Well, that's not what I expected," Griffin says. "They did make a deal."

Astral cuts in. "But they all died anyway. How could they be so naive? It was crazy."

Griffin shrugs. "It's easy for us to think so, knowing how it all turned out."

"Nobody even mentioned democracy," Kayko says, her voice small with disappointment.

"Edwards waved the promise of power in their faces, and most of their principles went right out the window." This is Astral.

"I think a lot less of them now," Kayko adds.

"But they didn't deserve to die," I say.

"No, they didn't," Astral agrees. "And neither did those eco-terrorists," he adds. "People shouldn't die for acts of vandalism."

I know one eco-terrorist who didn't die, but I keep that to myself for now.

24

This new protest movement, led by the Living Lost, is gaining momentum. We expect the Transitional Council to prove its commitment to democracy by taking these demands seriously.

—Editorial comment, *The Solar Flare,* October 7, 2370

The next morning, when Erica and I arrive at work, a larger group is gathered on the lawn, maybe fifty. Security officers are trying to keep them off the sidewalks. Some of the protesters hold signs. The sight of a mob like this makes me want to run away.

"Don't be alarmed," Erica says, "I'm sure they're peaceful."

I wish I could share her confidence. I take a closer look one of the placards. "*All of us are innocent, all of us are guilty,*" I read. "Those are my words. I said that."

"Isn't that her?" a woman cries. "Isn't that her over there?" She's looking at me. Now everyone is.

I grab Erica's hand. "Come on." I drag her up the steps and we burst into the building, startling the security guards until they recognize us. "What was that about?" I ask, as if Erica ought to know.

"It must have something to do with the interview you gave."

"Do you think they'll go away?"

"I don't know. This sort of thing should be part of Hanif's job. He'll still be on the minibus, but I'll ask him to meet us later."

In the media conference room, Kayko smiles. "You're famous."

"But I don't want to be. Do you know who those people are?"

"I don't, but Security will."

We settle into the difficult task of sorting through the remains of the hologram. Compared to the huge information gain we made yesterday, this work is slow and unrewarding. Griffin and I follow persons of interest through fractile after fractile while they talk about nothing. Yesterday, I would have hated to leave my work, but when Erica pages me to come to her office after a few hours, I'm glad for the break.

"Who are those people outside?" I ask as soon as I see Hanif.

"They call themselves the Living Lost," he replies. "The group emerged just after the Uprising. They're all people who suffered in the technocaust. They've been quiet until now."

"What are they doing here?"

"From the signs they're carrying, I'd say that interview you gave struck a chord with them. Have you looked out front lately? There must be a hundred people now."

I remember the day he rescued me with Spyker. "But you can get me in and out of here without being seen. If I disappear, they'll just go away, won't they?" It seems like the perfect solution.

Erica speaks. "Hanif and I discussed that option, Blake. It doesn't seem fair to them."

I'm trapped by our principles. "That's the sort of thing the Protectors would have done, isn't it?"

Erica smiles. "I knew you'd understand."

"This may pass quickly if we let it run its course," Hanif says. "I want you and Erica to take a private car and a driver for the time being, but you will have to walk past the crowds as you enter and leave the building, just so they can see you. That might be enough to keep them happy. And someone will be with you whenever you go out now."

"Someone?" I ask.

"A bodyguard. Mostly, it will be me. We'll be as discreet as possible."

Life is getting more and more complicated. "But, I don't understand why this happened. The Justice Council is about to begin the hearings. These people are getting what they want. What's their problem?"

Hanif looks to Erica, who nods. "You should tell her everything."

"The Living Lost is not exactly a typical victims' group. How can I say this? They cast a wider net. Anyone who suffered because of the technocaust can join."

"You mean people who were related to the ones who carried out the technocaust?" I ask. I'm slowly starting to accept the idea that some of these people might be victims.

There's an uncomfortable pause.

"Anyone who suffered," Hanif repeats.

"Blake," Erica says, "people's lives were ruined by the things they were asked to do. Families fell apart, men were psychologically broken."

"So, anyone?" I ask. "No matter what they did?"

"Yes," Hanif replies. "They even run a group inside the prison."

This almost knocks me over. I sit back in my chair. "I'm going to need time to accept this."

Hanif and Erica let me go back to work. I walk through the hall, seeing nothing, I'm so absorbed by my thoughts. A few weeks ago, even the idea of a group like the Living Lost would have made me furious. I can't feel that way now. Along with a lot of other baggage, I seem to have lost my capacity for righteous indignation.

"Did you learn anything?" I ask Griffin when I come back into the media room.

He grins. "A recipe for using up leftover chicken. It didn't sound bad. What about you?"

I tell him about the Living Lost.

"I can understand why they were drawn to you," he says when I finish. "You talked about your confusion with such honesty."

I realize this is my chance to ask him something I've wondered for weeks. "Griffin, where do you fit in to all of this? I mean, I know what happened to Astral and me, what didn't happen to Luisa and Kayko, but I don't know anything about your past at all."

"Both my parents died in the technocaust," he says evenly. "Monique and my mother were friends from university. Monique was given the chance to escape to Haiti in a cargo ship. There wasn't room for other adults, but my mother begged her to take me. A few months later Monique heard my parents had been taken, and eventually, she learned they were dead."

"But you're so normal. Compared to Astral and me, I mean. How did you do that?"

"I didn't. Monique did. She was sure my parents wouldn't have wanted their deaths to ruin my life, so she raised me not to hate anyone. I was only about four when she started talking to me about it."

I sigh. "I wish someone had done that for me."

"Blake, until a few years ago nobody did anything for you. What you've done for yourself is remarkable. You know that, don't you? Most kids who grew up the way you did are either criminals or dead by now."

I'm not good with praise. I blush. "I guess I know that, but I feel like I've only gotten halfway to being what I'd like to be, and now I'm stuck. I'm so tired of feeling angry and bitter. It's like I've been carrying this huge weight around, ever since I found out about the technocaust and what happened to my mother. I just want to put it down."

"Maybe wanting something is the first step to getting it."

"But how do I start? It's too late for me to be like you, Griffin. You were raised to be the way you are now."

"I guess that's true. But there are people like you who seem to have found a way to get over their anger."

I stare at him. "How do you know that?"

"Blake, they're standing outside carrying signs with your words written on them."

It takes me a moment to process this. "You think I could learn from the Living Lost?"

"I think so. It's your decision, though. Let's get back to work."

Until I spoke with Griffin, my only concern with the Living Lost was how to avoid them. His words stay with me for the rest of the day. Meeting with the Living Lost seems impossibly difficult, but I can't shake the feeling Griffin's right. They must know something I need to know. Still, I let the afternoon and Friday pass without doing anything about it.

One impossible task at a time, I tell myself. Because now, I have to deal with Prospero.

25

These eco-terrorists are a blight on our society. I won't rest until I've destroyed every one.

—Interview with Falcon Edwards, the *Johannesburg Times,* October 12, 2353

On Saturday morning, when I leave for the ghost library, a bodyguard shadows me. Not Hanif, he'll take over later in the day. The man is as unobtrusive as Hanif promised. No one watching would suspect he's following me. The Living Lost have not shown up at our home yet, but I might need him if I'm recognized at the ghost library.

The crowd on the lawn outside work grew again yesterday. I passed them on my way in and out of Queen's Park, trying not to meet anyone's eyes. They know me by sight now. They call and reach out to me from behind the barriers set up to contain them. There were new signs yesterday. One said, "No Victim's Voice Silenced." When I saw that, I felt a stab of sympathy.

I enter High Park well before the main entrance, hoping to slip into Prospero's encampment unnoticed. I'd like to see Sparrow, to know she's fine, before anything else happens. I might not want to stay after I've spoken to Prospero, or I might not be welcome. The air holds a chill this morning. I skirt the camp, scanning for children, dry leaves crunching under my feet. Wisps of smoke rise from cooking fires and the smell of frying food drifts on the sharp air. A group of children have already eaten, it seems. They're playing a complicated kind of tag involving monkey bars and not touching the ground. I watch for awhile before I recognize Sparrow, she's changed that much. The quiet, haunted waif is gone. In her place is a cheeky urchin, with glowing cheeks and flying hair, who taunts the "it" and squeals with delight when she escapes. Somehow, in under three weeks, Prospero's people have worked this miracle.

Seeing Sparrow like this gives me a surge of satisfaction. Very little of what I do pleases me completely; there's always a nagging feeling I could have done better. This time, I got it right.

"She's settled in perfectly." In the nanosecond before I recognize Prospero's voice, I startle. He laughs, not unkindly. "Easy there." He puts his hand on my shoulder. I shake it off without thinking. The laughter fades from his face. "What's wrong?"

He's caught me off guard, without time to compose myself. "I saw you," I say, "in a hologram. I saw you with Dido and the baby, outside the tent at that rally in 2353." My voice drops to an angry whisper. "I know what you were."

"What I was?" he says. "You mean a husband and a father, or an eco-terrorist?" There's no anger in his voice, only sorrow.

"B-both," I stammer. "You admit it?"

"I don't talk much about my past, but I've never tried to hide it, Blake. You might as well hear the whole story." He looks around. "Your timing's terrible, though. Let me delegate a few jobs that have to be done before the ghost library starts. Then we'll talk. All right?"

I nod, speechless with surprise. He leaves quickly, covering the ground in huge, energetic strides.

I turn back to watch the children. There's a lull in the game now, and they sit together on the ground. Sparrow's distinct, reedy voice carries over to me. "My father was as tall as a tree," she says, "and he sang me to sleep every single night." She pounds her fist on the ground as she speaks the last three words to give them the emphasis they deserve. I smile. She's already talking about the time before, something her Tribe would never have allowed her to do. I need to see her more than she needs to see me. I just sit and watch until Prospero returns.

"The rest of the work is taken care of for now," he says, sitting beside me. "It's been awhile since I've had to do this."

"Do what?"

"Explain myself to some idealistic young person who is disappointed by my past," he says. "It used to happen fairly often, but most people here know my story now. It's part of the lore of this place." He gives a deep sigh. "So, you saw Dido and Rosa. At least you know how much I've lost."

I wasn't expecting him to be so open. My anger vanishes. "How did it happen?"

"Dido worked with this environmental protest group, Save Earth Now. You probably know that. Swan Gil was the executive director, and Dido was the office manager, but in fact, they ran the organization as equals. Everyone else came and went. Swan and Dido were the backbone.

"And I was an eco-terrorist. You know that, too. It's not something I'm proud of. I was young, I was stupid, and I thought I was immortal. Really. I believed nothing could possibly harm me. We worked together as an independent cell, three stupid young guys. We started off with pranks, jamming communication lines, hacking into government holo-zines, harmless stuff. Only a few legitimate protest groups were willing to help people like us, provide information and sometimes funds. SEN was one of them. That's how I met Dido. She thought it was exciting at first. I think that's why she married me.

"But then we had Rosa, and Dido began to change. I did too, but in the wrong direction. My cell got more violent.

We never hurt anybody. Never. But we moved from mischief to vandalism, then we graduated to major vandalism. I still regret the Oak Moraine fire deeply."

"That was you?"

"Yeah, that was me. We'd planned it for months. We knew which night guards were careless and when they worked. We were just supposed to torch some half-finished houses, set the developers back a few million. But the night we'd picked turned out to be terribly windy. We talked about postponing, but the forecast called for rain. We thought it would be all right. We were wrong."

"I know. I saw the newscasts."

"So you know what we did to the forest. You couldn't replace those trees in a millennium. I was depressed for months after, pulled out of my cell for a while." He shakes his head. "Looking back now, I can't believe how angry I was. I guess being young lets you feel that deeply. But you have to understand, we were seriously concerned about the planet. You know the Dark Times happened because of changes caused by people. Because the Consumers couldn't stop consuming, even though they saw what they were doing. For more than a century, everyone had to live in horrible conditions right out of the distant past, until, finally, they began to recover.

"A lot of us felt we were reaching the same critical point they reached in the twenty-first century, where we were beginning to do harm on a global level. I was afraid we'd just repeat the same mistakes again, and send our children back into another Dark Time. Why is it so hard for us to think about the future? How often do we have to make the same mistake before we learn something?" There's so much passion in these questions, for a moment, he seems just as young as he did in the hologram. Then the lines of age and sorrow return to his face.

"The Oak Moraine fire was a turning point. The Protectors could not forgive. Of course, it wasn't the damage to the forest that bothered them. The money behind the housing development came from people in power."

"That's why Falcon Edwards was so upset?" I ask.

"Probably. After, the Protectors became determined to stop the eco-terrorists, and, along the way, a few other nuisances they wanted to get rid of."

"The environmental protest movement and the push for democracy?"

He looks impressed. "You've already figured out a lot of this," he says.

"It's been my job. We've been at it for weeks," I tell him. "Two of the people I'm working with are brilliant. A lot of the pieces are still missing, but I do know about the offer Edwards made, to limit the technology in exchange for eco-terrorists."

"Yeah," he says. "Most of our 'friends' went for that pretty quick. The protest movement took on new momentum that summer, so the government had to take it seriously for the first time."

"Because of the anti-regenerationists?" I ask.

"Right again. Those people were unlike anyone Dido had worked with before. They could whip up feelings in ways no one else could. The environmentalists thought they'd be able to handle what came next, but they were wrong. Fern Logos was able to tap into fear of technology at a very basic, very emotional level. Once those forces were unleashed, none of us could control them."

"But Falcon Edwards could?"

Prospero nods. "He knew how to channel that hate and make it do what he wanted. I've never seen anyone operate like that, before or since."

"So what happened to you, after that rally?"

"We knew I had to disappear right away. Too many people knew what I'd been up to. I tried to convince Dido to stay put with Rosa, but she wanted to come with me. We both felt the coalition might turn on SEN because of its links with eco-terrorists, so I agreed.

"We couldn't leave the prefecture without showing ID, so we were stuck in the area. We took what we could carry that same night and left everything else behind, just fled. We didn't tell anyone where we were going. Dido and Swan had a code, and we could send messages from public kiosks to let her know we were fine, but that was all.

"You can't get a job without showing ID. We rented seedy little places at the edges of the industrial zones and I started busking. I was already trained in clowning and mime. That was perfect in some ways, because I could work in makeup. I spent a lot of my time in disguise, and people gave me cash tokens. I moved around, taking the commuter trams in all directions—Hamilton, Oakville, even back to Toronto some days. So we were able to survive.

"But the situation got worse. Dido stayed at home, listening to a little radio obsessively, trying to find out what was happening. The other guys in my cell were arrested. Big media event, that was. Then Eric Wong was appointed Environmental Protector. Shortly after, Fern Logos became assistant deputy to the Medical Protector. In October, the government announced the list of restricted technologies, and people with specialized knowledge were told to obtain a 'technology registration number.' A few were actually given numbers, but most who reported to Internal Protection never came back."

"How do you know that?"

"During the winter, a resistance began to emerge. It didn't take me long to figure out how to connect. I'd been living a double life for years. Ironic, isn't it? Just a few months after

Falcon Edwards cut that deal, I was working with the very people Dido and I had been trying to restrict. The techies knew I was an eco-terrorist, but we didn't talk about it. I had skills they needed, and we had a common enemy.

"I enjoyed my years in the resistance. We rescued people from under the noses of officials and got them to safety. It was a lot like being an eco-terrorist—hating the Protectors, putting myself in danger, getting the same rush. But things were bad for Dido. The technocaust just ate at her soul. And I was too busy playing hero to notice.

"By spring, the technocaust was out of hand. Just a few days after Eric Wong died in that highly unlikely 'accident,' Fern Logos was killed, supposedly by eco-terrorists. There were no real eco-terrorists left by then, but the government used his death as an excuse to declare all members of environmental protection groups eco-terrorists. Suddenly, they were all criminals. It's hard to describe the climate. The military was helping the government, of course, but even gangs of ordinary people went door to door with lists, checking ID cards. The government only had to brand you an eco-terrorist or say you were involved in some sort of advanced technology. When key 'eco-terrorists' were caught, there were big media stories, with profiles of their lives and their supposed crimes.

"I was still moving Dido and the baby every few weeks to keep them safe, but not spending any time with them, not understanding how isolating that was." He stops and looks down at his hands. "I couldn't see what was right in front of my eyes." He stops and I wait, saying nothing because I can't think of anything to say. Finally, he takes a shaky breath and continues.

"The day after Swan was arrested, Dido took the baby and turned herself in. Just walked into an Internal Protection office and told them who she was. We were able to find that much out later, but we lost the trail after that." His voice chokes. "I couldn't find them, so I couldn't save them."

One hot tear spills down my cheek, taking me by surprise. I had forgotten myself and everything around us. I hesitate, then put my hand over his. "It wasn't your fault."

He shakes his head. "I've tried to tell myself that. It doesn't work." He gestures to the camp around him. "This is my life now. I take the children no one else wants. It doesn't make up for what happened to Dido and Rosa, but it gives me a reason to keep going. That has to be enough." He stands and pats me on the shoulder. "Don't worry about me. I've lived with this for a long time now." He looks past the bench to my bodyguard standing at a distance. "Tell your minder we're putting you inside a tent today, so you'll be out of sight. It's too chilly to leave the little ones outside. I've got a lot of work to do now. Are you all right?"

"Fine," I say. Then I cover my face with my hands and burst into tears.

Spending the day with the children helps me recover, but Prospero's story haunts me. By Sunday evening, I can't keep it to myself any longer, so I go to Erica and tell her everything. We're both crying by the time I finish, but I feel better.

"That's so terrible," Erica says, wiping her eyes. "But how strong he must be, to pull himself together and go on like that."

"Yes, and if I'd known about his past a few weeks ago, I would never have spoken to him. I'd have hated him. Just like Astral would have hated me."

"That's true," Erica says. I sense she's waiting for me to go on.

"I must be changing," I say, "because it seems to me I don't have the right to judge anyone any more." But I shake my head. "If every change is going to be this painful and confusing, I'm not sure I want to keep going."

To my surprise, she agrees. "It would be easier to stay the way you are now."

"No! No, it wouldn't. I can't stay like this." I remember what I said to Griffin. "I want to find some way to put all this anger and bitterness down and just walk away from it."

Erica smiles.

My mouth falls open in surprise. "You tricked me." Then, somehow, I find I'm laughing.

She laughs too. "I didn't trick you, Blake. It's what you said, you *are* changing. So, what are you going to do next?"

I've already made up my mind about that. "I guess I'd better meet with the Living Lost. Not all of them," I add quickly. "Just one or two to begin with."

She smiles again. "I'm sure Hanif can arrange that."

I shake my head in amazement. "I can hardly believe I'm doing this."

Erica puts her hand on mine. "It won't always be this hard, you know. Eventually, you're going to come out the other side."

I pretend to agree as I say goodnight, but when I'm alone, I allow myself to wonder how I can get to the other side without going past my father. Maybe this is just a way of stalling.

26

A person can only become a person through other persons.

—A Zulu saying

On Monday morning, I find myself sitting nervously in a meeting room, waiting to see who the Living Lost will send to me. I'm relieved when only two women appear. One is thin and nervous looking, the other is stout and serene. Both have skin the colour of chocolate. The stout one smiles broadly as she speaks. "Blake, child, it's such a pleasure to meet you. I'm Cadence Nkomo. This is Mimi Beaumardi." Her voice is low and musical. She makes no move toward me, but I feel as if I've been hugged. They seat themselves across the table.

I hardly know where to begin, but that doesn't matter. Cadence has everything under control. "We were so happy to see you on *The Solar Flare,* honey. So much of what you said was just what we've been wanting to say. But we've been going around in circles for so long, trying to decide how to tell our stories, if we should tell our stories, not knowing how people might react. Isn't that right, Mimi?"

"So it is," Mimi says.

"It took so long for us to all find one another, people of like minds, who want to put the sadness of the past behind them and just forgive. Not forget, just forgive one another and start to work together. Then you come along, just a slip of a child. And now, we have the courage to speak out. All because of you." She sits back in her chair and beams at me. Mimi smiles too.

"I'm nothing special," I start to say.

"Don't you say that. Don't you *ever* say that, child," Cadence says.

I change the subject to move the conversation away from me. "How did the Living Lost start?"

"Mimi and I were neighbours," Cadence says.

"Cadence was the one with the idea," Mimi adds quickly.

Cadence smiles her broad, ready smile. "That's right. During the Recovery, when the Dark Times were ending and knowledge was being restored, my great-grandfather came here from South Africa. He was a bio-technician, and he brought knowledge people here so desperately needed. But he didn't just bring his knowledge. He brought his wisdom, too. In my homeland, there's something called ubuntu. That's the foundation we used to build the Living Lost. That's our cornerstone."

I lean forward. "What is ubuntu?"

"In Africa, they say, 'A person can only become a person through other persons.' In this society, you would say, 'You can't respect others until you respect yourself.' But, if a person has ubuntu, she would say, 'I can't respect myself if I don't respect others.' Because we are all part of humanity. Do you see? If you offer disrespect to others, you diminish yourself. If you hate another, it's like hating yourself. A person with ubuntu is able to accept others and knows that we all belong together."

"I didn't know about ubuntu until Cadence taught me," Mimi says. "I have seen great sorrow in my life. Bad things were done. I didn't know how to find peace."

"And now you do?" I ask.

Mimi nods. "Should I tell her my story?" she asks, and Cadence agrees.

"Before the technocaust, Cadence and I were neighbours. We lived side by side. But I did not love this woman. She had a bigger house than I did. She wore nicer clothes. Her children did better in school. I pretended to be nice, but her happiness ate holes in my heart. My husband felt the same. He worked hard, in construction. He never seemed to get anywhere. Cadence's husband, he worked in genetic modification. He had a good job and he made more money.

"When the technocaust came, we thought, now, these people who are always happy, they will know some grief. As soon as the government restricted technology, my husband went to Internal Security and reported Cadence's husband. The military came and took him away."

"I had to take my children and leave," Cadence says calmly.

"And I had to stay and live with what we'd done," Mimi says. "Other neighbours came and looted her house, they took everything away. I learned the hard way, you can't make your happiness out of someone else's grief. Every time I passed that empty house, I had to look away. My husband joined a gang that went door to door with lists they downloaded from Internal Protection, rounding up wanted people. He thought this would earn him a job in the government. But later, the military came and took him away, too."

"What happened?" I ask, and Cadence answers.

"After the most violent part of the technocaust, the Protectors decided to cover their tracks. They took people like Grant Beaumardi and put them in forced labour camps in the industrial zones, so they couldn't talk about how the government had encouraged them."

"We got him back after the Uprising," Mimi says, "and he was a shell of the man I married. By then, Cadence had come back to her house. I couldn't speak to her, I was so ashamed. But when Grant came home, she showed up at my door to help me. I was too embarrassed to tell her my story, but I needed her help so badly. Finally, one day, I found the courage to tell her the truth, and she forgave me."

I stare at Cadence. "How could you do that?"

"When I came back to my house, some of my neighbours brought me things they'd stolen from us after we fled. 'We kept this for you,' they said, and I accepted that. It was then that I remembered what I'd been taught about ubuntu. I realized, if I was going to live among these people, I had to forgive them or I'd be asking hate to take a place at my table, to sleep in my bed. I couldn't do that to my children. I wanted them to grow up without hate. So I started to reflect on the spirit of ubuntu, and then I began to teach it to others."

"And that was how we started our meetings, and we grew into the Living Lost," Mimi says.

"We've been wanting to tell everyone this is what has to happen now, but we were afraid to speak," Cadence says. "Then I saw you on *The Solar Flare,* and you just opened up your soul. I looked inside, and I saw ubuntu there. I know you can show us the way to make things right."

This is ridiculous. I don't know whether to laugh or cry. Cadence must see that she's upsetting me because she stands. "We've taken up enough of Blake's time today, Mimi. We should leave her be. Besides, we have that meeting with Dr. Siegel soon." I'm afraid to ask them what that's about.

Mimi and Cadence hug me warmly as they leave. I hug them back, but I can't shake the feeling they are just plain crazy.

"You come and meet everyone when you're ready, Blake," Cadence says. "We meet every Thursday night at my house. Here's the address." She hands me a card. "We'll be waiting for you."

"I don't know if I can," I start to say, but the disappointment in their eyes is more than I can bear. "Maybe someday," I add, so they leave the room smiling.

After Mimi and Cadence go, I'm overwhelmed by a tangle of emotions and ideas. I can't deal with this now. I struggle to clear my mind as I go find the other aides.

They are not busy in the media rooms, as I'd expected. Instead, everyone is sitting in the conference room, looking gloomy. What do they have to feel gloomy about? Are crazy women making demands of *them*? I check myself before I speak. It isn't fair to blame them for my problems.

"What's wrong?" I ask, trying to sound as if I mean it.

"We're not getting anywhere," Kayko says. "I thought this hologram would tell us so much."

"It did," I say.

"It did, but now it doesn't. We haven't learned a thing since last Thursday."

"But I have." They all look at me in surprise. I tell them about Prospero and Dido, about Cadence and Mimi.

"You learned all that?" Astral says when I finish. "We've got to start talking to these people."

But Kayko shakes her head. "We can't. That's what the victim statements are for. If we talk to people before the Council does, it would be like putting ourselves before them."

"When will they start?" I ask.

"Another week or so, not long," Kayko replies.

"We're talking about things that happened fifteen years ago," Griffin says. "We can wait another week. In the meantime, we should pull together our report for the Justice Council."

"Griffin's right," Kayko says. "We can start by writing summaries of everything we've learned. No more than ten pages. Then we'll share what we've got and try to produce a coherent report."

Everyone agrees. So, without warning, we begin a new phase of work, dividing into our own offices.

The suite I share with Erica is full of people now. I hide myself away in a corner office. My only relief is lunch with the other aides. This is isolating work. It leaves space for thoughts to creep in. Thoughts about my father. Even if he has no access to the media in prison, he must know I'm alive by now. Why hasn't he asked to see me? What kind of monster wouldn't want to see his own child? These thoughts feed on one another, building, until I'm furious by the end of every day. At night, I lie under the skymaker, the wheel of anger turning so furiously inside me I can hardly think. When I finally sleep, my father is always lurking in my dreams, no matter what else is going on, somewhere in the background with his back to me. I wake up exhausted.

By Thursday, my distress is apparent. "You look terrible," Erica says at breakfast. "Maybe you should take a few days off."

"No!" I cry so forcefully, she drops her knife. "I'm sorry, I didn't mean to yell. It's just that going to work is the only thing that holds me together right now." I stop and take a breath. "I didn't mean that. It sounds too dramatic."

"Maybe it's not too dramatic. You've been pushing yourself so hard, Blake. I wish I could think of a way to make things easier for you."

I sigh. "I know what I've got to do," I say. "The Living Lost are meeting tonight. I should go."

In the morning, meeting with the Living Lost seems bearable, but by the end of the day, I would rather crawl under a rock than meet those people. How can I face their compassion and forgiveness when I find nothing remotely like that in myself? But Hanif has ordered a car and driver for me, so I let the momentum of his arrangements carry me forward.

Cadence's home is north, in a part of the city I've never seen before, very different from the quiet old neighbourhood beside High Park. Most of the houses are new, high-tech but cheaply made. Many have stores on the bottom storey. People line the streets, standing in groups talking while children play around them. The house we stop at is more sturdy than others, but it still bears scars that must come from the technocaust.

Cadence herself opens the door. "I knew you'd come," she says quietly. Her voice is filled with such warmth and dignity that my misgivings abate.

Cadence seats me beside her in a room that holds maybe fifteen people. It's comfortable, but the furnishings have seen better days. The meeting isn't what I'd expected, though. I'm braced to hear story after story about the technocaust, but the Living Lost turns out to be more than a simple support group. After introductions, they get down to work quickly.

"Everything set for the Saturday night patrol?" Mimi asks. "Who's collecting the blankets?" A burly-looking man raises his hand. "Good, Ray. Make sure they give you extra, it's getting cold out there now. What about the food?"

"I got that covered," an older woman says.

"Soup or chili?"

"Both, if you can get those big kettles from the Happy Mouth again. That worked really well last week."

Mimi nods. "We'll see what we can do. We should think about buying our own at some point."

I lean over to Cadence. "What are you planning?"

She whispers her reply. "We take food and blankets and some basic medical supplies down to those debtors at Union Station every Saturday night."

"What about protection?" Mimi is asking now. "Lolinda, can we rely on that big son of yours?"

"As long as he's finished by midnight, he says that's fine," a woman replies.

I remember the crowd that gathered around Spyker and me the day I found out about my father, and I shudder involuntarily. "That's dangerous," I whisper to Cadence.

She nods. "It can be. We don't take any chances, though."

I feel comfortable with these people. They remind me of Prospero and of the weavers at home, trying to deal with the problems around them. But I don't offer to help. The memory of that trip to Union Station is just too painful.

When they finish making arrangements for the Saturday night patrol, Cadence introduces me to everyone. I'm afraid she's going to ask me to speak about my past, but instead she says, "Everyone here is really interested in what happened in Terra Nova, Blake. Why don't you explain how you managed to get elections so quickly?"

I'm happy to talk about Terra Nova. These people listen intently and ask intelligent questions. By the time the evening's over, I'm more relaxed than I've been in days. People start to leave. Every one of them shakes my hand or pats me, as if I'm some kind of talisman, some kind of lucky charm. But I like them and what they're doing so much, it doesn't bother me.

I know the driver is waiting, but I don't want to go yet. This house is such a welcoming place, if I didn't know what had happened here, I'd never suspect. Somehow, Cadence has put her life back together. I wish I understood how.

"I'll help you gather up the dishes," I offer.

When the plates and cups are collected, Cadence turns to me. "Child, something's troubling you. What is it?"

I don't realize what I'm going to say until it's out. "I want to know why my father doesn't want to see me."

Cadence pats my arm. "Let's sit down and talk," she says. We sit at her small kitchen table. "What makes you think your father doesn't want to see you?" she asks.

I explain about my micro-dot and the information from Code Tracking. "He's been notified by now. He knows I'm alive, and he hasn't asked to see me," I finish. "Why?"

"I don't know your father, so it's hard for me to guess," she says. "But what would you do in his place? Would you want to see your child?"

A snort escapes from me. "If I'd done everything he has, I wouldn't imagine I'd be worthy to talk to my child." This stops me. "Oh."

Cadence smiles. "Maybe you just answered your own question."

I sit in silence for a moment, taking this in. It makes sense. "So what do I do?" I ask at last.

"If you want to talk to him, I'd say you have to make the first move."

"But what if we're wrong? What if he really is a monster and he isn't interested in me at all?"

"Do you know anything about your mother?"

This question surprises me. "Quite a bit. I even have a voice recording she made for me before we started to run."

"Does she seem like the kind of woman who would have married a monster?"

"No," I say. "But people change. *He* changed. He must have."

"If you have reason to believe there was good in his heart once, I think you'll find it's there still," Cadence says.

"What if I'm wrong?" My voice is small and miserable.

"If you're wrong, you have to hold your head up high and walk away. There's lots of people in this world ready to love you, child. You're a special person." She says the word "special" in a way that almost makes it possible for me to believe her this time.

27

To be free is not merely to cast off one's chains, but to live in a way that respects and enhances the freedom of others.

—Nelson Mandela, twentieth-century leader

The courage Cadence gives me may not last. If I wait long to see my father, I might change my mind. On the way home, I ask the driver to arrange a meeting with Hanif.

"You already have your security clearance," Hanif says the next morning. "I should be able to arrange this soon."

I was afraid it might take weeks. I'm amazed. "But they were so careful about letting the Justice Councillors in."

"Allowances are made for relatives," he says, and then he smiles. "Besides, you come highly recommended."

I'm supposed to spend the morning summarizing the broadcasts of RTLM, but I'm too stressed to concentrate. I keep writing the same sentences over and over. I jump when Hanif appears at my door a few hours later. "We can go now," he says.

I can't believe this. "To the prison?"

He nods. "I'll take you myself."

Erica is waiting in the outside office. "Do you want me to come?" she asks.

I hug her, then I say, "I have to do this alone."

Hanif and I travel in silence. I'm too nervous to talk, too nervous to think ahead. I've imagined meeting my father so many times, but never like this. Don't expect anything,

I warn myself. I'll get through this and get on with my life, like Cadence said.

We pass through several security barriers before we even approach the main walls of the prison. It's a huge, imposing structure. Then we leave the vehicle and go to a small door in the wall. Every door is unlocked to let us pass and locked again behind us. I'm beginning to feel trapped. Finally, Hanif says, "I'll wait here." I go through the last doorway alone.

The room is empty except for a table with two chairs, one on either side. There are guards by both doors, but otherwise, I'm alone. "You can sit," one says. His voice is not unkind. I do sit, but when the other door opens, I stand and lean forward across the table before I can stop myself.

The man who enters with a guard at either elbow is tall and dark, but otherwise unexceptional. No one I'd notice in a crowd. I sit down, propelled by the weight of my disappointment. I feel no spark of recognition.

He keeps his head down until he's seated. Then he raises his eyes and looks at me, reluctantly. And he pales. "You look . . ." he begins, but his voice falters. He tries again. "You look so much like Emily. Do you remember her?"

I shake my head. "I was too little."

He agrees. "You were very little." I hope he'll say more, but there's just a long, uncomfortable silence. I consider telling the guards I want to leave, but then he speaks again.

"Do you know what happened to her?"

"I do," I say, and I tell him everything we learned. He listens without moving, staring down at his hands. When I finish, there's another long silence.

Finally he says, "Thank you for telling me." Then he adds, "Suppose you tell me what brought you here." I can't read his voice. It could be empty of emotion, or filled with all emotions, in the way the colour white is really composed of all colours.

"I want to know how this happened," I say. "I want to know what happened to you."

He looks startled. Then he looks scared. "I guess you have a right to know," he says finally. "My area is—was—remote sensing. I designed tracking systems. Before all this happened, I was possibly one of the ten best in my field. Not in Toronto. In the world. That must sound arrogant, but it's true.

"I lived for my work; it was everything to me. I never expected to marry. Then Emily came into my life. Her brother, Tony, worked in my lab. We met at his wedding." For the first time, a ghost of a smile flits across his face. "I almost didn't go, but that's how I met her. Most people, when I mentioned remote sensing, their eyes would glaze over, but Emily was interested. She knew very little about it, but she listened and she asked intelligent questions. She was pretty and funny, but what I really loved about her was her intellectual curiosity. We shared an almost insatiable hunger for knowledge. We were so lucky to find one another. The first years of our marriage, I used to lie awake at night and wonder, 'Why me? What did I do to deserve this happiness?'"

I wonder the same thing, but I don't say so. I just wait for him to continue.

"When you were born, I designed the chip for you myself. I thought it would let me find you anywhere." There's bitterness in his voice, but I can't tell if it's because he lost me, or because his design didn't do what he expected.

"I didn't pay attention to politics," he continues. "People were talking about hostility toward technology, but I thought they must be exaggerating. I expected it to pass. But Emily didn't. She was the one who made plans. By the fall of 2353, everyone was nervous. We agreed then that she would take you and run if anything happened to me. I was so sure I'd be able to track you.

"And then I was taken. It was a big sweep, lots of people were picked up that week. We were all held in the Hippodrome for questioning. Once they latched on to me, they didn't let go. Have you ever heard of a man named Falcon Edwards?"

"I have."

"Edwards wanted me for Internal Security. I was held in his 'private suites' he called them, his own personal prison. At first, I refused to cooperate." He sighs. "He was a clever man. He pretended to be friendly, learned all he could about me. It didn't take him long to realize that you and Emily were my weak spot. He told me you were gone, then he promised me access to long-range tracking systems if I cooperated. They wanted me to develop a system that could track down people they wanted to find without their knowledge."

This piques my curiosity. "But how? You'd need to plant some sort of homing device on them to begin with, wouldn't you?"

For the first time, he looks at me with real interest. "A lot of these people had security clearances. Their retinal scans were already in the database. I was supposed to develop a tracking system for a retinal scanner that could be hidden in public places. In ads on the public transit, for example. The scanner would capture the retinal scans of anyone who looked at these devices long enough to read what was written on them. If we got a match, we'd know where that person was."

"You'd know where they had been," I say. "That wouldn't let you catch them, would it?"

"It would if we found patterns in their movements. A lot of people take the same routes every day, even if they're in hiding. Edwards expected to pick up enough fugitives to make it useful."

I've been so caught up in the originality of this plan, I let myself forget what it was used for. Now he's reminded me.

"How could you agree to help?"

"I wanted to find you and Emily more than anything," he says. "And I was arrogant about my abilities. I thought I could design a system that would look as if it should work, but build in enough bugs so it would never really be functional. I thought, if Internal Security invested enough time trying to find people with a system that wasn't working, some of them might escape."

"So you never really cooperated?" I ask. For the first time since I've entered this prison, I feel a faint hope.

"Never is a long time. You'd better let me finish.

"I agreed to develop the system. I took as long as I reasonably could to design it, hoping people still on the run would escape in the meantime. It took eighteen months to get everything in place. I had hoped they'd let me access the tracking systems I needed to find my family when that was done, but Edwards said my design had to work before he'd give me the passwords. Alone, I could have hacked into the systems, but my access was always closely monitored. Of course, the scanning system I'd developed didn't work. After three months without a single match, they figured it out. I tried to pretend the flaws were accidental, but that didn't help. 'Fix it,' Edwards said. I took as long as I could, but you have to understand, I was frantic by then. I had to know where you were.

"I held them off for almost two years, but finally, I gave them a system that did what they wanted. Some key people were captured. People who might have escaped without me." He pauses again. "When that happened, I was finally given access to the long-range tracking systems. Edwards wasn't around by then. They told me he was dying. But when I looked, it seemed as if you were dead. And without you, I could never hope to find Emily. After that, I lost interest in everything but my work. I hardly noticed when the technocaust ended. I stayed on at Internal Protection. A real collaborator, because that was the only life left to me.

"I deserve to be here. I don't expect forgiveness. When I found out you were alive, they told me about the work you're doing here. You shouldn't be burdened with a father who's a criminal. That's why I didn't ask to see you. There's only one thing I wish I knew," he continues. "How were you declared dead? Did your chip fail?"

"No, it still works perfectly. They've been using it to track me here."

A smile of satisfaction flickers across his face. "I knew it," he says.

"Security says someone must have removed my code from the system."

He frowns. "That's hard to believe. The security around those systems was amazing. The Protectors knew people they were looking for had the ability to break into most systems."

"I was told it must have been done internally, by someone who had access."

He looks at me in amazement. "If they let me into the system, I could tell who did it."

"How?"

"I designed it so no one could make changes without leaving a signature code. If the person who deleted your code had a security clearance, I can tell who it was." His face lights for a moment, but just as quickly his excitement fades. "I'd never get to talk to anyone who could let me do that," he says. "The paperwork for an interview alone would take years."

I stand up and go to the door. "I think the man who can give you permission is right here."

28

No employee of the Transitional Council, or any of its related bodies, may contribute to policy-making with knowledge that there is an opportunity to further that person's private interests.

—*Ethical Guidelines,* Transitional Council of Toronto, May 2369

Hanif sends for me a few days later. "It wasn't difficult to convince the Transitional Council to give your father access to the code-tracking system," he says. "They want to unravel this mystery too. But he won't be allowed to work inside the prison. It's too much of a security risk to take the equipment in there."

"But that makes it impossible for him to do anything, doesn't it?" I ask.

"Not if we bring him here. He can use secure equipment while I monitor his activities."

"They'll let you do that?"

"He committed no violent crimes, and he's always cooperated fully. We think it highly unlikely that he'd try to escape, and our building is secure."

"That means yes, doesn't it?"

"That means yes. Do you want to see him while he's here? That would require a higher security clearance, but I can get it for you."

I hesitate. My father seems more interested in his tracking systems than me. Still, I want to know what happened. "I'd like that," I finally say.

"Do you want to watch him work on your code?" Hanif asks.

"Could I? Thank you." I'm so grateful to Hanif for doing all this for me.

I look for Kayko in her office to tell her what's happening.

"So you might actually figure out who took your code out of the system?" Kayko says. "Do you think you'll ever know why?"

I hadn't thought that far ahead. "It doesn't seem likely, does it? My father knows a lot, but I'll be surprised if even he can unravel that."

"Blake, how do you feel now that you've met your father? I've been waiting for a chance to ask you."

"He's not what I'd hoped for before I knew he was a collaborator. But he's not as bad as I was expecting him to be after I found out. Erica said he was just a person who got caught up in things beyond his control, and she's right." I tell Kayko how he tried to sabotage the tracking system he was forced to design.

"Most people would understand it wasn't his fault," Kayko says when I finish.

"But who will ever hear his story? It may be years before he comes to trial. Anyway, even if he resisted, he's not the father I was hoping for. He's more interested in remote sensing than people."

I find life easier this week. I'm not so angry and I'm not working alone. We've come back together to produce a report from our summaries. In the halls, I sometimes pass Cadence and Mimi, who smile but pass without stopping. The Living Lost have stopped demonstrating outside the building. I wonder what they're up to now.

Over the next few days, Kayko's ability to take our disparate bits and fit them together into a coherent whole amazes me. I'm not alone. "You're a born editor," Griffin says to her one afternoon, and it's true.

The work is so satisfying, I've almost put my father out of my mind by the time Hanif sends for me. I follow his messenger through the maze of tunnels and security checks, deep into the sub-basement of the Security building, until a door opens, and I find Hanif with my father in a small room jammed with equipment. Hanif gestures to a chair. My father is hunched over a console, lost to everything. He barely acknowledges me.

"You can start now," Hanif says. I'm grateful they waited for me.

My father enters the code-tracking system. "Here's Blake's file," he says after a moment. Then he hits a few keys and the display changes completely. "This is the programming code," he says. "Anyone making changes would work at this level." He hits a few more keys and the display changes again.

Hanif looks startled. "What's that?"

"This is the sub-code. It's my system for tracking changes," my father replies. "When I started to cooperate, they finally gave me a security clearance and some freedom. I wasn't really expecting this layer to be useful, I just did it because I could."

"We didn't know it existed," Hanif says. He sounds stern.

"I'm sorry. There was so much to communicate, it escaped me. I'll give you the access codes before I leave and explain how it works," my father says as he continues to search the screen.

"You didn't check her file when you were told Blake was dead?" Hanif asks.

"No, I just accepted the news at face value. So many people died in those days; I'd been expecting it so long. It never even occurred to me it might not be true.

"I'm switching back to code now, so we can see where changes were made in Blake's file," he says. "This is where the micro-chip was brought online, just after Blake was born. That predates my sub-code system, but I know who made that entry. I did. I wasn't working directly for the government then, but I designed the system, so I knew everyone in Code Tracking. They let me come in and make this entry. That was such a great day."

For the first time, I hear warmth in my father's voice, real human emotion. I lean forward involuntarily, to catch what he's going to say next, but he's focussed on the screen again. He frowns. "This file has been vandalized. Here's the change that took Blake out of the system. Let me switch to sub-code." The screen changes again and he sits back, staring in disbelief. "I should have known."

"Known what?" I ask.

"Who took Blake out of the system?" Hanif says.

"Falcon Edwards. This is his security code. The date is December 21, 2355. That's odd," he adds. "I'm sure he wasn't working by then." He turns to Hanif. "Can you check his death date?"

"I have it right here," I say, pulling my scribe out of my pocket. I do a quick search. "January 12, 2356."

"Just a few weeks later," my father says. "This was probably one of the last things he did."

"But why?" I ask.

"To punish me," my father replies. "That's the only logical reason. I was never sure Edwards believed I couldn't make that tracking system work. Sometimes, I was almost certain he was just pretending, as if he was playing a game with me."

Nobody speaks for a long moment, then finally, my father says, "What about Emily?"

He must be losing his grip on reality. "I told you about my mother," I remind him.

"Not your mother. Your cousin Emily. Tony's daughter."

"I have a cousin named Emily?"

"She was born about a year before you. When I designed your chip, we had one made for her, too."

"What happened to her?" I hardly dare to ask.

"I don't know. I lost contact with everyone during the technocaust. I didn't dare try to track anyone. That would have given them away. After . . . well, nobody from my old life came looking for me. I couldn't expect them to."

"But, could you still find her?" I'm trying to absorb this. It seems unreal.

"If the chip is working, yes. We should be able to track her. If there's time, I can do that now"

"Not today," Hanif says. "Time's almost up, and I need you to show me everything about that sub-code before you leave. This is a major discovery." Hanif turns to me. "I'm sorry, Blake. We'll follow up on this, I promise, but not today. Someone will be waiting outside the door to show you back."

So I find myself in the hallway again, stunned and confused. I can't quite feel angry with Hanif. He was generous to allow me to watch at all, and what my father can show him about the tracking system must be important. But where is Emily? What if she's living with some Tribe, like Sparrow and Spyker were? She might need to be rescued.

I need to talk to Erica, but when I go to our offices, the new receptionist refuses to contact her. "The Justice Council is in meetings with the Transitional Council. We've been instructed not to interrupt them for any reason," she says. Her tone makes me realize it would do no good to insist. But what could be so important?

"That was so fast," Kayko says when she sees me. "Didn't you learn anything?" Everyone else crowds around so they can hear.

"We learned a lot," I say, and I tell them about Falcon Edwards removing my code to exact revenge on my father. I don't mention Emily yet. I'll tell Kayko when we're alone.

Kayko's frown deepens as the story unfolds. "That's horrible," she says when I finish.

Astral says nothing, but his face darkens with fury.

"I think we should add this to our report," Griffin says.

"It tells us as much about Edwards's character as anything we've seen in the holograms," Kayko agrees.

"I tried to talk to Erica, but I was told the Justice Council and the Transitional Council are in meetings. It sounds serious. What's going on?"

"It must be serious. I can't get a peep out of Uncle Kenji," Kayko replies. "We should wrap up this report by the end of the day." She grins. "Then I'll see if I can find out what's happening."

We're just putting the finishing touches on our report a few hours later when a message comes through, asking us to join the Justice Council upstairs.

"It's too late in the day to start a meeting," Astral says. "Something's happened."

We find the Justice Council waiting for us with Dr. Siegel. "Tomorrow morning, we will be making a major policy announcement," Dr. Siegel says. "We want you to hear this first, because it has implications for the work you'll be doing in the future." He nods to Daniel Massey.

"We came into this process uncertain how to proceed," Daniel says. "Some of us, specifically Paulo and myself, wanted traditional forms of justice to prevail. Our difficulties in reaching a consensus have slowed our work and made it more difficult.

"I'm not sure Paulo and I had a good sense of this place or the complexity of what had happened. We wanted to set high standards of innocence. We didn't want our work to be clouded by ambiguity. Then, the story of a certain girl became public." He nods in my direction, and I feel myself redden as everyone looks at me. "Blake's statement helped us to realize that even an innocent victim could be associated with those who were guilty. Perhaps more importantly, the publicity surrounding Blake's story brought the Living Lost to our attention." He smiles. "Cadence Nkomo is difficult to resist. She helped us understand that our ideas about justice might not provide the best solutions for this situation.

"So, we are completely revising the work of the Justice Council. This will be made public in a press conference tomorrow. Monique, I think you've offered to outline the changes?"

Monique smiles. "I have to tell you, before I begin, how happy this announcement makes me. I won't be able to talk like this in public, of course. But I feel this new process we're adopting will bring us much closer to the reconciliation this society so badly needs.

"Cadence urged us to consider how South Africa dealt with justice at a similar juncture in that country's history, near the end of the twentieth century. Violence and oppression had dominated that political system for decades under something called apartheid. Like the technocaust, apartheid left few people without some kind of stain on their hands. The Living Lost helped us realize that many people who seem guilty are victims too. So everyone who wants to make a victim statement will be allowed to do so. Blake, that includes you."

The room erupts into cheers. Even Astral looks pleased.

Monique holds up her hand. "Before you celebrate, there's something else you need to know. We're not making this public yet. Cadence has caused us to seriously revisit all our ideas about justice. The people of South Africa appointed a commission for truth and reconciliation. Anyone who made a complete statement of wrongdoing was granted amnesty. We want to explore the idea of implementing that sort of process here. We're not sure it can work, but it's worth considering, especially for some of the more complex cases where threats against family members and other forms of coercion were used to force people to collaborate."

This announcement is greeted more soberly. I glance at Astral to see how he's taking this. He shakes his head, but he looks skeptical rather than angry. I realize what this might mean for my father.

We're reminded to keep this information confidential, then told we can go. I rise with the others, but then Erica speaks. "Blake, we'd like you to remain behind for a few minutes, please."

I sit back down, wondering what they could possibly have to say that's too serious for the other aides to hear. Kayko gives me a worried glance as she leaves. Then, the Justice Council focusses on me.

"This isn't a punishment," Erica begins. "We want you to understand that. We've had to make a very difficult decision, but we're only doing this to protect the reputation of the Justice Council. You've caused a huge shift in our direction, Blake. We're all very happy this happened, but it's inappropriate for someone in an aide's position to have exerted this kind of influence."

"I didn't exert," I say, "it just happened."

"When it comes to conflict of interest," Dr. Siegel says, "appearance is as important as actual occurrence."

"This a conflict of interest?" I ask.

"I'm afraid so," Erica says. "It's so unfortunate. If you were an ordinary citizen, like Cadence, you'd be fine. But an aide cannot appear to wield this kind of power."

"So what are you going to do?"

Erica is too upset to speak. Monique continues. "We have to ask you to resign your position, dear."

"But you're not really asking me at all, are you?" I say.

"Please don't make this difficult for us," Dr. Siegel says. "We'd like your resignation now, before you make your victim statement. I can promise you'll be at the very top of the list when we decide who's going to appear." He's treating me like a child. I don't want to reinforce that view of myself by making a scene.

I push my chair away from the table. "Very well," I say. "I'm offering my resignation."

29

These startling new developments are being attributed to a movement called "The Raintree Rebellion" after the young girl whose story started it all. Blake Raintree is a true hero.

—Editorial comment, *The Solar Flare,* October 25, 2370

"So I gained the right to present my victim statement and lost my job in the same moment," I say, finishing the story. "The work that mattered to me, contact with my friends . . ." My voice trails off because there's no way I can finish that sentence, it's impossible to name everything I've lost. I'm sitting on a bench inside a huge tent in High Park, talking to Prospero. Not far from us, children in a small class bend over their books, Sparrow included. It's too cold for them to be outside now, but the tent is made of self-heating fabric so we're nice and cozy in here. It will be a good place to spend the winter.

He shakes his head. "What are you going to do now?"

"I don't know. Yesterday was my last day of work. At least they let me stay to help present the report about the technocaust we've been working on all this time."

"How was that received?"

"Really well. They want to make it public. It shows pretty clearly that technology wasn't the real target of the technocaust, that people were manipulated so the Protectors could maintain their dictatorships. Everyone said we did a great job. Then they showed me the door. Now, I have to wait a few days to make my victim statement. Maybe after, I'll go home."

"Home?"

"Back to Terra Nova, I mean. I've always intended to go back to school. I'm going to be a scientist. Changing the world is just a sideline for me."

He chuckles. "You do a pretty good job with your hobby. How about staying on until Erica's ready to go back? You could work with me."

"Helping out with the ghost library, you mean?"

"I was thinking of something more serious. Somebody's got to do something for those debtors living around Union Station."

"Somebody's trying." I tell him what the Living Lost is doing.

He smiles when I finish. "Great," he says. "You can start by hooking me up with Cadence Nkomo and Mimi Beaumardi."

"There's something you should know. Mimi's husband went door to door with a gang during the technocaust, rounding up people the government wanted. He's still alive. Maybe you wouldn't want to work with her."

"I can't let something like that stop me, Blake," he says. "If we're going to put things back together, we need everyone who's willing to help. How about you?"

"Thanks for asking but I don't think so. I've always been a bit of a coward. Those people were really scary." I stand to leave. Prospero has work to do, even if I don't.

"Consider it an open invitation," he tells me when we say goodbye.

It's not the first offer I've had. Kayko wanted me to work on her holo-zine with her. I had a terrible time talking her out of quitting her job with the Justice Council. Erica too. Convincing people they shouldn't resign because of me has been my main occupation for the past two days.

Of course, Astral was the worst of all. "I'm quitting too," he said. "It's not fair."

My reply surprised even me. "Actually, it is. They used a set of rules that would apply to anyone in this situation. That makes it fair."

I could see I'd stymied him. "Life isn't fair," he sputtered. "It should be."

"Astral, life *isn't* fair. It never was and it never will be. Only people can be fair. The Justice Council is trying. They need you. Keep your job." I could see I'd won him over. That gave me the first real happiness I'd had in days.

Then he said, "Blake, when this is over, you could come to British Columbia with me. Why don't you?"

He'd caught me completely off guard. I looked at Astral and I knew I was drawn to him. But then, I tried to picture myself living in a Truth Seeker community. Visiting divining parlours. Astral will spend the rest of his life looking inward. "I can't," I told him. "I'd never fit into your world. Besides, I have to take care of something in Terra Nova."

"Something or someone?" Astral asked, but I knew from his smile I hadn't really hurt him.

It's much colder outside the tent. I pull the collar of my jacket up around my ears. I've spent a lot of time lately thinking about my father and how remote he is from everyone, how finding my mother seemed like a miracle to him. Maybe the distance I put between myself and others isn't because of everything that's happened to me. Maybe I'd be like this anyway. But, if my father could fall in love, there might be hope for me. I have to go home to find out. My school is in St. Pearl, and that's where Fraser is now. I'm still not sure I can love anyone, but if I could, it would be Fraser. We both want to make things better. What was it Erica told me a wise man said long ago? "To live in a way that respects and enhances the freedom of others." We both want to do that, and it matters.

When I look ahead to the park gates, Hanif is waiting, exactly where he was all those weeks ago when everything was just beginning. I'm surprised. I still have bodyguards because of my association with Erica, but Hanif is too important to be one of them.

He starts to speak as soon as I'm within earshot. "Your father reconstructed your cousin Emily's tracking code today. I put it into the system an hour ago."

My heart starts to pound. "And?"

His smile is like sunlight bursting through clouds. "It works. The micro-chip is still active."

"Where is she?"

"I thought we could find out together. She's outside the prefecture. I told Erica not to expect you back soon. Is there anything you need to do first?"

"Not a thing. Let's go."

Hanif drives to a maze of huge hangars at the airship docking port by the mouth of the Humber River. Finally, he stops by some small fixed-wing devices. "A pilot is waiting," he says.

We take off abruptly. This noisy, flimsy aircraft feels as if it might shake to pieces in the sky. For the next half hour, my excitement about finding Emily is quashed by my fear of sudden death. Below us, towns and bio-farms give way to a more rugged landscape of grey rock outcrops divided by lakes and ponds. I feel a powerful tug of homesickness. It looks like Terra Nova. The big lake to our left could almost be the ocean. Suddenly, we make a sickening dive. I'm sure we're going to die. But the pilot touches down so lightly, I barely feel the landing.

"We still have to drive some distance," Hanif says. "A hovercopter would let us land close to where your cousin is in half an hour, but we have no way to let her know we're coming, and I don't want to alarm her. You'll have to use the tracker while I drive. A car is waiting."

"Where are we?" I ask as Hanif drives away from the airstrip.

"North of Georgian Bay, about a hundred and fifty kilometres from where we started."

"Are there any cities around here?"

"No. This area is rural."

"Are there Tribes? I've been afraid that Emily might be with a Tribe, the way I used to be."

"Not out here, Blake. The Tribes are strictly urban."

I let out a breath I didn't even know I was holding. Maybe it's absurd to care so much about someone who is barely more than an idea, but I do. The tracker shows the map of this area, and the tiny blip that is Emily. We have a long way to go. I have time to think about micro-dots and tracking systems.

"Why did Falcon Edwards remove my code?" I ask. "My father had been cooperating for a long time by then. Making him suffer didn't accomplish anything."

Hanif thinks for a while before replying. "I read the report your group prepared about the technocaust. You paint a vivid picture of Edwards in it. He thought he was protecting a way of life. He hated anyone who stood in his way so much that he felt he had the right to destroy them."

"There it is again, hate. It seems to be at the heart of everything that's happened," I say.

"Yes, it's like a toxin. I don't think we'll ever achieve democracy if we can't get rid of it."

I'm surprised. "Why is that?"

"In a democracy, everyone takes turns. Sometimes, the other side gets power. Everyone has to be included, even people whose ideas are repugnant to you. If you hate the other side so much you can't bear to let them take control, democracy won't work."

This is such a thoughtful reply. "Hanif, maybe I shouldn't say this, but you don't seem much like the other people in Security."

He laughs. "I feel that way myself, sometimes. When I was taken off the streets, I was trained to work in security. That was the only chance I got. Until the Uprising, I worked for private firms. Being so close to government has opened up a whole new world for me. Maybe, when everything settles down, I can do something else with my life."

When things settle down, I think, we will all do something else. The idea of getting back to my real life is starting to sound more appealing. We drive on in silence until the daylight begins to fade. The forest outside grows darker, but there's nothing threatening about it. The land looks profoundly peaceful. "This is so much like Terra Nova," I tell Hanif. "It feels like coming home."

The last road is just a dirt track, not even on the map. Branches slap the vehicle as we bump along. Very little traffic comes this way. The road ends in a grassy field edged by low-tech wooden houses. Dogs of all shapes and colours rush the vehicle, barking. I pull back instinctively, but then I notice their tails are wagging. These are not watchdogs or strays.

In response to the commotion, people pour out of the buildings. Someone whistles and the dogs withdraw immediately. My blood is rushing in my ears. I can hardly think. "What should we do?"

Hanif smiles. "We should get out."

The crisp evening air carries the scent of woodsmoke and fir. A crowd has collected now, maintaining a cautious distance, waiting to find out what's happening. I scan the faces and latch onto one, a girl with dark hair. We don't really look alike, but there's an unmistakable sameness to our features, our hair, the shape of our bodies. An older man beside her follows my gaze. He looks at me, at the girl, then quickly back to me. When he speaks, his voice is soft with wonder, but it carries as if he'd spoken in my ear.

"Blake," he says. It's not a question. It's an answer.

30

Never doubt that a small group of thoughtful, committed citizens can change the world. Indeed, it's the only thing that ever has.

—Margaret Mead, twentieth-century anthropologist

Diffuse, golden light glows all around me. I see it, even with my eyes closed. Every muscle has settled into blissful relaxation. I have been scrubbed, I have been pummelled. I have been shown how to stretch and bend my body in ways I did not know it could stretch or bend. I search for the sound of the wheel of anger and realize it's gone. The silence left behind is sweeter than any music. There will be room for other feelings now.

I'm lying on a mat on the floor of a huge hall in a bio-spa. Dozens of other people lie around me. This should remind me of sleeping with my Tribe. It doesn't. Instead, it reminds me of a poem. Without thinking, I begin to recite.

Ah! Sunflower, weary of time,
Who countest the steps of the sun,
Seeking after that sweet golden clime
Where the traveller's journey is done.

From her mat on the floor beside me, Kayko smiles. "William Blake," she says. Her voice sounds as relaxed as I feel. After a moment she adds, "That poem has a second verse."

"I know, but it doesn't seem appropriate somehow."

Kayko nods. The second verse of that poem is about ghosts. "The time for ghosts is passing," she says. Silently, I agree.

"Blake was the poet my mother named me for," I say. "But he wasn't her favourite poet. She loved Shakespeare best of all, but she couldn't figure out a way to name me after him."

I know all these things now. My Uncle Tony even managed to bring his scribe with him when they fled, so I have pictures of my mother with me as a baby and toddler. We are always hugging one another, always smiling. He has pictures of me with my father, too. I'm not ready to ask for copies of those yet.

"You learned a lot about your mother from them, didn't you?" Kayko says.

"I did, and I'm going to know even more. Erica says I can stay at the commune with Emily and Uncle Tony as long as I want."

"When do you go back?"

"Tomorrow morning. My victim statement is the last thing that's keeping me here in Toronto."

Kayko rises on her elbow. "Blake, I wish things had turned out differently. We really miss you."

I smile at her. "Kayko, if I had to stay here now I don't know what I'd do. Emily and her father can't leave the commune, they don't have enough people to do all the work as it is. I've lived that kind of life before. I'll be useful to them. And I have to be there now. When I met my father, I thought I'd never be related to anyone I could love. Emily and her father always kept a place in their hearts for me, even though they thought I was dead. Being with them is so different from being with anyone else."

"Family," Kayko says. "I think I understand."

"I can't stay with them for very long, but I want to know them as well as I can before I go back to Terra Nova."

"What about your father?" Kayko asks.

"Uncle Tony and my father went through school together, they worked together. It sounds like he was the only friend my father ever had. That first night when I found them, we stayed up all night, talking. I told them what happened to my mother, and what happened to me, and then I told them about my father. The whole story. When I finished, Uncle Tony said that he didn't blame my father for anything. He said, that day in the Hippodrome when Internal Security came to find people from the remote sensing lab, my father stepped forward before anyone else could. 'I'm the one you want,' he said, and he went with them before they had time to consider who else they might take."

Kayko's eyes widen. "He saved them?"

"That's what my uncle says. But my father didn't tell me that. Uncle Tony says he wouldn't. He said it's like my father to blame himself for everything. He said, 'Evan has got to learn to forgive himself.' He's asked to visit my father in prison."

"Will they let him?"

"Hanif says it can be arranged. If anyone can bring my father out of his shell, it will be my Uncle Tony. He even said he'd testify on my father's behalf if he comes to trial."

"The way things are going, that might not be necessary. The South African process is gaining a lot of public support. People like your father might get amnesty."

I haven't allowed myself to consider what I really want for my father. Suddenly, I realize I'd like him to be free. Maybe, in time, we could forge some kind of bond. "That's a long way ahead."

"We should go soon," Kayko says. "Everyone will be waiting."

"Soon," I agree, but I lie back in the light of the artificial sun a moment longer. "I'm glad you brought me here. Now, I finally know what fun is."

"Actually," Kayko says, "I consider this therapeutic. The next time you come back to the city, we'll tackle fun." She stands up. "Come on. We really do have to go."

We shower and dress, and Kayko's driver takes us to Queen's Park. We have to show our security passes before the car is allowed anywhere near the building today. Hundreds of people cover the lawns, and huge projectors have been placed around so they will be able to see the proceedings inside.

People recognize me and cheer. I walk up the red sandstone steps, turn, and wave. The crowd roars. I cringe inwardly even as I smile. I'm not a hero. I never will be. But they want to think otherwise and I know I have to let them. Hanif is waiting inside the door. "I'll escort you in," he says. We walk into the big room that once held the parliament. The victim statements are being presented here.

Hanif leads me to a table at the front of the room and I sit facing the Justice Council members and their aides. All except for Kayko, who rushes through a back door and quickly takes her place behind her uncle with an impish smile of apology. The room behind me and the old visitors' gallery above it are completely full. But there's nothing solemn about this occasion. It's like a party. The clamour in the room falls to a hush as soon as Dr. Siegel stands.

"I want to welcome everyone today," he says. "We have a huge task ahead of us, but if the energy in this room is any indication, we are ready to meet the challenge. Before we begin hearing victim statements, the Transitional Council has an announcement to make. Six months from today, we will hold general elections for a new parliament. It will be the first in over two hundred years."

The room erupts. It takes a long time for people to settle down. Finally, Dr. Siegel continues. "Before we can look to the future, we have to put the past to rest. It seems appropriate to begin these hearings with Blake Raintree. As most of you know, Blake came here to serve as an aide to the Justice Council. Because she drew attention to the needs of everyone who suffered in the technocaust, she was required to leave her position. We placed her first on the list of victims because of the sacrifice she made."

Dr. Siegel sits down. Everyone looks at me. I can't believe he said that. I don't feel like the most important victim. This isn't right. But I start to read the words in front of me because I don't know what else to do.

"My name is Blake Raintree," I say. "I was born on July 14, 2352. For the first sixteen years of my life I didn't know those things about myself. Not my name or my birthdate or my age. I didn't know who my parents were, or how I had been separated from them. I didn't know if I was lost or thrown away. I want everyone to know how this happened to me . . ." My voice falters, then stops. I've waited so long for this moment, and now, it seem meaningless. I don't need to make a victim statement. I'm not a victim any more.

Everyone is watching me. I read the concern on the faces of my friends. Erica looks like she's ready to stop everything. "Don't worry," I say softly. "I'm all right."

I raise my voice again so it connects with the amplification system, including everyone in the room. "Most of you already know my story," I say. "I don't want to talk about that any more. The past is over. I have more important things to say, about what I've learned since I came here, about letting go of hate." I push my scribe away. I don't need notes now. I take a deep breath and free-fall into the future.

Also by Janet McNaughton

An Earthly Knight
Catch Me Once, Catch Me Twice
To Dance at the Palais Royale
Make or Break Spring
The Secret Under My Skin